ALL
THE
WORLD
BESIDE

ALSO BY GARRARD CONLEY

Boy Erased

ALL

THE

WORLD

BESIDE

*Garrard
Conley*

RIVERHEAD BOOKS NEW YORK 2024

RIVERHEAD BOOKS
An imprint of Penguin Random House LLC
penguinrandomhouse.com

Library of Congress Cataloging-in-Publication Data
Names: Conley, Garrard, author.
Title: All the world beside / Garrard Conley.
Description: New York : Riverhead Books, 2024.
Identifiers: LCCN 2023050153 (print) | LCCN 2023050154 (ebook) |
ISBN 9780525537335 (hardcover) | ISBN 9780525537359 (ebook)
Subjects: LCGFT: Gay fiction. | Romance fiction. | Novels.
Classification: LCC PS3603.O53566 A78 2024 (print) |
LCC PS3603.O53566 (ebook) | DDC 813/.6—dc23/eng/20231103
LC record available at https://lccn.loc.gov/2023050153
LC ebook record available at https://lccn.loc.gov/2023050154

Printed in the United States of America
1st Printing

Book design by Alexis Farabaugh

For Shahab

"Indeed, we are but shadows; we are not endowed with real life, and all that seems most real about us is but the thinnest substance of a dream—till the heart be touched. That touch creates us—then we begin to be—thereby we are beings of reality and inheritors of eternity."

NATHANIEL HAWTHORNE, LETTER TO
SOPHIA PEABODY HAWTHORNE

"The unendurable is the beginning of the curve of joy."

DJUNA BARNES, *NIGHTWOOD*

ALL
THE
WORLD
BESIDE

Hull, Province of Georgia,
January 1, 1765.

Sister,

Perhaps you will not be surprised to receive a letter from
Nobody. It must seem I have always defied the expectations placed upon the boy once named Ezekiel Whitfield,
your brother, and in writing to you now, I am once again
defying the role of the exile I am meant to play. In truth,
I never intended to defy even one soul, certainly not
yours. This life of exile came upon me gradually, then all
at once when the fatal blow was dealt our family and our
lives altered forever.

Gradually, because even from the first I knew I would
never follow Father's vocation. Never have I been suited
for the sort of life where others must listen to the wisdom
of my words. You must know this. You know that since
the age of four, Sister, the very year the awakening came
to our town, I have not spoken. This has not been by

design. I do not know the reason for it, though I believe I must have known even then that no one wanted to hear what I might have to say, and that it was best to avoid all trouble by never saying a word.

Writing must suffice.

After leaving you, I traveled thousands of miles from Cana, working from one mill to the next, following rumors of more work and better pay. I do not know where my feet shall land, but this town, Hull, has offered me a few months' work.

You would be surprised to see your brother working so industriously. Allow me to paint it for you.

On any given day, I roll up my shirtsleeves and strip bark. I carry logs to the yard for decking. I pray a silent prayer over the lost tree if I remember. Some days are too cold to remember, wind sharp with ice from the river's spray. The men give me a look every now and then. Curiosity tells them something. I shrink before their eyes. At the age of five and thirty, I am the size of their wives, even their older children. In fact, if children live in the house where I am boarding, I am claimed as a playmate and my second workday begins. The food in these houses is always better because someone else cooked it, though it is never as good as the memory of your cooking, Sister. Fresh bread from the mill, a porridge of some sort. The best evenings are silent. We gather round a table, fire blazing behind us, heads bowed from overwork——a benediction. On days like these, it is almost as though I am home.

Inevitably, someone will spoil the moment by asking questions. I do not answer these questions. If they continue to insist, I write out my answers, though I do not tell them much. If they ask where I am going, I write the truth: I am a pilgrim in search of a place where I may be free. If they ask about family, I lie: I say all of you are dead. This never fails to quiet them.

In these quiet moments of astonishment, I remember the dress you leant me, Sister, the day I felt truly one with you. I was sick, and you wished me better. You dressed me in blue silk with the lace stomacher, your childhood favorite. You held me up. You propped me against you. You wanted me pretty then. You must have seen the smile upon my face as we gazed into the looking glass at our twinned features, red cheeks you pinched for me so I would appear beautiful beside you. That was when Nobody was born, Sister. Ezekiel Whitfield left us. You gave me that gift all those years ago, and it has taken me two decades of living to receive it fully.

I think of you often, and miss you, and pray you are safe with Mother in Boston, far from the Pharisees who brought our family to ruin.

I do not think of Cana, not the place itself. What happened in Cana has made it impossible to think of it as a real place. I must think of it now as an idea, Father's idea of a better world, and perhaps that is how it was always meant to live. Father believed the best in people, and they destroyed him for it. I know you see things differently. Do you continue to blame him? I will not lie to you, Sister. I want you to see things as I see them. I want you to see how circumstances made it impossible for him to find a path forward. The same was true for all of us. We did not always comfort each other through our sufferings, but we may do so now, though it is late and much that has been done cannot be undone. Will you turn to me now, Sister, though I may seem a stranger to you? I shall always remain

your brother,

Nobody

I

NIGHT WATCH

1730

1.

Spring

The shore of his mother, her warmth sheltering his infant body from the cold. The shore of his sister, pressing her nose to his. Lavender and orange on Sabbath mornings when the women pass him round amid psalm-singing. Violet and musk and wheat as the women take turns grinding grain on working days, the sound of stone against stone, the room filling with fire. Then, after their work, the cold on his face as his mother carries him home in her arms, her breath a raft of white cloud, his hand reaching to catch it as it passes between them. Do not cry, little one. There will always be more clouds. So long as I am here to breathe, ye shall have more clouds.

His father is a darkness between these bright shores, the man's voice a thunder that shakes his bones. After the singing on Sabbath mornings comes his father's sound, loud and booming from the pulpit. The man's eyes are sharp, searching. They find Ezekiel within the flock. After the service, when his father holds him, Ezekiel grows frightened. He cries out for his mother. The smells are wrong, musty wood and tobacco, no trace of milk.

"What is wrong, child?" his father says, gripping him too tightly. "Does he not seem touched by some devil, Catherine?"

"Do not cry," his mother says, reaching for him. "You are mine, little one. You belong to eternity."

Nuzzled against her neck, head full of rosewater, he forgets his father. Each time he lands upon her shore, he forgets the man, again and again, until one day, in the spring season after his first birthday, Ezekiel remembers his father even in the midst of his mother's embrace, and in spite of it all—his bones' fear of the man's unfathomable darkness and the knowledge that he may be swallowed whole by this darkness—he desires his father. He cries out for his father. He cries for so long and with such force, his entire body aches. Soon come the waves of nausea. His flesh grows hot, sweaty; his mother, fearing typhoid, carries him to the new physician's house. There, he cries out once more for his father, sensing the darkness he craves is even farther from him now. The physician places his cool hands upon Ezekiel's belly. Ezekiel grows calmer; he has seen this face before, half-cloaked in shadow, with the sound of the forest at night. His father had been there, too. This man is like his father but not, with softer, kinder eyes, a wide smile.

The physician feeds him a bitter milk that falls against his throat like a scalding coal. Ezekiel closes his eyes.

"He is a beautiful child," the physician says.

"After his father," his mother says.

"Yea," the physician says, placing a trembling hand upon the child's brow.

"I've done everything," his mother says. "I've done everything, and nothing works. I cannot guess what the source of this trouble may be."

"Wait and see," the physician says. "There is no fever at the moment. You've no need to fear typhoid."

"I am tired."

"It is sometimes hard with boys this age. They start to sense the world is not all mothering. Does he still sleep in your bed?"

"On occasion. Though I am determined not to spoil him as I did my firstborn."

"Oh, spoil him for a while yet. He'll soon grow stronger on his own."

"You are a kind man, Arthur. I am glad you are here with us."

"Tell this to the others in Cana. I fear only you and your husband are glad."

"The rest of the flock will be glad when they have need of your services. Give it time."

When Ezekiel opens his eyes, his mother is carrying him home under a pink sky. He wants to cry, but the potion has made him too weak.

"Look, little one," his mother says, bringing them to a stop. "The first bloom."

He follows the tip of her finger. At first, he cannot see anything beyond it. Then, slowly, a burst of white against the pink sky. The white dances. In its center, a pink circle with tiny white spindles.

"Your father planted these trees. Soon, in summer, you'll eat of this tree's fruit. I shall bake it in a pie and feed it to you. Do you see? The world has been made for you."

Sarah hears them enter through the garden door. Her brother is quiet now, but her mother's loud sighs tell her the problem has not been solved. He has been crying for days, ever since their father left for Stockbridge, less than half a day's journey yet far enough to keep him there for the week it will take to set up the Mohican mission. Something always goes wrong when their father is away. It is a law in Cana. She rushes to the kitchen to see if she can be of any help.

"No, Daughter," Catherine says, shifting Ezekiel to one hip. "It is only that I am tired, and worried."

"I shall prepare a supper," Sarah says.

"You are too young."

Sarah holds up both hands with palms facing her mother, spreading her fingers wide. Ten. Soon the number will move past her hands, and she will have to remember her age as something outside of her body, alien to herself.

"Well," Catherine says, relenting, looking about the kitchen for any hazards. "Do you remember our lessons, girl?"

"Yea," Sarah says, nearly leaping across the room to embrace her mother. She forces herself to keep still. Any movement might put an end to her sudden adulthood. Sarah knows her mother has coddled her, protected her from the duties of womanhood; by the age of seven, her friend Abigail Jacobsen had known how to set a table, sew a dress.

"A simple beef and pease stew then," Catherine says. "Your father won't be home for another day."

"Should we not send someone for him? He might know what to do with Ezekiel."

"Arthur Lyman has given the child a potion. It should last through the night. I'll take an hour to bed while he sleeps. Wake me if you need me, Sarah. Do not hesitate."

Sarah presses her mother's arm and kisses the top of her brother's head, always so warm and sweet-smelling, with something of the gristmill about it. She scurries out the door and to the side of the house, where the tinder pile awaits. With each movement, each exhale, she adds another word to her prayer: Please, Lord, please, yea Lord, keep us safe.

Two years before Ezekiel's birth, before the new physician arrived in Cana, Sarah had lost her friend Abigail Jacobsen to an outbreak of typhoid. Before that year, the world had been composed of wonder. She and Abigail had spent hours with Catherine in the garden, naming the plants anew. Hyssop, lemon balm, sweet woodruff became Tall Man, Lady of Green Fans, Sweetly White.

Catherine had clapped for them. "That one does look a little like a lady overburdened with fans. And yea, this is our dear Sweetly White, who must always be protected from too much rain."

When Sarah's father once teased them about their game, insisting God had granted Adam alone the power of nomenclature, Catherine had said no such record of plant naming existed in the Bible.

"Adam named only animals. There is but one named plant. And it was quite lengthy, that name. Do you remember it, Sarah?"

"The Tree of the Knowledge of Good and Evil."

"Yea, quite lengthy. We women shall content ourselves with naming all the others."

Her father had laughed, a rare sound. "A group of Anne Hutchinsons, in my garden," he said. Anne had been banished, that woman, and later scalped by the Siwanoy of New Netherland. This had happened almost a century before Sarah's birth, but the lesson was clear: stray too far from your station, and God will punish you.

Sarah thinks of their game now, pausing before the garden with tinder in hand. The rooms of the Whitfield house stand before her in miniature. She is a giant who has ripped off the roof to peer inside. Her father had built the garden in this way, in honor of her mother's curious cravings when she was with child. The effect is magical and curious: for the parlor, borage; for the kitchen, spearmint; for Sarah's chamber, strong-smelling sorrel, apple-sharp and fresh; and all about the garden, to serve as decorative walls, the yellow tufts of marigolds. The garden was a gift, a rather impractical gift since it did not always suit their kitchen's needs, but Sarah felt it was as much a part of herself as her own beating heart. All one had to do, when the house became too oppressive, was to stand before the garden and imagine the rooms behind you transformed into something far more alive. It seemed one could not be unhappy in such a place.

Now, however, as she counts the green shoots rising from the soil, Sarah finds her spring joy tempered by the memory of Abigail's illness. Sarah had been forbidden to sit beside Abigail's sickbed. She had stayed awake every night of her friend's illness, praying the

prayer she now repeats for her brother: Please, Lord, please, yea
Lord, keep us safe. After Abigail's death, Sarah's father had preached
a sermon on God's will, his eyes lighting on her several times during the service, as if to say, *Your mourning is sinful, child.* And how
could she argue with such words from such a father? He had been
called by the Lord to spread His gospel in this New World. Whatever words he uttered from the pulpit had been passed down directly
from Heaven. Perhaps it was a sin even to pray her prayer, to ask
God to intercede on her behalf. Could it be His will that her brother,
her sweet-smelling baby brother whose first birthday is but a few
weeks past, be condemned to suffer and die as Abigail did?

She had discovered she would soon have a brother when she and
Catherine had been playing their game, renaming the plants. It had
not been the same without Abigail, but she could not bear to to see
her mother lose the one entertainment that seemed to bring a genuine smile to her lips. They watched the sky grow dark, and in only
moments, a heavy rain began to turn white and hard. The hard
white knobs filled the garden and struck at the plants, tearing at
their leaves, weighing them down. Sarah witnessed a vision of their
house overrun by these intruders, each room overcrowded, the inhabitants beaten beyond recognition. She buried her face in her
mother's dress and cried.

"Hush, child," her mother said. "What have you seen?"

"I do not know," Sarah said, though she did know. She had seen
death once again—death that had seemed impossible before Abigail's illness, now gathering its forces to invade their house.

"All of this will pass," her mother said. "The plants. The trees.
Even this house and the people in it. The Lord hath made it so. Yet

He hath also asked of us—each of us—to give names to life while we live. Name what you see, child. What shall we call this thing you have never seen and which terrifies you so?"

Sarah parted the curtain of her mother's dress and willed herself to open her eyes. She saw an ugly mess before her where earlier she had witnessed order. The plants she loved to name were no longer familiar. She remembered a verse from one of her father's sermons: *Thou shalt plant vineyards, and dress them, but shalt neither drink of the wine, nor gather the grapes; for the worms shall eat them.*

When Sarah looked into her mother's eyes, she saw something new inside them, a depth of feeling she later learned was her new brother. She reached for her mother's stomach, placed her palms there.

"I do believe you possess the gift, dear," Catherine said, sliding one hand to meet her daughter's. "You mustn't tell another soul or they'll call you a witch. Not until it is time."

Catherine closes the curtains, leaving a small gap through which she can watch her daughter. The girl stands rigid before the garden with a pile of tinder cradled in her arms, lost to the world. She has coddled the girl too much, it is true, but she had wanted Sarah to love her, to come to trust her, in a way she had neither loved nor trusted her own mother. From the bedroom, she can admire the simple braid she fixed for her daughter this morning, a ritual she finds comforting especially on these terrible days when her husband is gone.

Soon the girl will have to remember to cover her head even in the yard, to watch after the state of her undress. Soon it will be time to hide her from the boys, from the temptations of the forest. There is always much to fear, much to worry over.

Ezekiel sleeps soundly on the bed. She joins him there, lying in such a way that they might breathe the same air. He is still hers, and she his. Arthur was right; spoil him for a while yet while she can. His tiny hand finds her finger, grasps it tightly. His closed eyes wrinkle with effort. She is a giant beside him. She is far too large for this delicate creature. The world is far too large.

Since his son's birth, her husband has entered a new era of restlessness. At first, he had watched over the boy incessantly, peering into the crib as the child slept, asking her if she noticed anything odd about him. He had not done the same for Sarah. Catherine told herself it was because the new child would be an heir, someone to one day take his place, but she had come to believe there was something far more profound in her husband's worry. He began to ask her if the child might be possessed, if there might be some devilish tendencies in her sweet boy. Then, as though he had confirmed it, he began to avoid Ezekiel, to leave the room when she entered the parlor with the child in her arms. The result, it seemed to Catherine, was that her second-born was afraid of his father.

A grunt, sweet and quiet. He wants to fight the potion's effects. For a moment she worries the drug might kill him; she pictures his face turning blue in the dim. Then she remembers how Arthur has not lost a child since he came to their town a little more than a year ago, in all the months of her pregnancy. She closes her eyes, breathes in the scent of the potion on his breath—an unnatural sweetness, like overripened fruit.

"Wait and see," Arthur had said. "There is no fever at the moment. You've no need to fear typhoid."

"I am tired," she had said.

Some time later, after the child had fallen asleep on the table: "And his father? How does our Ezekiel take to him?"

Then those horrible words that issued from her mouth without warning. "I do not believe he loves his father." Where had they come from? Why had she told them to Arthur?

The man's eyes as she said this. Fear. Shock. Something else, perhaps. It was hard to say what disturbed her most about his reaction, but she knew it had something to do with his interest. As though Ezekiel were his primary concern, not hers. She had felt this before when in his presence, what she had told herself was a natural consequence of his preternatural gifts as a healer. Why had it bothered her this time?

She breathes in tandem with her son, sleep spinning its wool blanket over them. She listens for the faint sounds of her daughter preparing supper below. A bowl placed on the worktable. The scrape of ladle against pot. Quiet, careful sounds. The susurration beside her, the boy's lungs so small in comparison to the riot of his father's snoring. She can hear the wind outside picking up, a hollow probing as it seeks entry, then a low mournful moan as it turns back on itself in defeat.

Her childhood house had never been silent. Always her bedridden mother calling out for some task to be dealt with immediately, and Catherine, eldest of three daughters, was the one forced to carry out the woman's every wish. Catherine now craves silence within her own house. The groaning floorboards she quiets by sprinkling flour into their joints. Her mother's china, stacked in the entry sideboard, no longer clatters when someone descends the stairs, thanks to the cotton she has placed beneath the plates and cups. Even the birds have no place to build their nests in her eaves ever since Catherine strung up the netting Anne Lyman had lent her. She has taught her children to respect this silence, raised Sarah to speak only when she has something important to say. In this way she and Nathaniel have always been well matched. Better to save up one's thoughts, toss out the unimportant bits, and deliver one long, dazzling, and brilliant sermon brimming with the wisdom of the Holy Spirit. And oh, those sermons! When he is inside the house, she can feel the low rumbling of his thoughts collecting, a calming vibration that passes through her, gathering strength, awaiting the perfect moment— God's moment—when she will look up from the midst of the crowd to see her husband beatific and exalted, perfected. She can cope with all of his moods, his long bouts of coldness toward her, so long as he transcends his earthly shell to become this other man on Sabbath mornings. Yet, as of late and in this present moment—his long trips elsewhere, the neglect of his son, these hours she spends alone in the house—this she does not think she can abide much longer.

"I am sure that cannot be true," Arthur had said. "The heart is not always so simple."

In the physician's house there are many jars, glass jars of all sizes, lining the walls of his workroom. An additional lean-to for his growing collection of rare ingredients, many of which, truth be told, he simply wished to collect on account of his interest in botany. In the jar on his worktable is a fine powder made of cascarilla, often used as a tonic, a plant found only in the tropics, procured from a seaman who had taken a liking to him down at Long Wharf when he and his family had lived in Boston. The seaman had passed by Arthur, who was pretending to admire the waves lapping the piles; then, in a swift motion Arthur had come to associate with these assignations, the man returned, permitting his arm to graze Arthur's hips. Arthur waited a few moments before following the man down a narrow alley. When they finished, and the seaman surprised Arthur with a tender kiss on the neck, a promise was made: a sum of money for the cascarilla, a trade, for when the seaman next traveled to the West Indies. Always it had been this way with the men Arthur met at the wharves. Whatever pleasure he found there had soon been eclipsed by the trade, and he was able to tell himself the animal moans that escaped his mouth as the men entered him were merely part of the price of his science.

Lizard tails, fish scales, and ambergris he had collected by less complicated means. Though he gave up the wharves and the men and all that came with his previous life when he moved to Cana, he could not give up these rare ingredients. Here they sit beside pots of mint and juniper berries, a reminder that other flavors, other essences, continue to thrive on other shores.

Nathaniel had asked after the jars. It has been a little more than a year since then, a year that feels like an eternity. Sitting now at his desk not long after Catherine and Ezekiel Whitfield paid him a visit, Arthur wonders if none of this would have happened, none of this fine mess, had Nathaniel never asked.

Always a curious man, the reverend had gazed into the jars with his nose nearly touching the glass. His earnestness, his helplessness before the unknown, was so very handsome, so real. He had come for a salve, having injured his hand while repairing the meeting-house roof. The nail had not gone in too deep, Arthur saw. They barely knew each other at this point; it had been less than a few months since the Reverend Whitfield spoke before the stocks on Summer Street in Boston, where men were punished on a scaffold before the public, a fitting place for a sermon on freedom from sin. Arthur had gone to see him, this man people said had once led five hundred souls to be saved in one meeting.

The rest is now part of Cana's story: a wealthy physician leaving his comfortable post in Boston to join a small town, hardly a town really, of roughly two hundred souls who had all been converted thanks to Reverend Whitfield's words. As Nathaniel spoke, Arthur felt the hinges flying off their joints, the boards cracking, his limbs freed of their shackles. He did not have to do what he did at the wharves; he could simply love this man—a divine love, a Christ-love.

Arthur had added a handful of juniper berries, some beeswax, and a sprig of mint to the mortar. As his hands moved, he felt the rever-end's eyes upon him. "It won't hurt," Arthur said, trying to ease the familiar tension creeping through his legs, up his back. He felt if he turned away, he would soon feel that hand brushing his back. He dipped two fingers into the salve and held them up. The reverend held out his palm, and Arthur slid his free hand beneath the man's, steadying it so it no longer trembled. The reverend let out a small sound at this, something like a laugh or a cry. Carefully, Arthur pressed the salve into the wound. Once or twice, the reverend's hand jerked back, as though expecting pain, but Arthur knew there would be none; he knew there would be only a cooling relief, so he gripped the reverend's wrist to hold him fast. "Our Savior endured the whip and the cross," the reverend said. "Your reverend cannot endure a sting."

"There is no sting, reverend," Arthur replied. "It is your mind playing tricks."

Arthur must have known then. It would take some time, another month of dancing around it, but finally, one night when Arthur had seen the windows of the meetinghouse lit from inside and decided to pay his friend a visit, it had happened. He walked into the door where none should enter but the minister and discovered Nathaniel kneeling beside the pulpit, his wig cast aside, his natural hair pasted to temple and brow. A man afflicted. He walked to the minister's side and listened to the sound of their breathing in the cavernous hall. When his hand reached the minister's shoulder, faint words escaped the man's lips: "I discovered Catherine here, upon a pulpit much like this. She fell into my arms, and I kissed her before all the people of Hingham. I did not know why I had remembered it just now, why I felt such a powerful desire to pray this evening. Now I understand. The Lord was preparing me."

Arthur had heard the story, a famous one. Catherine crying out for salvation, the minister delivering her not only to God but also right into the arms of marriage. For once, Arthur did not choose his next words carefully. "Will you open your arms to me, reverend?"

And when it happened, he understood the Reverend Whitfield's words had not been freeing him from sin but rather leading him toward something more mysterious and binding, a love that felt divine. He had seen but a spark of that love when standing before the stocks on Summer Street, yet he had not understood it. He had cloaked it in a language incommensurate to the highest reaches of their bond, which exists beyond all human languages save, perhaps, that of touch. Some part of him had known he wanted this all along, all of those other men were leading him to this man, the one who spoke directly to his heart.

The knowledge that he is responsible for their coupling no longer troubles him. He views his predicament from afar, with a detachment he usually reserves only for his studies. Perhaps he should be fearful; perhaps he should worry after the state of his soul, but all that matters to him now is this love, keeping it alive, ensuring the reverend does not turn him away from the source of his happiness. He knows they view it differently, of course. The reverend believes their time together in the meetinghouse was but a slip, a mistake, perhaps a natural reaction to their close brotherly bond, but one the Devil has corrupted in order to drive them away from God. It is for this reason they have only come together in that way once; each time Arthur tries to draw closer, Nathaniel pushes him away. Arthur cannot understand this thinking; or rather, he cannot understand how this thinking can be so close to the reverend's heart, when all that drives Arthur, in the wake of their union, is desire, not thought. A desire that, in his case, makes him feel closer to God than ever before.

Could it be anything but a heavenly sign that Ezekiel Whitfield was born almost exactly nine months later? Could it even be possible that the seed spilled between them that evening had remained with Nathaniel as he lay with Catherine later that night with renewed vigor, lust carrying over from one body to the next, uniting them all? The only evidence he needed was the boy's features, which inexplicably resembled both of theirs and also Catherine's: a divine miracle. The Lord was known to work in such mysteries. None believed Mary at first; none would have her at the inn, yet see how she was blessed, see how she was vindicated.

He stands. The room tips, swaying. He steadies himself on the edge of the desk, waiting for the dizziness to pass. They had been here. He had pressed his hands upon the child's belly, soothed him as a father might. After his father, Catherine had said. Something had unlocked inside of him with her incantation. He had stared into those eyes so like Nathaniel's and seen himself reflected there, right in the center, where he belongs. He wanted to return with them to their house, care for the child in Nathaniel's absence, but he forced himself to remain calm. The child is not sick with fever, but something does indeed ail him. Even if it is not serious, his father must know. Yes, that is the right thing to do. Arthur must leave at once so he can tell Nathaniel. Less than half a day's journey to Stockbridge, but he can make the trip much sooner if he takes one of the Griggses' strong pacers. He banishes from his mind, as soon as it appears, the thought that he is fabricating an excuse to see Nathaniel again.

A few moments of slow breathing, and Arthur is calm. He heads up the stairs to tell Anne and Martha of his plan. No one in the parlor. The kitchen empty as well, the spout of Anne's teapot still steaming. He places one hand upon the side of the scalding teapot and holds it there a second too long. They had been here. His wife and daughter had been here and left him.

"Who is this stranger?" a voice behind him says. His wife's.

Arthur paints on a smile to hide his pain, tucking the injured hand into his coat pocket. He turns to Anne, who stands in the kitchen doorway with a genuine smile upon her lips, one hand on the frame. She is still young, thirty-one to his forty, and playful. Today she wears her market dress, an ugly sack that on her delicate frame looks like a costume, a smudge of dirt streaked across her reddened cheek for added effect. It is her day to stand beside Deborah Inverness, the merchant's wife, and assist that stern woman in Cana's unique system of trade, a system designed by all for the good of all, where none shall want for goods or money. She is proud of her task even as Deborah keeps her at a distance, even as the other inhabitants of Cana eye her with suspicion, as though she might be a popish spy.

"I saw you eyeing that teapot, stranger," she says. "My husband does not permit tea in this house, so if you wish to have some, you should have it now before he returns."

"How long have you been home?"

"An hour," Anne says. "Deborah brought in Goody Munn so she'll have someone else to spread her vile gossip with. I'm afraid I am lacking in that particular grace. But it was so quiet here—I thought you had gone out. What were you doing down there?"

Arthur feels caught out. Had he voiced any of his thoughts aloud?

"The tea, Arthur," Anne says, after a pause. "Would you like some tea?"

His palm has begun to pulse with each heartbeat. "We shouldn't be keeping tea. It is too expensive, too lavish. They'll think we haven't adapted to life in Cana, that we are too good for them. I hope you don't offer it to the other women."

"What other women?" Anne takes a seat at the table, propping

herself up by the elbows like an eager pupil. "There is no one to offer it to."

"The town will come round when they have need of our services,"
Arthur says. A parody of Catherine's words, for he doesn't yet believe them. Though he and Anne have given up their life in Boston
for Cana, there is something the flock seems to detect in them, some
worldly sheen lingering within their mannerisms and habits of
speech that keeps them separate from the rest. Though they store
their money in the city and rarely spend it on anything aside from
what is required of Arthur's practice, it seems nothing can wash
away the scent of their past.

"And what is my service to these people, Arthur?" Anne says,
staring longingly at her nails. He had helped her overcome the urge
to bite them, that nervous habit: a simple solution of kitchen pepper
and clove applied to each nail. "We've been here more than a year,
and still no one calls upon me. If I am to sit here every day in this
house by myself, I shall have my tea. Besides, Martha has given up
too much already. She is too young, Arthur, to give up every comfort."

"And what of Catherine for you? And Sarah as a companion for
Martha? There is some symmetry in the arrangement, after all."
Arthur places his good hand upon his wife's shoulder. "Are they not
someone?"

"Indeed, we must labor diligently, my dear husband, if we are to
finish your fine painting, for who shall be companion to Ezekiel?"

Arthur is glad his wife cannot see his expression. "Please be serious, Anne."

"Is the notion of welcoming another Lyman into this world not a matter of significance? It has been quite some time since we made the attempt." Anne presses Arthur's hand with her own. "Besides, they are the minister's family. They must be kind to everyone. It hardly counts as anything more than Christian charity."

"I believe Catherine at least sees something of herself in you. We are quite alike, the Lymans and the Whitfields. Oddly, I think we are all outsiders here."

Arthur sees the back of his wife's neck tense.

"You are indeed a stranger, husband," Anne says. "Are you so full of philosophy today?"

Arthur frees his hand and takes a seat opposite her. He must look a dandy with one hand still in his pocket, but Anne has not seemed to notice. "Catherine came to the house this morning with Ezekiel. The boy is sick."

"Oh dear. Is there anything I can do?"

"It seems I shall have to fetch the father," Arthur says, as casually as possible. "I do not believe it is anything serious, but one must always be cautious."

"Well, what is it then, if it is not serious?"

"I hesitate to call it a spiritual affliction. Yet it cannot hurt to ask the reverend to pray over him."

"Of course," Anne says, nodding. "But Arthur—isn't he due back tomorrow? Soon it will be a week, will it not?"

"I believe so," Arthur lies. "I've not kept count of the days. But you know how these men tarry. Stockbridge is a very busy place, and I wouldn't wish him to think he had leisure where he had not."

"Of course," Anne says, and Arthur must struggle not to hear the hint of irony. He turns to the kitchen window. Outside, the alders tremble, a buzzing of green. A thrush calls out four cheerful notes. He hears his wife move from the table, the scraping of the teapot, then a sharp sound as she pours out the precious brew.

The reverend does not waste time in Stockbridge. Every day, to maximize efficiency, he wakes at dawn, prayer poised on his lips. He opens his diary to the marked page and adds another prayer, a meditation on God's greatness. Miraculously, even as sleep lies coiled at the back of his mind, the reverend creates something beautiful with his words. It is his life's glory, these words; they come to him unbidden. Sometimes, after he finishes, he allows himself to marvel at the pages, at the strange consistency with which his mind has focused on the natural world. Here lies the spider, spinning string from its abdomen, launching into the great unknown in search of a home made of air. How close he brings us to Heaven, to a world made of gossamer which catches the morning's dew, spinning it into pearls which, in the right breeze, tremble like lost bits of sunrise, morning stars. Yet even as the spider is the perfection of the Lord's beauty, he is also the symbol of the world's evil. This home of his—this heavenly pattern—exists only to usher in death, to entrap his prey. Thence you are led astray by beauty, by the trappings of this world, soon to be sucked to a dry husk by a venomous foe. The reverend has taken to calling these natural portraits Shadows of Divine Things. Shadows, because what you first mistake as the purely divine in nature turns out, on closer inspection, to harbor the danger, the rot, the death and slow decay of this wicked world.

At seven, the reverend takes his Indian pudding and cider with the other white men and one Indian minister in the great hall of the newly built Mission House. As he eats, careful not to swallow too quickly, he admires the view from the windows on either side of the room: maples of startling abundance, their crisp greenness held by the sturdy bones below. The wooden spoon never scrapes his teeth.

The other men know to give him space. They congregate at a separate table, speaking in the hushed tones of young boys. During the past several years of working at the Stockbridge mission, all of them have felt, at some point in their tenure here, that the man must hate them, only to discover, a few days later, a gentle hand upon their shoulder, their name uttered sweetly in prayer, a surprise visit to one of their chambers during which Whitfield listens attentively to their many sorrows and tribulations. He is an odd man but an exceedingly kind one. There is something of a mixed nature in him, the light and the dark, the playful and the dreadful—a tortured soul if there ever was one—and yet perhaps because of this, because of his tortured life, his words are always powerful. And none will deny the power of his words, for when he does speak, all must listen. The reverend's mere presence at this newly established Indian mission all but ensures its success. When it was first proposed by Reverend Mathew Colman, Whitfield's venerable mentor, the very man who had first convinced Whitfield to travel to the colonies and pursue a life of itinerant preaching, there was never any doubt they would have need to call upon the extraordinary gifts this young man, now a man of forty, might use to persuade the local Mohican tribes to send their children to be educated by Christians.

The other man Mathew Colman chose for this mission is Reverend Thomas Alcom, the Mohican minister sitting at the opposite end of Whitfield's table, who hardly looks up but once or twice to glance at the other men. Thomas wears a black gown that pinches his wide shoulders, and he wears his hair naturally, long and black, eschewing the white wig that to him symbolizes popishness, corruption, and, though his criticism is careful, the white settlers themselves. He is self-assured, entirely independent; one might even say aloof, but the kindness of his eyes, his general air of tranquility, and his gift of speech place him solidly at Whitfield's table.

From the hours of eight to ten, Nathaniel and Thomas survey the progress of their mission. They climb the narrow Mission House stairs to the schoolrooms and listen as the schoolmaster reads from the primer and the Mohican children echo his words.

In Adam's fall
We sinned all.
Thy life to mend,
This Book attend.

The two men speak with the jointers and carpenters who have set about expanding the mission to other houses. They speak with Colman about funds, adjusting for minor changes and setbacks. They nod their heads slowly, with great sobriety, as numbers are recited. These two naturally taciturn men rarely speak to each other during these hours, but there is a conviviality that can sometimes be found

in their overly polite mannerisms, when Whitfield allows Thomas
to walk ahead of him or when Thomas holds a door for Whitfield.
Theirs is a God-given duty; they are brothers in Christ.

Much later in the day, after they have written their correspondences and tended to other pressing matters, when the schoolchildren have gathered round to hear first Whitfield then Thomas
preach the gospel in English then Mohican, the two men admire the
way the other speaks, the elegant pauses and surprising metaphors
that could never be anything but divinely inspired. Whitfield has
learned enough of the language to find it beautiful, and he must re-
strain himself from casting his hands into the air, from crying out
with pleasure at the sound of the gospel in this native tongue, the
glory of God's goodness reflected in these new sounds.

Except on this day, at the hour of four in the afternoon, something
unplanned has arisen in Whitfield's meticulously planned day. Stepping down from the wooden stage where he has just delivered his
sermon, he follows the children's rapt gazes to where there emerges
from a coppice of trees the outline of a horse with a man astride it.
Even before he can see the man's face, Whitfield knows at once who
it is. He sees it in the way one hand holds the reins with such easy
authority. He sees it again in the erect posture that seems held by an
invisible rope. He sees it in the bulk of the man, the way his largeness seems to dominate everything around him, though somehow
this largeness does not suggest clumsiness but rather a hidden elegance, as though this greater sense of scale has taught him to be
careful. And in this moment, when he sees the man before seeing
the man, Whitfield sees also the curve of Arthur's bare shoulders,
the dip between ribs and waist, the beautiful shock of hair traveling

from navel to groin. He sees his hand moving across the expanse, feels the sweat there, the subtle movement of breath so soft in that one spot of belly where Arthur is not muscle. He feels his head falling against this pillow of flesh, Arthur's fingers combing his hair, then the scent of Arthur's skin after it has been washed in his seed. All of this comes in the instance of recognition before recognition, a swelling of the bones. His face, without warning, has broken into a smile. He cuts through it with action, with speech.

"Arthur! What brings you to Stockbridge?"

The children have already gathered round this man on his horse, pulling him into the preaching circle. They ask him questions they have learned in English: Where are you from? What do you do? Why are you here? Arthur seems determined to answer each one, stepping down from his horse to squat beside them. Whitfield watches with pride as his friend pours his undivided attention upon each pupil. It is the touch that has already helped so many in Cana, has helped Whitfield a great deal more than any could imagine. He is happy to see Arthur. Simply happy. Yet soon, within a matter of seconds, he finds his body weighted with worry, his neck aching from the old tension. Arthur notices the change and draws nearer, parting the schoolchildren.

"It is nothing serious, reverend," Arthur says, nodding to Thomas, who has already begun shepherding the children inside the house. Thomas takes one long, hard look at Arthur, a look that could mean anything, and yet, knowing Thomas so well, Whitfield interprets it as curiosity. And curiosity, he has learned, is always dangerous.

Whitfield lowers his voice. "What can have happened?"

"I did not wish to interrupt you."

Whitfield leads them to the edge of the forest where the carpenters have begun constructing a new house for one of the schoolmasters, dappled shadow stretching for miles around.

"It's too late for that, friend. Say it." Even as he sees the shadow passing over Arthur's face, he knows he will only render those shadows deeper the longer Arthur stands before him in this public place. It is far too odd, showing up like this. Perverse, to almost wish something sufficiently terrible to have happened in order to account for his friend's visit.

"It is Ezekiel," Arthur says, stepping across the threshold of the future house, pausing in what will soon be the entry. Whitfield follows. "He is sick."

Despite dreading for these first few months of Ezekiel's life that this moment might come, Whitfield cannot hide his reaction, the sharp wince that, as though he has been cut, ripples across his features. So the Lord has finally decided to take this child from him, to remove him from their pernicious influence. There need be no marking or sign of the Devil's hold; Whitfield had been searching all these months for such a mark in vain. No, only this swift judgment while he is away from home, as clear a sign as any of his guilt.

"It is not serious," Arthur says, seeming to sense Whitfield's worry. "But I believe he misses you."

A moment for Whitfield to take in Arthur's words. The child is not sick, not really. He remembers to breathe.

"Misses me?" Whitfield laughs out his relief. "Why did you frighten me so, friend? I shall return tomorrow."

Arthur turns, a look of such pleading in his eyes that Whitfield must look away.

"Ah," Whitfield says, shaking his head. "I see."

"No, it is not only that," Arthur says. "Of course I miss our friendship. But it is not only that. I felt it significant Catherine should come to see me."

"Catherine came to your house? With the boy?"

"Yea."

Whitfield steps over a pile of lumber. He waits for the image to leave his mind, the thought of Catherine seeing the look on Arthur's face as he gazes down at the boy. What might she have witnessed there?

"What good will it do to spoil the child if he is not sick?"

"I do not see it as spoiling," Arthur says, echoing his friend's laugh. "We're learning a great deal about the human animal. Philosophers are now saying humans are primarily driven by the passions. We must, to a certain extent, indulge those passions at an early age."

"That is precisely the problem, Arthur. The boy was conceived almost to the day—"

Arthur places a hand on Whitfield's shoulder. Whitfield shrugs it away.

"Is it my fault you chose to lie with her so soon after?" Arthur had been riven with jealousy when he discovered Catherine was pregnant, almost as though she had stolen the gift of their coupling from him. Then, as the months passed, he began to see the unborn child as a miracle, a sign the boy was in some part his as well; since Nathaniel would no longer permit their union, Arthur was at the very least able to live and feast upon the product of their love. When Ezekiel was born, the resemblance was unmistakable; even Whitfield admitted privately to Arthur, while in a state of paternal giddiness, that the boy shared all three of their features.

"What I am saying," Whitfield says, his tone softening, honeying into the sounds Arthur loves to hear more than all else, "is we must be careful with Ezekiel. We cannot allow our influence to alter him. I want him to have every opportunity. I want him to become the best minister this world has ever seen, to live freely in such a way that he does not doubt himself on account of the temptation we both feel."

"Yet he will face some temptation, reverend," Arthur says. "Even Christ was tempted in the wilderness. You cannot prevent it from happening. It is the way of all flesh."

"Arthur, you and I both know any temptation he might face will be far better than the one we feel for each other."

Arthur reaches out once more, this time with his injured hand. And this time, Whitfield allows it.

"No," Arthur says. "I do not know this, reverend. I'm almost certain I wouldn't trade this temptation for another."

"Quiet," Whitfield says. Yet even as he says this, he presses his hand against Arthur's. When he is near his friend, even in public, he feels himself drawn in, magnetized by the pull that makes him want to run his fingers over every part of the man, commit to memory every dip and dimple, every blemish. The knowledge of this man's body: a kind of gnostic scripture. The touch: an exquisite burning.

"Thank you for that," Arthur says, pressing harder despite the pain.

Whitfield steps into the yard, leaving the house behind. Arthur remains standing in the future parlor.

"A house made of air," Whitfield says.

"What is that?"

"This morning I was thinking of the spider. How he spins a house made of air. All of that beauty merely to entrap his prey."

Arthur clenches his hand into a tight fist, digging his nails into the tender flesh. "We humans are not so different," he says, stepping closer to the invisible wall.

Awakening from a void later that evening, Ezekiel hears his mother say, "I have done everything. I have done everything, and nothing works. I am frightened, husband." He opens his eyes. His father's hands swoop down to cradle him. "Let me try," his father says. "You need your rest. I'll care for the boy tonight." Ezekiel falls against the man's solid chest and cries so hard his breath catches. He might die of happiness. He hiccups into half slumber, drowning in the unnamable scent of his father.

Now comes the time when he remembers them both—the shore and the darkness between each shore—and he longs for them both. A soul flickers to life in his chest.

His father carries him down the stairs to the parlor where the heirloom clock ticks its loud seconds. The light has faded from the windows, but there is the low fire and the glowing orange tongue of the hearth, shadows sculpting strange creatures all about. Man and child make one, their forms melded into an ungainly beast.

"You missed me, my sweet one?" his father says.

Ezekiel lifts a hand to touch his father's face, but it is too distant. His father draws him closer. Fingers trace the man's chin, hard and full of stubble. He wants to be pressed against it, but his father lowers him once more to his chest. There is a loud thudding as his ear meets the surface, an angry life there, powerful and proud. He listens as its thudding grows louder and faster. He listens and listens as his father holds him to his chest; he listens until the sound is no longer frightening, until the sound becomes his sound, part of his own chest. The sound is unlike any he has heard before—or perhaps, yes, he has heard it before, only it was a different beating. It had once been his entire life, this sound, then it was taken from him, only to rarely hear it. How he had missed it. How he had missed it without ever knowing it was missing.

Ezekiel closes his eyes and forgets his fear.

"You missed your father, boy?"

Ezekiel opens his eyes to a brighter room. Another fire, this one far more powerful. His sister scrapes at a plate. She smiles at him. Her braid has unraveled from the heat and toil, and now two perfect waves fall on either side of her face. He sinks with his father to the worktable, holding fast to the man's neck, his feet tumbling into the soft part of the man's stomach, a spongy bed that makes his toes tingle.

"Are you the woman of the house now, Sarah?"

"And why not, Father?" Sarah places a bowl of pease stew before them. Ezekiel marvels at the colors: orange swimming in a yellowish broth with bits of meat like floating planks.

"I suppose it is time," his father says, sighing.

"You and Mother are always complaining about your duties, but I find them quite easy to manage. Mother has been asleep nearly all afternoon."

"You say so only because they are new to you. Give it time, Daughter, and you shall complain."

"I shall never complain so long as I live. It is unchristian to do so. We must be humble, and charitable."

"Not only are you now the woman of the house, but you have also taken my position. I see we shall soon have two more preachers in the family, isn't that right, Ezekiel?"

At this, his father places a hand on the back of Ezekiel's head. Ezekiel leans into the hand, then falls once more onto his father's chest. As his father eats, Ezekiel can feel the man's chest moving, each spoonful passing somewhere beneath him.

"And your mother?" his father says, his voice changing, cautious now. "Did she complain of anything?"

"She only said she needed a sleep."

"She went with the boy to the Lyman house?"

"Yea, Father. It was a precaution. But he is better, now you are here. We are all better when you are here."

A long pause. His father's breathing grows shallow. "And did you notice any change in her when she returned?"

Another long pause. His father's chest rises and falls, rises and falls.

"Why do you ask? Is something wrong with Mother?"

"No, child. Do not worry."

Ezekiel lifts his head, and here is his sister, beaming down at him.

She presses her brow to his, spreading her warmth. Though she is smiling, he feels her worry.

"He grows so quickly, doesn't he?" his father says.

"If I should ever have one of those, I'll not let it grow. I'll keep him at this very age when he is perfect."

"And what will you do? Bind him?"

"If I must."

"It is not very becoming in a mother to practice such cruelty."

"It is only cruelty if one presumes that this is a child, not a cherub," Sarah says, the worry leaving her once more. She lowers her head, nudging Ezekiel with her nose. She smells of garlic and ash and something earthy. He leans back into his father's arms and giggles. "Let us hope he also remains our quiet saint, Father, else I shall have to bind his lips. You were not here for the worst of it."

"I leave you for one week, Sarah, and you've already developed the sharpest tongue in Cana. If I didn't know better, I'd think you were truly set on replacing me."

It is past midnight by the time Sarah drifts to sleep. She has said her prayers three times, one for each member of the Whitfield house. Always, when she arrives at herself, she pauses. She cannot think what to pray for, what to request, what she must be forgiven for doing. Her mind becomes blank, a fog drifts over her, and the nightly visions return. Sometimes they are of forest animals nosing their way into her chamber, wild beasts tamed to mildness for her enjoyment: a wolf lowering its head in deference, a buck with towering antlers sinking to its knees. Other times they are of people in the town, changed somehow by sorrow or immense happiness or by age, worry, distortions of the flesh. Tonight she sees Arthur Lyman with a wide smile upon his lips, made more handsome by the moonlight. Then she sees her mother, oddly proud and confident, head high. Her mother's form lowers to the bed, and soon she is beside Sarah, already asleep, in such a deep slumber her eyelids twitch with her own visions.

The packed straw at Sarah's back needles her awake again. She is surprised to hear quiet, a quiet she has not heard all week. Ezekiel asleep in his crib. All week it had been Sarah and her mother holding him in the middle of the night, rocking him until the sounds of his crying quieted but never ceased completely. Mostly it had been Sarah. She had not wanted to wake her mother, her sleep so rare as of late. Sarah would take him in her arms and carry him to the window, quietly opening it to the dark where trees could be felt but not seen, a blind mass that seemed to grow larger in the imagination the longer she stared into its blackness. Sometimes it seems to Sarah that the forest will swallow their town if she is not watching, that her father has carved Cana out of a wood seeking its original form, wishing to be united with its dark brethren. She does not know why such visions assault her, why she cannot see the natural world as simply as her mother sees it. She stood at the window with Ezekiel in her arms and tried to see the darkness as a babe might: a place where things are quieter.

Tonight there are no sounds. The afternoon wind has died, the moon returned with its icy glare. Sarah turns on her side, relishing the soreness of her limbs, the new weight in her neck from bending low to stir the pot. She is a woman now with a woman's duties. Her mother has told her there will soon be a change in her body, but she had not told her there would be this change in her mind. For once she is too tired to worry about the forest outside her window. Perhaps soon she will be cleaning and washing at the river and speaking with the other women in the market, at the looms. A sharp pain somewhere in her chest as she remembers Abigail Jacobsen, how they had wanted to do these things together, to have a partner in all the tasks women do, so none of it would be truly scary, all of it exciting. Now Sarah must become a woman alone. Even so, she wants to do it. She wants to move past what she has known and see things from the distance of maturity. Perhaps then she will no longer find the forest and its visions so frightening.

She cannot see Ezekiel in his crib, but she can feel him, the quiet life there, just as she can feel her mother and father sleeping above her chamber. When her father is not here, the house loses meaning, the rooms narrow, the air seems less abundant. It is not so much that she misses him, for they do not speak but once or twice a day; their conversations are often labored, and she has learned over the years that he is uncomfortable around children, yet he is the one they all turn to for guidance. Even when he does not know the right path for them, his stern, proud voice tells them there will be a solution sooner or later, even if the solution is that nothing can be done. Then, at the end of the week, when she sees him ascend the pulpit, Sarah knows whatever path they are on will be guided by God's wisdom; God has chosen to bless them with His voice. She has more than once been angry at her father's distance from her; she has even viewed him as a weak man with petty concerns, but always she returns to this assurance that God is speaking through him.

A creaking now in the hallway. A loose board, one her mother has forgotten to sprinkle with flour. She makes a note to tend to it tomorrow morning before Catherine notices. Much of being a woman is rendering all effort invisible. She thinks of her mother's worried face this afternoon, how she had seemed changed after her visit with Arthur Lyman. Her father had asked after this, and Sarah had not told the truth, perhaps because she had not noticed the change until her father asked. She had been too preoccupied with making supper. She thought it simply had something to do with days and days of tending to a crying babe, and perhaps that is the truth of it, nothing more. Her mother only needed sleep.

The creaking grows louder, loud enough to alert Sarah to the fact that someone is outside her door, moving through the hallway. The steps are careful. She thinks of the story her father once told her of the Dark Man who stalks the forest at night with his Red Book. He is the Devil's incarnation, bidding young children sign their names in blood in exchange for infinite delight, forbidden pleasures. Perhaps he has come for her tonight, and she will have the chance to deny him, to prove her worthiness before God. She opens her eyes as wide as they will go so she will see him enter. Though the Word of God is not beside her, she knows her prayers will keep her safe; God will not abandon her. It may not be the same for Ezekiel. Perhaps it is possible to corrupt one so young, one who has not yet understood the Word. The thought pins her to the mattress. She wants to rush to the crib beside the door and wrap Ezekiel in her embrace, protect him with her prayers, but she finds she still cannot move. With each creaking of the boards, her muscles tighten.

When the figure emerges in the doorway—this tall man, his natural black hair grazing his shoulders—she does not recognize him at first. It is rare to see her father without a wig even inside their house. Rarer still to see him out of the black gown he wears even at supper, stiff white tabs always spotless. In his shirt and breeches he is thinner, with long arms and legs. She has never seen a man like this, never so much of one. Here is a strange beast.

Her father. This stranger.

She watches him approach the crib and lean over the lip. Worry written upon his face, the fear of what he might see there. She thinks of the words she had heard him ask her mother: *Is the child not possessed by some spirit? Is there not some affliction within him?* Sarah had been in the room when her mother gave birth to Ezekiel, hidden behind a curtain. She had seen the babe emerge a bloody terror but had seen also how the midwife, Mercy, cleansed him with water from an earthenware bowl, how perfect he looked when he returned to lie upon his mother's breast. Her father could not stop searching for marks, some sign that something was wrong. Mercy told him to cease all of his rough handling, to marvel at the beauty of a perfect birth. The town had not known Mercy had come to their house, but her mother insisted on having a midwife all the same, since Sarah's birth had been long and painful. Sarah remembers this woman with a witchy clove scent entering their house with her strange ways. Does he feel Mercy has corrupted the boy, or might there be something else?

He stands, peering into the child's face. She cannot tell how long. She worries that if he turns to her she will scream. The hollows of his eyes are shadow. The intensity of his silence a loud clanging. He reaches into the crib, picks Ezekiel up, and carries him out of the room into the darkness of the hallway.

Sarah wills herself to move. Her head swims with the sight of this stranger her father has become. The floor shifts beneath her bare feet. She turns right into the dark hallway, hurrying up the stairs, making her way to her parents' chamber. Through the cracked door she can see her mother asleep on her side, arms curled round her front as if to protect herself, her face free of wrinkles, pale and soft in the moonlight. Sleep has carried her to a better place.

Once downstairs, Sarah pauses within the parlor. The heirloom clock ticks loudly, its ormolu trim now silvered like sunken treasure. She cannot tell where they have gone, but there aren't many places to go, and something tells her the black forest, site of her visions, has already taken them. Into the kitchen, then out into the garden where, just beyond, the pale figure of her father stands beside the well, head tilted to sky.

"Shall we go, Ezekiel?" he says.

The night air is cold, the moon winking above like a polished coin. Sarah's shift is too thin to protect her, the ground beneath her feet still wet from yesterday's rain, but she has no time to return for her boots. Her father has entered the forest path with Ezekiel. Soon she will lose them to the thick branches. She follows at a distance, careful not to make a sound. The steps go on for so long that her eyes begin to grow heavy; she worries she may succumb to sleep before they reach their destination. Before long, however, a wandering flame appears in a meadow beside them. It is her favorite meadow in the daytime, one her mother has taken them to on many occasions, a place where they might gather cardinal flowers in the spring, shocking red petals opening to the sun like a beckoning hand. Now, with the flame casting its orange glow upon these scarlet flowers, there appear two rivulets of fire, with a man standing at the center of it all, holding a lamp aloft for her father's passage. The Dark Man. He has already taken them.

"Arthur," her father says.

The man comes closer, close enough for Sarah to see his face. The man does indeed resemble Arthur Lyman. She watches as he places the lantern upon a rock at his feet and takes Ezekiel in his arms.

"You shouldn't bring him outside without a blanket," the man says. "The season is still too cool."

Her father remains silent.

"He doesn't cry in your arms any longer," the man resembling Arthur Lyman says.

"He never cried in yours," her father finally says.

"When I saw him today with Catherine, I swore he recognized me."

"Perhaps it was the drug."

"No, it was before that. I believe Catherine may have even noticed. You are cold as well, reverend. Come closer."

To Sarah's great shock, her father obeys the command without hesitation. His head sinks to the man's neck. With his other arm, the man resembling Arthur Lyman presses her father closer to him. Her father looks so small beside this large man in his leather duster.

"Does he not look more like me every day?" the man says. "My sweet one. He looks more like both of us."

"Your words carry some truth."

"How I have missed this."

Her father sighs. The sigh is louder than anything he has said. "Why couldn't you see him again in your house, Arthur? The boy has every reason to call upon his physician. I could have brought him tomorrow when Anne and Martha were out."

"I wanted to meet here once more before things change. It has given me such joy, meeting you with him here these past months."

"It is nice."

"And you've enjoyed our times here?"

"We'll see each other every day, Arthur. Ours is a small town. There's no need to be so—"

"Will he think of me when he passes this place? Will he see Martha as a sister, do you think? Perhaps they'll be good friends, our children. I spoke of it to Anne just today. If you can believe it, she even wishes us to try for another child. Perhaps it may be the same as with Ezekiel—"

"No. We cannot think in this way."

"Yea, friend, you are always right, of course. Even so, our children may grow close."

"They may sense something without knowing it. I do not think it entirely possible to hide every effect of our union."

"Thank God for that."

"There is no other path, Arthur. We must stop meeting here. We must stop thinking of ourselves as a family."

"This is my home. You are my family."

"Arthur."

"Don't go on," the man says.

"I cannot hear it, Arthur," her father says, weeping softly. "I cannot bear to hear it."

Her father frees himself from the man's embrace, Ezekiel in his arms once again. She can see he has made up his mind to leave; soon he'll discover her. Fearing for her life lest the Dark Man steal her soul as well, Sarah takes one last look at the figures, the three of them huddled together, the word "family" still ringing in her ear. She does not understand what she has seen and heard here, but she knows she was never meant to see or hear it; what she has witnessed will forever change the course of her life, of all their lives, has already changed it.

Back in bed, Sarah tries to slow her breathing, feigning sleep. She hears her father enter, the same careful creaking of the board. She feels him pause beside her, feels almost the touch of his hand upon her brow.

"Pray for me, Daughter," he whispers.

Then he is gone, and all is quiet. She keeps her eyes closed, hoping to render all of it a mere dream. None of it was real, all of it a dark illusion sent from the Enemy to snare her. Another vision of hers and nothing more.

By morning, when she kicks off the bed sheets, her mud-caked toes glare up at her.

2.

Summer

In the first few weeks of summer, Catherine says to Sarah: "More ashes. Move your hand like this and scrub. You are too easy with it. Vinegar won't hurt your soft hands. Scouring paper will do the trick before long, and you'll be grateful since fire won't bother you then. This is called rosemary, not Thee-of-Little-Hands. Rosemary is a girl's name. You steep it here, in this. Months. Many months."

Sarah's knees burn from the work, heat bathing her hair in sweat. Drops scatter upon fresh-polished wood, mocking her progress. From the kitchen window she can see the garden and its milk-green light teasing her, asking her to step into the yard where, not many months ago, she had seen her father crane his neck to the band of stars, and say, "Shall we go, Ezekiel?" She lowers her eyes.

Since she began learning from her mother, her body aches every night, her back feels older than her age, knots crawl up her shoulders into her neck, so each night she must spend an hour digging at the hot cords. And each night, after she has tended to her neck, she prays a new prayer: Lord, help Mother to be strong, help Ezekiel to be strong, help Father to be strong . . . but when she reaches her own name, she cannot utter the words. She does not know how to be strong, not in this way, not after what she has seen. She cannot look at anyone the same way again. In the square when she greets Deborah Inverness or Goody Munn or any of the other women, she imagines them joining her father and brother and the Dark Man in the forest clearing at night, their faces altered by flame, by the surrender she had witnessed in her father's face. Sin has always seemed distant, impossible, something only those outside of Cana could fall prey to. Now she knows this is a lie. Sin lives in her own home.

Her mother sits behind her on an old stool that wobbles each time she crosses her legs. Sarah cannot tolerate the sight of such childish disorder, as though her mother has suddenly forgotten herself. She tries to hide her irritation. Only recently she had wanted to learn everything from this woman, to take up her duties in this house as a grown woman would. Now she feels as though her mother has betrayed her, for she must have known something of the reverend's secret life. Sarah has been played a trick on, coddled so she would never understand the truth of this world. A woman must hide all effort, but must she also hide all sin? Is this but another duty Sarah must learn? If only Abigail were here to help guide her through this maze.

After Sarah has cleaned the kitchen floor, she begins making a humble pie. This is her favorite moment of the day, for she is a natural cook. As she beats at the clove and mace, the sheep's heart a glistening ruby at her elbow, her hands move by instinct, ease.

Afternoon sunlight inches its way across the room to her, and though it is hot, she welcomes the change, the way she can glimpse her progress anew in each surface's reflection. The house will never be clean, but for a moment she will know she has done right. If she can keep this house clean, she may prevent the evil from crossing their threshold, from sneaking into her chamber and stealing what remains of Ezekiel's soul.

More wobbling behind her. She glances over her shoulder to find Ezekiel climbing onto her mother's lap, latching himself to her breast. Ezekiel's hair has grown to a fine shade of chestnut, his cheeks red and full. He is fat and healthy, with greedy, searching hands that cannot get enough of life. He presses into her mother's pale skin, marking her. As Sarah continues watching, it is as though a transparent curtain has been peeled back to reveal another scene behind this one: Ezekiel closes his eyes, suckling, his fingers pressing deeper into Catherine's flesh, and Sarah cannot but think of an incubus waiting for the perfect moment to corrupt her mother. She returns to the sheep's heart, the swell of angry red. She must banish the vision from her mind. He is an innocent child; there is no proof he signed his name in the Devil's Book. It is entirely possible she has imagined it all despite the mud on her feet. The Devil has been known to play such tricks, turning family against family. This vision might be no more real than the animals she sees entering her room at night. If she can forget this feeling, she may save herself from the snares of the pit. She may return to seeing her mother as a wise woman. She may even be able to sit through one of her father's sermons without the odd sensation that someone else is watching him with such intensity that no one else's gaze may rival it. She may convince herself that those intent eyes do not belong to Arthur Lyman, whom, when once she turned to follow the source of her discomfort, she discovered with head uplifted and eyes wetted.

"Sarah, remember to melt the butter first," her mother says. "I've told you not to rush it. Your father does not return until much later. Much later these days. He avoids us. He avoids the sight of his son, which pains him for reasons I cannot comprehend. Take the edges up, just so. You must cover it all. Do not be afraid to cover it all."

"I will cover it," Sarah says, biting her lip, trying not to imagine her father at the Lyman house without them, living some other life with this man.

"Does he speak to you?" Her mother's voice is soft now. "When he comes to your chamber at night, does he tell you why? Sometimes I wake up, Sarah, and he is not there. I know he must be walking the child to calm him or else tending to his duties as night watchman. That is why, I suppose, isn't it, Sarah? Now we place it—we place it—here, ah, yes, that's done now, only a little leak, now we will see if he keeps it down."

Sarah wants to ask more, but she knows she must wait. Her mother will tell her what is on her mind if she will only pretend to be uninterested. She picks Ezekiel up and tugs his arms round her neck. She wipes his mouth with the edge of her sleeve. He gurgles up at her, half frown, half smile. She runs her fingers through his hair, aging him comically with flour. He falls upon her breast, and for a moment she imagines having a child of her own, watching him age through the years. How strange it would be, perhaps even wondrous. Yet even as she kisses his cheeks, smiling into his soft skin, she feels this is not for her; God has other plans for her life. It seems to her now that her lifelong duty is to watch over her brother, and no one else; he is far too delicate a creature for this hard world.

"Has he told you, Daughter?" her mother says, joining Sarah at the worktable. She is livelier, more awake than she has been in days. Sarah has tried to ignore the long afternoon naps, the promises that she would be only a few minutes when, in reality, she is always more than an hour. "Has he told you our story? The real story, not the one he tells the flock. It was not always like this, coming home so late in the evening. No, not always. Before you were born—even when you were born—he was a different man. You should know this, Sarah, now you're becoming a woman. Men possess the power to change. Women cannot change, not truly; they have no such luxury. Come, help me with the bedpans while we let that rest."

Sarah follows her mother to her parents' chamber. Each bounce up the stairs draws a happy sigh from Ezekiel. Once in the chamber, Sarah is surprised to find the curtains still drawn, this darkness her mother has permitted during the day. Even the air smells stale, cramped, not unlike a sickroom.

"Hold it level or you'll spill it," her mother says, pointing to the space beneath the bed. Sarah passes Ezekiel to Catherine, then gropes beneath the bed, fingers searching cautiously for the bedpan. She wonders how long it will take her mother to tell the story of who her father was. She cannot imagine any story will explain the reverend to her, yet she must know more. She must be patient. Her investigation must not reveal too much, for then she can be sure her mother will not tell her the truth.

"The things you don't see," her mother says, almost as though answering her thoughts. "Did you even know I did this for you every day? Did you think some faery swept into your room? Now hold it steady, child, and we shall carry it to the garden. But first you must read it aloud."

Sarah has never taken notice of the words written along the sides of the pot, symbols that had always seemed mere decoration. Her father has insisted she learn how to read; all of the girls in Cana learn alongside the boys. Cana is a place of equality, he preaches. No servants or slaves, and no making slaves of women, but an equal division of labor for all. Her mother has told her these truths are not always realities in Cana; the men often fall short. Sarah is beginning to understand just how far from the ideal they have fallen. Still, she does recognize these symbols. If she sounds them out . . .

"You-s-s-s-s me well and k-k—"

"Keep."

"Keep me k-k-k-line."

"Clean."

"Clean. And I will not tell w-h-hu—"

"What."

"What I ha-ve su-su—"

"Seen. Now together: Use me well and keep me clean . . ."

"Use me well and keep me clean . . ."

"And I will not tell what I have seen."

"And I will not tell what I have seen."

Sarah follows her mother into the garden. She does not look up toward the well and the forest path beyond it. It is a dark blur at the edge of her vision.

"Now toss it here. This will help them grow. Life works in this way. What we do not need we give to the plants. Don't make a face, Daughter. It is good and natural. One day your body will be food."

"Yet my soul will be elsewhere."

"Yea, Daughter. You say your prayers at night. 'Now I lay me down to sleep.' What did you think those words were for? Words have meanings, dear. 'If I should die before I wake . . . '"

"'I pray the Lord my soul to take.'"

"Yea, girl. There is life, then there is death. That is why your father spends his time concerned with people's souls. Everyone's souls but ours. He was not always this way. He was a different man. Yea, he does indeed care for this little one right here, though he cannot tolerate being in the same room with him for very long. Would you hold him a moment, dear? Just a moment while Mother plucks these nasty leaves. You should be glad for the practice. This will be you one day. Not every little girl learns it before her time. I didn't. No, Mother didn't shield me. She hated me. She wasn't protecting me. She was crippling me. She was too bitter to live, and I was too much life. You should be glad you never met her. I studied what she did to me and I did the opposite to you. Maybe I did too much, protected you from too much, since now you seem shocked by everything. What really troubles you, girl?"

Her mother gestures toward the forest path, the one place Sarah won't look. "Is there something here which troubles you?"

Sarah pauses, cautious.

"No, Mother," she lies.

"I'm not certain I believe you, Sarah, but let us go inside and tend to the pie."

Sarah follows her mother up the path. After a long silence, she says, "How different?"

Her mother stops in the doorway. "How different what?"

"How different was father?"

Her mother does not answer for some time. Then, as though she has not heard Sarah, she says, "Oh, but we've forgotten the hens, haven't we?"

They walk to the far edge of the yard where the coop rests. The hens are loud, as always, when Sarah approaches. When she was younger, she had taken some delight in pestering them, chasing them about the yard with her favorite walking stick, and it is as though their blood remembers her cruelty. Sarah cannot stand the desperate sounds they make, a cry she imagines people will make when the world is ending. Ezekiel reaches a tiny hand out to pet one, and Catherine lowers him to the ground, steadying him on his feet. He toddles forward with her help, fingers grazing feathers. The hen arches her neck, cautious but permissive. He has a way with animals. It is something they first noticed when a stray cat appeared at their front door. Catherine had opened the door to chase it away since it had been such a nuisance in the past, stalking the chickens, meowing late at night beneath their windows. Ezekiel in her arms, Catherine kicked at the creature as always, yelling for it to leave, but this time the cat pressed itself against her leg, and when she very carefully sat Ezekiel next to it, the cat began to purr. Sarah has more than once suspected that the child possesses a special connection to the natural world. It is one of the many reasons she is so protective of him; he is so trusting, and thus far the world has answered back in kindness. Sarah now knows this will not always be the case.

"We check the eggs this way," Catherine says, shooing away a hen. She lifts one of the eggs and shakes it a little, close to her ear. Ezekiel tugs at her other hand, arms outstretched, ready for another pet. Sarah follows her mother's instructions, forcing herself to feel nothing when she sends another hen on her way, trying not to think of stealing another animal's baby. Arthur's words: *Does he not look more like me every day?*

"When he came to my town, more of a village really . . ." Catherine says, drawing Ezekiel back to her side. "When he came to Hingham, there had only ever been one itinerant preacher before him, a sad little old man who didn't stir up much of anything good or bad. Our village assumed that was what he would be, too, because he also came from London, and none of those Londoners could seem to stop staring at our primitiveness long enough to see us, though some of us, like my own mother, had come over from England not long ago and still laid claim to a fine title. So here comes your father looking like another sad little old man, only in truth he wasn't little or old. He was but thirty then and I not yet seventeen. Though to a young girl, to someone like yourself, he would have seemed plenty old."

Sarah removes two spotted eggs from the nest.

"Fold up your hem, like so." Catherine makes a little pouch with the bottom of her dress. "Place them carefully inside, one by one."

Sarah copies her mother. She places the eggs inside the pouch, careful not to clack them together.

"How did he look, back then?"

"Much the same. He wore a thick black robe even in the hottest summer I've ever known, and a white-powdered wig, and a pair of dark iron nose glasses he kept in his left hand all the times I saw him, save when he stooped over the Bible, which I came to find was often. I might not have taken any notice of him had it not been for his eyes, unusual in a young man. Deep set and dark, night dark, so dark I thought his pupils must have burst. He kept a spike of golden rye in one corner of his mouth. I watched him cross our mangy little street from my mother's chamber window. I remember thinking even then a man like that belonged in a better place, a town of his own. I even liked the way his shadow looked on the ground behind him. There was something inside that shadow. Mother sat behind me in her sickbed, asking why my spine shot up so straight. 'Nothing,' I said. 'Nothing?' she said. 'I've been on about your posture since you were born and now you decide to sit up straight?' She was angry, always. Her speech may sound funny when I repeat it but, Daughter, believe me, she'd a way of stringing words together so full of hatred you thought the walls might catch fire."

One of the eggs drops to the ground, cracking open like a tiny, accusing sun. A hen clucks disapprovingly at Sarah's heels. She had not been paying attention, so engrossed was she in her father's story.

"What must you do?" Catherine says.

"Keep it clean." Sarah squats down to scrape up the mess. Ezekiel wobbles over to help, falling to his knees. He does not cry. His days of relentless crying seem to have come to an end, at least for now.

"'Claim him,' my mother said to me from her deathbed. 'Or some whore will.' She respected Reverend Nathaniel Whitfield's air of the Old Country. More than that, she knew he was the best man I could find, since I was the plainest of three sisters. The dress I wore to the meetinghouse was white, simple, but I embroidered it with fine lion's tooth. Hair done up in a plain bun. Nothing I could do to my face without looking like one of those whores Mother always seemed to imagine everywhere, though I did bite my lips just seconds before entering the sanctuary. I have wonderful lips. I have always been very proud of my lips. Look at your sweet mother's lips when she bites them. You, too, have them. Father's stern frown and Mother's lips. Vanity is the Devil, so don't spend too much time thinking you're special. Just a nice little thing to know. Whose features, do you reckon, young Ezekiel shall favor? I see your father in him, yea—the rest is a mystery, I suppose, until he is older. Here. Bite them like this. Not too hard. I stood in the back of the sanctuary biting my lips, for it was far too crowded to sit in my usual place beside Father, and I watched this London minister tilt his head back to the ceiling and sing God's praises. I felt something in my belly—here, right here, this is where you'll feel it one day—as I watched him pound the pulpit with his fists, his face red, tears streaming down his face. It was strange to see such emotion in a man. He cried before us all, but it had the opposite effect it usually had. You might see a man crying on the street at night, usually a drunk. You know Hiram, who lives in one of the public house's cabins."

"The man with the cane?"

"Yea. No doubt injured himself from some drunken fall. Your father has worked on that man's soul more than any other, and all for nothing. Some men are beyond the Lord's dominion. I do not like to say it, but there isn't a sliver of a chance he is of the Elect. Yet the Reverend Nathaniel Whitfield gives up on no soul, save those of his family. He'll be home even later today, I guarantee. You see a man like Hiram and you feel nothing but pity. But you couldn't pity your father. No, his tears were his strength."

"Is crying not weak?"

"You could say his weakness leant him strength. His was another form of weakness, one I had never seen before. Certainly not in my father, who was weak but never showed it. Father squandered most of Mother's money, for she was the one who married down. She was foolish and mean, and her foolishness and meanness are what I believe brought on her sickness. She wanted to be better than everyone, better even than her own title and her family's rank, but when she became poor, she realized her mistake. I could never believe she was truly sick. She suffered in limbo, a woman too dignified to live and too proud to be dignified. Yes, yes, I think it is time for a very short rest, don't you, Sarah? We'll bring in the eggs and move to my chamber, and you shall keep me company while I rest my eyes for a moment. I shouldn't have used the word 'limbo.' Limbo is for papists. Forget the word. It has no use, since it does not exist. There is only life and death, Heaven and Hell. Though, yes, it is a helpful word for that feeling, the feeling that sometimes comes in the afternoon, when your mother must lie down for a spell . . ."

Sarah follows her mother inside. She has never heard her speak this way about her side of the family. In fact, Sarah has heard almost nothing about the rest of her family. There are some cousins in Boston and Northampton, and an aunt and uncle on her mother's side she has seen but twice, yet she has heard nothing more than a few passing comments about her grandparents, and certainly nothing from her father's side. It is as though her parents had arrived in Cana fully formed, and because Sarah's life has always been here, she has never questioned this fact before now.

"You were at the meetinghouse," Sarah nudges, once they have entered the dim chamber. Her mother stands beside the bed, loosening her cap. Ezekiel crawls to his favorite spot on the bed. "Father was crying."

"Why are you suddenly so interested, dear? What has your father said to you? Has he frightened you? You've never before this day wanted to know. Or have you discovered some clever way of getting out of today's work?"

Sarah watches her mother climb into bed, the relish with which she surrenders her body. She helps her mother secure the gap in the bed-curtains, then sits on the edge of the bed with hands folded in her lap.

"'Another town tomorrow.' That was what your father said to me when I first spoke to him outside the meetinghouse. 'Another town tomorrow.' He was always looking ahead. I was done with silly trysts in the forest, with fumbling hands. I wanted a man who looked ahead, somewhere far away from my mother's house. He walked me home that evening. 'Another town tomorrow,' he said. 'I've yet to write my new sermon and already it is too late to make a good one. Perhaps you will be my inspiration.' I told him I wasn't the type to inspire a man. I don't know why I said it. Then your father said something very surprising. He said to me, 'Each man sees a Helen in the woman he loves.' A Helen! 'Why, you're a pagan preacher,' said I. 'I am no beauty, but I'm no simpleton either. Best not to utter an untruth, minister.' Are you following, girl?"

"Yea, Mother."

"He smiled at my words, but it was a cold and wooden smile, a minister speaking to one of his sisters in Christ. I do believe I frightened him with my mention of paganism. I began to see him as a challenge: push too hard, he becomes cold; too cold, he becomes hot. There are all sorts of tricks you must learn, Daughter. All sorts of tricks for each kind of man. I believed I could induce fire and ice in him as I pleased. I was wrong, of course, for your father is an unpredictable man, governed by his own secret thoughts. You know our clock on the mantelpiece? That ormolu clock with impish cherubs scaling the dial? You've never taken much notice of it because it has been a part of your fixed world since you were a babe, but it is highly unusual to have such a clock in a minister's household. Highly unusual. We have taken to hiding it during visits. I'll tell you its origins before this tale is finished, but I mean to show you that your father has allowed in me—and in himself—a certain degree of permissiveness when it comes to beauty. You could say it is what most unites us even as we both worship the same God with equal enthusiasm. Do you see others in Cana with flowers in their gardens such as ours? Foxgloves, daylilies, and peonies alongside our vegetables?"

"Sadeye, Yellowneck, Smellnice," Sarah says, recalling their secret names for the flowers.

"Enough with that, girl. Proper names. You could say he saw my love of beauty and coveted it for himself. Only a woman can allow a man to feel this. The design for the garden was his idea but it lived in me, in all those hours I sat in Mother's wretched house craving a better view. Little squares for each room of our house. Two gardens growing at once. It has delighted me to no end. You've no idea how these small touches can change the day-to-day, things only the two of us may notice. It has been a relief to possess even the smallest bit of beauty after Mother. All those years of Mother's bedridden illness, there had been only this ugly head with no body beneath. How she had gone on and on, as if the walls of a sea had parted to make passage for years of her bitterness but had never closed upon it. She warned me I would end up bedridden like her if I married a man like my own father. Her sickness would fossilize in my bones if I didn't marry a man of sense, of enterprise, so I wrote to your father. And at first it seemed nothing would come from it. Oh, things were rough then, after I received no word from him. Mother let me know I was a stupid girl to have lost my only chance at a man. She no longer cared what happened to me. Do you understand why I am telling you this, child? I'm telling you because I want you to know I'll never make you feel as my mother made me feel. Do you understand?"

"Yea, Mother," Sarah says, though she cannot help picturing the horrid old grandmother lying in the same position as Catherine. Better never to marry, better never to have children, if the deathbed is to come early for her. The room grows darker; the clouds outside must have overtaken the sun. Catherine closes her eyes. Ezekiel makes his way to his mother's side, curling into her as usual, hands clutching her shift.

"Here's the part with the clock on our mantelpiece." Catherine's voice is far away now, half in sleep. "Mother had Father take out the clock from a case beneath her bedstead. She placed it beside her in the bed and said to me, 'This is the only piece of wealth you were to inherit, the last thing I have left to bequeath you. And now you have lost it.' She had me look closely at the clock as she explained each detail. It was the most beautiful thing I had ever seen. I thought I was staring into the Old Country, into all of the marvelous estates she spoke of in my youth. After she showed me this clock, Mother had Father place it back inside the case. 'You are too plain for it anyway,' she said, settling the matter. She refused to speak to me for several weeks after that. I decided then that I could be silent, too. As the weeks passed and no letter arrived from your father, I fell into a silence for so long I became somewhat invisible. I felt I could escape notice. It was nice after a while to hide from the world. Soon, however, people began to regard my silence as an act of great faith, and they respected me for it. Everyone but Mother, of course, who thought it foolish, though she was herself silent with me. Oh, how I wished for her death. I never prayed for it, but I allowed myself to wish for it. I am ashamed to admit it, Sarah, but you are old enough for the hard truths. You must know what evil thoughts will plague you as you grow older. Do you harbor such evil thoughts against your mother, dear?"

"No, Mother," Sarah says, beginning to feel she cannot breathe in the stuffy room.

"I was silent the rest of that year. I still crave silence, as you know, dear. Remind me that we must add more flour to the hallway boards; they have grown loud again. After that year of silence, your father returned to preach once more in our assembly hall. By then we had already heard of his miracle. During the year-long

itinerancy when he never once wrote to me, he had on a single afternoon led five hundred souls to the Lord. Five hundred in a single
meeting! We had never heard of such a thing before. They say his
speech placed such guilt in their hearts, and was spoken with such
deep emotion, that the crying lasted several hours. People fell out of
the pews and broke into violent paroxysms upon the ground. We
had no word for it then. Now we call it an awakening, a revival. The
awakening you see happening now in towns all about us. Back then
no one had heard of such a thing. Of course, some saw it as devilish,
all this crying and flapping about as though people had wings, but
most of us were excited to have the chance to see it in our own town.
I never once thought he might be returning to Hingham on account
of me. Pay attention here, child, for this is important. Some two
hundred of those awakened souls had dedicated their lives to your
father's mission and followed him everywhere he went. He had told
them he'd soon find a place for a new town which he would one day
populate only with those who had been awakened, those who could
rightfully call themselves part of the Elect. You've heard this part
before, yea, in our history of Cana?"

"Yea, Mother."

"When your father preached for the second time in Hingham, he
seemed to have grown a foot taller. I saw his strength and his weakness at once. And all along the walls of our sanctuary and gathered
round the windows outside stood his two hundred awakened souls,
his disciples. His words were so beautiful to me then, his tears even
more so. I sat beside my own poor father, no longer ashamed of him,
because I was now invisible. Nevertheless, your father seemed to
see me. Out of everyone gathered there, he saw me. He called out

for me to read the scripture, something you don't do with women. The crowd turned to me, for I was silent and a girl, two things which made his choice—"

"Women never read scripture?"

"Women do not read scripture aloud."

"Why?"

"There are verses in the Bible which some believe explain it. But your father has always done things differently. I was silent and a girl, two things which made his choice odd, so everyone turned to me with wide eyes. 'Speak, Sister,' his voice commanded. So I gathered up all of my strength and used my voice for the first time since he left. And as I read the scripture aloud, I sensed a new kind of heat passing through me. My words mixed with the echo of his words, as if there were no one else in the room but us. The heat swam into my head. My vision left me. A loud ringing filled my ears, and in that ringing, I felt I could hear the Lord's voice commanding me toward a new life. When I could see again, I was being held in your father's arms before the whole assembly in that church. I thought I might be imagining it, but your father's steady arms against my back convinced me otherwise, and even with all eyes upon me, I gripped his shoulders and pulled myself up and . . . and . . . kissed him on the lips! Can you imagine your sweet mother doing such a thing in church? Can you see it, Daughter? Imagine your father standing before the flock and kissing your sweet mother on the lips, holding her in his arms. That is exactly how it happened. The flock was so loud with shouting I couldn't hear the words of marriage he spoke to me, and though many found it wrong to witness such a passionate display in church, there was no denying the minister had found his helpmate. It was as though the Lord had ordained it—and who was I to question such a thing, for hadn't I ended up in your father's arms with a desire to kiss that frown of his?'"

Sarah closes her eyes, picturing the moment. Only once had she seen her father kiss Catherine on the neck when they thought they were alone, and she had been shocked at the informality of it, as though their formality were simply an act for Sarah's benefit alone, though now she wonders if any of it was real. But a kiss before a crowd of people, a kiss in a church, an intimate kiss on the mouth—this she cannot picture. Instead, what she sees swirling in the darkness behind her lids is the image of her father pressing his lips to Arthur's neck, the complete surrender in his face. She opens her eyes to rid herself of the sight, but in this room there is only more darkness.

Sarah suddenly remembers her mother is waiting for her to speak. "What did your mother say?"

"Your grandmother. Thank God you never met her. We walked home to call upon Mother, Nathaniel bowing before her deathbed to declare that the Lord had seen fit to make Catherine one of His own. I had been saved from the pit. The Lord had also seen fit to bring him a wife that day. I was calm as I stood beside him and watched my mother's face turn sour. She had already given up on me, and she was far from happy to find herself proven wrong once again. 'My daughter can no longer speak, I'm afraid,' she said. She looked at me as though I were no more than a mouse that had wandered into her room. So I gripped your father's hand and kissed it, a gesture so unspeakably intimate in that airless room, with so much life passing through it, that my mother seemed to wither before us. 'Very well then,' she said, turning from the sight of our love. Your father asked for my hand in writing before he set off in search of a promised land where he could lead his two hundred faithful followers. Mother's dowry was far from sufficient, but when she died, not long after your father set off, she bequeathed to her plainest daughter the most ornate clock in the New World. And when your father returned, he found the household in mourning, the coffin propped on wooden stilts in the parlor, the clock with all its trimmings perched atop the lid like a final joke. 'Where we're going we have no use for such things,' he said. 'Ours will be a new way of living. There will be no servants, no slaves, for we are all God's servants.' 'Grant me this one indulgence,' I said. His face turned red, for he knew ours was a shared desire, and he nodded. 'What will this place be called?' I asked. 'We shall call it Cana,' he said. 'In honor of our union.'"

"Why this name?"

"You don't know where the name comes from, Daughter? How is this possible? We shall have a reading of the scriptures after your primer today. I can see I have sheltered you far too long. C-A-N-A. The jars of the wedding feast, Christ's first miracle—what was once only water turned, suddenly, to wine. A conversion. A great conversion. Your father named this town after our holy union. It was a great honor. It remains a great honor to this day, for all who live here know why he named it so. Now, head downstairs and make the fire as I've instructed you. We shall eat our supper at the regular time, with or without your father. Leave your mother to a short sleep. I'll be but an hour, no more. Do not worry your head about it. I can see the worry in your face even in the dark. You can be certain all will be right, Sarah. All will be right in the end."

———

Later, after returning from the kitchen, Sarah watches her mother sleep. She stands before the bed, feet frozen.

"What else, Mother?" she says quietly. A whisper. "What else is there to explain it? That cannot be all. That cannot be all there is."

A low moan, but no answer.

"Mother, I must confess something. Something I saw in the forest."

Still no sign of wakefulness. Ezekiel is the only one to stir. She waits for him to cry, but he is quiet, so quiet.

"I saw father and Ezekiel in the forest with Arthur." A blade runs through her middle. She has never fully confessed it, not even to herself.

"I don't know what is right. You must help me, Mother. Please, wake up. Please, you must wake up."

3.

Fall

Anne Lyman waits for Deborah Inverness to signal to her from the vegetable stall. Foolish, to stand at the edge of the square beside the jointer's cottage and the barber's shop as people move about her, waiting to be allowed to do a job she does not in the least enjoy doing. She smooths her fluttering cap, tucks her hands into her dress pockets to feel the silk there, a little secret she stitched into her garment: the sensation of cool water trickling down her palms. Deborah does not look in her direction. The woman stands beneath a wide gray canopy at the other end of the square, whispering something to Priscilla Griggs, whose scarlet wool cloak is spotless despite the dusty fields that surround her house. Between the two women sit cheerfully bright harvest mounds delivered this morning by Priscilla's husband, Judah, who tends these fields with his five sons. Though the women do not look at her, it is clear to Anne that they are aware of her presence, that their every mannerism, every movement, has been designed with Anne's exclusion in mind.

If they but knew what Boston was like. If they knew, they would feel ashamed of their provincial concerns, of mocking someone like Anne. She hates herself for this thought, for judging them as they judge her, but the longer she stands here looking foolish, ignored by these women, the angrier she grows at being reduced to such indignity. They had been known, the Lymans, they had been known and respected, and they had given up their lives in service of the Lord.

But here in Cana, Anne must know her place, and her place is always one rung below the rest, for she and Arthur are not of the original two hundred souls. They arrived to this town a little more than a year ago, long after Reverend Whitfield had already found a home for his wandering flock, and no one here will let them forget it. No one, perhaps, save the reverend himself, who has always treated her as an equal. He has always been kind to the Lymans, so kind that Arthur has grown quite close to him, the two men sharing one mind in nearly all matters concerning God, though there seems to be some tension between them of late. She has not asked Arthur about it, not yet, but some part of her has begun making a plan, conjuring up a dinner, perhaps even some light entertainment for the Whitfield family and themselves, something to show off Anne's skills for the one family in this town who might appreciate it. Arthur's suggestion that the two families might be linked as outsiders had struck her as another of his mollifying tonics at first, but she hadn't been able to get it out of her mind. Though Catherine is indeed plain, she carries herself well, and Anne now feels that they might share a great many things, for she has heard Deborah gossiping about

Catherine's lethargy, the way this woman has sealed herself off within the Whitfield house, ignoring calls, even sleeping during the day, behavior Anne finds bolder and much more interesting than what she'd expected from a minister's wife.

The barber nods to Anne as he makes his way to the public house for his morning beer. Outside, on the steps of the house, Hiram suns himself, already drunk. Hiram is a clock, a rather harmless clock, Anne thinks, though everyone in this town is of the opinion that a drunk is intolerable. Soon someone will come by to take him inside, likely to one of the cabins in the rear of the house where he may sleep through the afternoon. Deborah says something in a low voice to Priscilla, who has begun to look in Anne's direction from time to time.

Anne places one hand on the low railing beside her, careful of splinters. The wood is pleasantly cool. A breeze sends the maple leaves rustling overhead, drawing a patchwork curtain of shadow all about her. The scent of something sweetly rotting mixed with ash from distant fires: a signal the season has changed. Her gaze follows the breeze across the square to where the other maples answer back with one long red wave, leaves cleaving like a dropped kerchief. She has just begun to contemplate the white cross at the center of the square for the hundredth time when she hears a sound behind her, someone clearing a throat in expectation. She turns to find the Anderson widows walking arm in arm toward her, their long matching black dresses cinched sharply at their narrow waists, clogs sounding loudly on cobblestones.

"Mrs. Lyman," Humility Anderson says, nodding.

"Humility," Anne says. "Constance."

Anne has learned to tell the difference between Humility and Constance because Humility is the one with the scar from cheek to jowl. Anne has never heard the story of this scar, but she associates it with the dead husbands, whom the sisters seem glad to be rid of, having both reverted to their maiden names. The widows hail from New York. Their story, now a part of Cana lore, is that Reverend Whitfield once stayed at their inn during one of his itinerancies; after one conversation with him over dinner, they were convinced to dedicate their lives to God.

They, too, are not of the original two hundred, and like the Lymans, there is still something worldly about them despite their outward devotion, something that seems to spark in their eyes as they turn to Anne, a knowing look suggesting they see in her another sister.

She watches them make their way up the steps, the kindness as they move carefully around Hiram's sprawled limbs. To be so loving, so understanding, one must have already had one's life obliterated. She wants to call out to them, to tell them she is indeed one of them, but to do so would be to throw everything in her delicate life out of balance. Anne still has too much to lose: a good family, a good name, a hidden fortune in Boston to secure her future if need be. She had come to this town because she feared she was already on the cusp of losing it all. She had seen the change in her husband, the way he stayed out later each night, the smell of him as he lay beside her—sawdust and saltwater, sweat and musk, sometimes even the stench of the privy pit, something she could only imagine issued from a forbidden act—the way he no longer touched her without an excuse. They had once been so close, but he had lost all passion for her. Even their daughter, Martha, whom he once doted over, he now neglected. So when he came to her with that look upon his face, so bright and beautiful once more, she had wanted to believe him. She had wanted to believe the Reverend Whitfield was the answer to all of their prayers. She was willing to give up the practice, and her life, for this dream, just to see Arthur happy again, for his happiness was her happiness.

Nevertheless, here she stands, mocked by these townspeople, as distant as ever from her husband, who spends his time in the workroom or visiting patients or, until recently, engaged in some project with the reverend. But Anne is ever resourceful, ever hopeful. Yes, she will find a way to bring them together within her house, the Whitfields and the Lymans. She will prove an excellent wife, the Whitfields will come to love her, and she will secure her role within this town. Arthur will come to see her as an asset once again, as he did when he first set out to become a physician, for she had entertained all of his best clients, the best families; when people in Boston discussed Arthur's success, her name was the first to be mentioned; everyone had agreed her charms were the rarest of his rare spices, more essential to his practice than any of the miracles stored in his workroom. Let the women of Cana gossip, let them find her haughty and rude, let them discover every fault within her that it is possible to discover within a woman; they will come to respect and even fear her.

Anne's thoughts have gone to her feet, daring her forward into this new future.

Deborah does not move when Anne arrives. Her eyes do not leave the pile of apples before her. After a long silence, she says, "Tell us, Anne, since you are newer to Cana than the rest of us: Do you believe our little town shall experience an awakening like the one in Northampton? Dozens of our youth converted?"

Anne pretends to arrange the dusty potatoes before her, stalling like a thief. They seem to have been plucked from the fields only recently; Martha might have harvested them with the other children, who, as the reverend has decreed, must dabble in all the trades of Cana before they are assigned their separate tasks. Martha is only ten and can be spoiled, Anne thinks, tossing out a black leathery potato she plans to trim later; in fact, Anne had had to bribe her with a new dress in order to convince her to join the children in their labor—but she is a perfect little girl, made the way a little girl should be: a true terror. Anne was herself a terror, yet being a terror taught her to be graceful later in life. Martha is in no need of awakening; no, she is in need of a childhood, a rarity in Cana it seems. She knows she cannot say any of this to these women. Instead, she says, "I have always believed I would live to see another of Reverend Whitfield's miracles. It is part of the excitement of living in Cana."

Anne hears the falseness in her voice, but it is a falseness answering falseness, no more avoidable than the wind moving through the trees. She must pray for forgiveness later when she is alone.

"We've not seen a miracle here in some time," Deborah says, turning at last to Anne. "Some might say there's a reason for it. A town must be free of certain impurities, I believe, before it may be saved."

"Oh yes," Priscilla says, drawing her hood about her. Anne cannot fail to notice the message, for Priscilla has shifted ever so subtly away from her. "Yet one cannot rush God's plans. 'For a thousand years in thy sight are but as yesterday when it is past, and as a watch in the night.'"

"Speaking of the night watch," Deborah says. "I hear they've grown quite lengthy these past months."

Those long nights of Anne waiting in bed for Arthur to return, nights when he stayed out well past three, fulfilling his duty to excess. The night watch in Cana is something of a formality; only on the rarest occasion might someone discover a valuable has been stolen, and only once has there been a fire. The Mohican tribes around the area are peaceful, perhaps because of the reverend's work in Stockbridge, his close ties with Reverend Alcom, yet it is as though Arthur has become ever more vigilant in spite of this fact, as though peace is not to be trusted.

"Arthur likes to think all of his big thoughts on the watches." Anne dares herself to look into these women's eyes once again.

"Actually, I was thinking of our reverend," Deborah says. "But now you have brought me to it, Anne, they do both seem to be taking much longer walks these days. I suppose we should all feel very safe."

"Perhaps that is the first condition of an awakening," Priscilla adds. "A town must be safe before it may be saved."

Anne cannot understand where these women are directing their irony, but she fears it has something to do with her marriage. She must say something, anything, to draw attention elsewhere. "It seems to me a town composed of so many converted souls might not be in need of much awakening."

The women grow quiet. She shouldn't have said it. She shouldn't have spoken her mind, but she had to say something. Anne stares at the white cross at the center of the square. No, she shouldn't have said it, but it is just that she belongs here with the rest of them. She is just as much a Christian as these women, as anyone else in this town. She and Arthur had stood before the flock and answered dozens of questions about the state of their faith, their relationship to God, to each other. They had recited all of the verses, proved doctrinally sound, never once faltering before the crowd of eager eyes. And when she grasped Arthur's hand at the end of it, after they were declared members of Cana's church, she had never been prouder of herself, for out of all the tests society had given her, after all of the rules and subtle machinations she had had to endure in Boston, this one had been the most trying; this one had been about her soul, her essence, something beyond the surface of her life. Anne and Arthur had proved they were ready to move beyond whatever temptations had snared them in the past.

What does Deborah mean by suggesting the two men now spend longer hours on the night watch? She cannot understand it. A few months ago, it was the two men together on the watches, as is often the custom, but lately they have begun to go about them separately. Perhaps that is all Deborah means, that there is some noticeable rift between these two, a rift that threatens Anne's standing within the town. Well, that is one thing Anne will soon solve.

As morning turns to noonday, as she meets with Cana's families, speaking with them about their concerns, their family illnesses, promising to relay their symptoms to her husband, she begins to picture it: her and Arthur sitting across from Catherine and Reverend Whitfield at their largest table, with Martha and Sarah and Ezekiel at the other end, two families framed in the window for all to see. Then, when the time is right, she will introduce the tableau. The Whitfields will be scandalized at first by the mere mention of theatre, but Anne will draw them out, loosen them up a bit, show them there can be fun, too, in Cana. Afterward, of course, the two families will grow closer, and the town will see the Lymans are one of them.

When Anne had first come to Cana, she had not yet understood the town's strange ways, how one came to fit within certain slots that were supposed, at least on the surface, to be of equal value. Some members of the flock arrived with a ready trade, like Arthur, and others, like many of the women, were asked to dabble in various trades until they discovered their calling. That Anne had been incapable of doing just about anything worthwhile for the community had come as no real surprise to her, but it had come as a surprise to everyone else, for they were not used to women like her. Now, it seems, even handling fruit comes with further instructions, further difficulties she must navigate.

When next she looks up at the cross, Anne finds Sarah Whitfield standing before her, a sign if there ever was one that God has sanctioned her plan. Prim and tidy, fairer than her mother, in a plain white cotton dress and cap that nevertheless renders her every bit a woman. She has matured much faster than Martha; the change shocks Anne, for she had not noticed it, and she sees almost at once how Sarah would make for an excellent companion during this trying time in a young woman's life. Anne had heard from Arthur that

Sarah's friend, Abigail Jacobsen, had been taken from her not so long ago. Perhaps now is the time to remedy that loss.

"Why, Sarah," Deborah says, rushing to embrace the girl before Anne has the chance. "Are you to tell me you are now the woman of the house?"

Sarah blushes. "I am in charge of a great many tasks now, Mrs. Inverness."

"Are you certain you can carry everything with you?" Deborah says. "It is far too heavy a burden for a girl to bear."

"I am quite strong," Sarah says, and now the woman in her has risen to the top, tracing her fair features with the outline of someone defiant, proud, brow lifted in subtle agitation.

"I must believe you," Deborah says, patting the girl's shoulders. "For I know your mother would never send you here if she did not think you quite capable. And how is your mother, dear? Is she getting her rest now that you are in charge?"

Sarah's eyes do not falter, but Anne can sense her hesitation. She wants to push Deborah aside and speak to Sarah herself, save the girl from gossip.

"Mother is doing quite well," Sarah says. "It was time for me to learn the household duties."

"Indeed it was," Deborah says. "She certainly took her time with it. I believe it may be time for Martha, too, to learn some sort of skill, wouldn't you say, Anne?"

Anne does not answer. She has already begun to fill Sarah's basket with everything the Whitfields will need for the week. She returns the basket to Sarah, who does her best to appear unburdened. Strange, however, how the girl will not look into her eyes.

"In the meantime, dear girl, you must keep clear of the forest. The forest is what possessed those Northampton children, I assure you. It is where the Devil stages his greatest seductions."

There is no need, Mrs. Lyman," Sarah says.

The road to the Whitfield house is longer than ever with this woman by Sarah's side who refuses to hand over the basket. Despite her dark mood, Sarah had been excited to tend to the stalls for the first time, to act every bit a woman in public, but now she looks like a child indulged by a mock task. What makes it worse is that it is Anne who walks beside her. Anne, a foolish woman, not the kind of woman Sarah would ever want to become even with all of her outsize beauty, or perhaps because of her outsize beauty. Sarah should not be angry with Anne; she does not know this woman, but she cannot help but feel agitated by Anne's forced cheerfulness, those broad gestures that ring false, even falser now that Sarah can imagine her as the keeper of her husband's secrets.

"You are quite Martha's opposite, Sarah," Anne says, offering a smile.

Sarah looks away, moving faster now. Red on either side of the road, wine-red waving branches of the plum trees. Martha she has spoken to but once or twice, a girl with no more sense than her mother. When the Lymans first arrived, everyone had told Sarah she was to have a new companion. They had used that word, "new," as though all it took to replace Abigail was a warm body, never mind the brains.

"You wish to do the work others would do for you, whereas Martha wishes to do no work and would be quite content to live her life without an ounce of independence."

"I only wish to be helpful," Sarah says coolly. "I wish to do as the Lord commands."

"Then perhaps you may help my Martha, who is far too idle to do as the Lord commands."

Sarah slows, allowing Anne to catch up. She must learn to be more careful in her judgments. She no longer knows who her allies truly are, who her enemies might be. Perhaps Anne knows nothing of Arthur's doings. Tutoring Martha would grant her the opportunity to study the interior of the Lyman house, to search for signs of—what, exactly? She has already snuck into her father's study, pretending to clean it one afternoon, only to find a stack of letters hidden inside the pages of a book, letters she could hardly read, the script so small, the language so ornate. She had only been able to make out the name and a few phrases. Edwin Sharpe of London. A man who called himself her father's benefactor. There had been one phrase in particular that stuck out: *I pray you have saved yourself from my influence.* Those words have remained with her, a taunting clue with no clear answer. Sarah had never heard of Edwin Sharpe of London. Her father had never spoken of a benefactor. When she asked her mother to tell her more about her father's life in London, Catherine had been unusually quiet. "There are parts of your father's life which remain a mystery," she had said. "I know only that he does not wish to speak of it."

"Would you ever consider it, dear?" Anne says. "Martha has much to learn, but she does possess her own talents. If a pianoforte is to be found in a place like Cana, I am certain she will teach you."

Sarah does not know what to say. She does not wish to appear overeager after her coldness, but she does not want to lose this opportunity to discover more about Arthur Lyman and his family.

"I shall have to run ahead to ask if Mother can see you," Sarah says, answering Anne's smile with what she hopes passes for warmth. "I am sure she will be delighted, Mrs. Lyman."

Lucky that Catherine had been standing in the parlor, rooted to the same spot for more than an hour. Lucky because she had not been in bed; she had managed to resist its pull all morning, so that now, as this woman sits across from her on the divan, she can brighten her smile with ease, as though she has been alive this whole time and, after all, she has been. Today, at least. Today is a good day. Some days are better, sunlight peering in at the proper angle, Nathaniel kissing her cheek before leaving for the meetinghouse. He has been better to her of late, returning home earlier, spreading out his night watch duties with the other men. Sometimes, before he wakes, she feels his arms around her; she wakes in the night and he is holding her.

"Oh no, thank you," Anne says, shooing away Catherine's offer of a repast. Catherine tries not to stare as Anne tucks her hands into her pockets. A nervous habit; she seems to be caressing something there. This may be the first time Catherine has ever seen something of herself in the woman.

"I apologize for staring," Anne says, eyes darting once more to the mantel. "It is truly a remarkable piece."

Catherine had forgotten to remove the clock from the room, but she is not sorry for it, for here is one person who might appreciate its value.

"An heirloom," Catherine says. "My husband permits me this one indulgence."

Anne starts. She wishes to say something, then seems to think better of it. Just when Catherine is about to offer up some trifle for conversation, the woman adds, rather timidly, "I must confess I have also kept a few things from my old life, though they are mostly old costumes from when I held parties. I hosted tableaux vivants, you know, in Boston."

Catherine pictures the glittering rooms, the plates stacked just so one atop the other, the polished silver. Her mother's exhaustive descriptions of wealth, how they had burdened her. In some ways it would be hard to live such a life, harder still to walk away. Yet there seems to be no bitterness here, at least not of the sort that makes targets of others.

"Your husband is already something of a historical figure," Anne says. "Perhaps he could play himself in a tableau."

A sound from the hallway. Catherine does not turn to look. Sarah, no doubt, spying on them. It is the girl's own fault she can be heard; Catherine had asked her only yesterday to spread more flour upon the floorboards.

"Oh, perhaps it is a silly idea," Anne says, shaking her head.

"Pay no attention to Sarah," Catherine says, loudly enough for the girl to hear. "Last week I heard her sneaking into her father's study. She wants to know how the adults live."

"I should like to know as well," Anne says quietly. "I cannot seem to get the hang of it."

Catherine does not say what she wishes to say: the two women share this problem. No doubt Anne has already heard rumors of her mysterious decline. Mysterious even to Catherine. Something has changed, something since her pregnancy with Ezekiel, and her husband changed with it, yet she cannot point to any singular cause. Catherine sits up straight, bracing herself for an act of charity.

Instead, she hears Anne say, "I've always the sense something isn't quite right." The woman's voice trembles. "I've the sense everyone knows it but me, only I alone am too dull to comprehend it. I thought it had to do with the bustle of the city, how we weren't really suited for it, Arthur and I, despite our successes. But now the feeling has followed us to Cana. I was hoping your husband would be the answer. Oh—but I've burdened you with this, Mrs. Whitfield, when we barely know each other. I fear I've spoken out of turn."

"Not at all," Catherine says. So Anne is here out of charity; charity for herself. Catherine hides a dawning smile.

"I must ask you something or else I shall be very disappointed with myself."

"Please."

"I was going to ask if you and your family might join us one evening for dinner. Sarah might get to know Martha better, and we might even have a bit of fun with my old tableaux. That is, if such a thing is not too sinful for the minister."

Catherine rises. She makes her way to the mantel, turning from the woman. It had seemed, only a moment ago, that the two of them were on the cusp of some revelation. A little light had been let into a dark corner by Anne's confession, and Catherine had seen there a glimpse of the fragments coming together, something to do with the Lymans leaving Boston, how Arthur's arrival had changed everything.

"I don't see why one night of fun would do us any harm," Catherine says at last.

"Oh, that is very kind of you, Mrs. Whitfield."

"Catherine."

When Catherine turns to face Anne, something unexpected happens: Anne rushes to embrace her, as though the two have been friends for ages. Catherine bristles at first, but the hold is so earnest, so eager, she can do nothing but relent. The scent of orange flower and cassia, soft hands on the nape of her neck. Anne's cheek falls upon her shoulder. Instinctively, Catherine pets the top of her head. Whatever awkwardness Catherine felt has vanished. In its place curiosity, even warmth. It is as though the two of them have just avoided a gaping pit; they have left something awful and mysterious behind by never naming it.

"Thank you for being so kind to me today," Anne says. "You've no idea how terrible the others can be."

"I've some idea. Deborah Inverness and I were once close."

"But the two of you are so very different."

"Thank you for the compliment, dear. I was once close with many of the women. Deborah and I spent a great many of our days together, though I imagine she looks upon those days as wasted now that the minister's wife has turned out to be human. I've the feeling she sees me as the reason my husband has not brought about another awakening."

Catherine has said too much already; Anne has drawn her out, but she cannot stop; she has shared these thoughts with no one but Sarah. "I have always wished for my husband's success," she says. "But I am not him. I do not think it a fault in me."

"Yea," Anne says. "Though our husbands do seem similar."

Here they are again, toeing the pit, dancing about with careless abandon.

Anne adds, "Have you noticed a change in them? In their friendship, I mean? They were so close before. In the spring, after you and Ezekiel visited our house, it was quite unusual for Arthur to make the trip all the way to Stockbridge. He is known for his manners, certain, but I found it very touching how deeply he cared for your family's well-being."

Catherine must be careful. Every part of her wants to rush out of the room at the mention of Stockbridge. Nathaniel had failed to tell her why he had returned so hastily. Why had he omitted this detail, that Arthur had been there, if not to hide something? She will not even think to herself what she now suspects to be true, for it is unthinkable; it is unknowable, impossible. She has never heard of such a thing, not really, only rumors of court cases with that horrible word, "sodomy," so redolent of filth, of dirt, of that Old Testament story of fire and judgment.

"Nathaniel has spent far more time at home these past few weeks." Catherine is careful to hide her agitation.

"I fear something must have come between them. I would hate to see that happen. The reverend has always been such a positive influence on Arthur's character."

"I am sure whatever you feel has happened between them will be mended the minute we sit together at the table. A fine meal can heal all things."

"I hope you are right, Catherine."

"Leave it to me. I'll convince the reverend." As Catherine says these words, she feels safe once again, certain all of her suspicions will lead to nothing; they are merely the product of a mind slowly wasting away beneath the tide of excess sleep.

Anne seems embarrassed as she collects her cap, so Catherine proffers a hand on her elbow. She guides her to the entry.

"Next Friday?" Anne says.

"Next Friday," Catherine says. "I look forward to it."

Before leaving the doorway, Anne takes one last look at the clock on the mantel. "It really is a beautiful piece. I shall think of it sitting there, all by itself, counting the hours in this town. It shall bring me great pleasure to think of time in such a way."

Nathaniel Whitfield returns home by way of the forest path, his legs weak, his breath shallow. He has been fasting for days. Fasting and praying, and keeping a daily diary of his thoughts, his resolutions. As he steps over the roots blocking his path, the hunger draws him deeper into Christ's pain, ever closer to the mortification of His flesh. He pauses to rest his shoulder against the soft coils of a birch. A low sun filters through the honeyed leaves, prismed like precious quartz.

Above the tops of the trees, tufts of silvered smoke rise like mist, so distant as to seem part of the fabric of the sky itself. Eyes unfocused, he begins to see the world behind this one, the one waiting for him in the next life, just beyond reach. A sweet taste floods his tongue, so sweet he might retch. He bends low, hands on knees, his gown straining against his legs. When the fiery dots swimming before his eyes begin to recede, he sees he is looking into the clearing. There is the circle of pines spaced so uniformly they might have been planted by a man. There is the even ground, a nearly perfect circle where red flowers bloom in spring like a blaze. And there is the fallen branch he has never moved, gnarled and twisted with twigs pointing upward like a dead spider's legs, marking the place where the two of them stood when he had allowed himself to meet Arthur with Ezekiel in his arms.

He has not given in to temptation since they made their pact, yet on certain lonely days he has not been able to resist walking past this clearing. To his great surprise, Arthur kept up his end of the promise; he had stated things so plainly and carefully that Nathaniel had not even had to fight him on a single point. They had been standing in the middle of an empty street around midnight, the new moon their sole companion on the night watch. They had been walking together all night, an intimate quiet between them, when Arthur finally said, "I shall agree to your conditions, reverend, because I want more than anything for our friendship to survive. That is my sole concern, far greater than anything else I feel for you. I wish to help you in this struggle of yours, for though I may not share the same struggle at the moment, I do understand it. The question rests between you and God, and the two of you must be free of all distraction." As Arthur's speech drew to an end, Nathaniel felt closer to him than ever, grateful for the freedom this selfless man had granted him. He wanted to kiss him in that moment, but seeing as they had reached such a sound agreement, he resisted, and in the resistance, he realized he was disappointed, angry even, that Arthur hadn't fought back. Where were his tears, his fists? Was it all so easy to give up? And then the next day, when Nathaniel saw Arthur talking to Judah Griggs, the physical ease between the two of them, doctor and patient, the cold lightning passing through his veins as he thought of the many opportunities Arthur might find when calling upon these men in their houses.

He shakes his head clear of such thoughts. A breeze caresses the sweat of his neck, his brow. To the Shadows of Divine Things he adds the wind's cooling touch, God's breath. His vision fully returned, he heads up the path, careful again with his feet. Ahead, through the crimson leaves, he sees the well and the garden beyond it, a sliver of the house he built with his own hands, its every clapboard another memory of the days he and Catherine stood together outside these half-built walls and envisioned a future in this town. As he draws nearer, the candlelight from the kitchen window fills his path, swelling as twilight descends, igniting the garden plants here and there with tiny sparks. Sarah passes before the window, her face aglow, so bright and youthful, as though the light issues from the surface of her skin. Catherine sits behind her at the worktable, Ezekiel toddling slowly upon its surface with arms outstretched, Catherine's hands moving at something in her lap, a bit of stump work no doubt, those lips that have always drawn him in now pressed tightly in concentration. He pauses beside the well, a solitary figure in the dark, a shadow, a stranger. He watches them, this family he has made, framed within the leaded lights. Has he ever once considered what it is they do when he is gone? Has he ever imagined their lives without him? The answer comes suddenly, like the boom of a musket: no, he has not. A deep shame rises in his gut; again he tastes the sweet rot on his tongue, feels as though he might retch. He has led them here, to this house. It is his job to keep them safe, never lead them astray; yet in this moment he is a stranger to them, this happy family.

He sinks to the ground beside the well, one hand clutching its cool stone lip. Lord, he prays. Lord, grant me the strength to guide them. Within the silence of his mind, a vast chasm appears. Somewhere deep within it, deeper than the deepest well, far from any light, rests his soul. He knows he cannot call it forth; it will not answer to his voice; it will answer to one Voice alone, the Voice that first created it. And though he feels it might be lost completely, eternally, he does not sense it is dead to him yet. No, it is aware of his presence, of his desire, as an animal who senses the stirring of a bush might sense imminent danger. He means it no harm; he wants only to know if it is still there, but he is dangerous all the same, dangerous because he is still alive to his sin; it remains a part of him no matter how long he fasts or how often he tries to ignore it. He cannot even know if it is the sin of his desire that has brought about this danger or if it is his pride that has created this desire in him, if the root cause is much deeper and much more stubborn. He has believed in God. He has believed in God since he left his father's house at sixteen to live a different life. He knows this to be true; it is this belief that has sustained him, provided him a new continent to live upon, a new Father, and a new family, this life, this gift of saving souls. Yet what if belief is not enough? What if, despite everything he has done, despite the miracle of saving so many souls, he is still lost, never chosen by God, never one of the Elect?

The chasm closes. His soul sealed away once again. As he rises to his feet, a feeling of great consolation courses through him. His chest expands, as though a warm hand were reaching inside, pulling him toward the light where his family awaits him. This is the hand of God leading him forward, guiding him to happiness. He pauses at the doorstep, listening to the sounds of their voices. Will he still be a stranger when he enters? He shakes away the question. God has given him his answer. All he must do is open the door and become the man he was always meant to be.

Once he is inside, Sarah greets him with a steaming bowl of pottage. He takes a seat at the head of the table. Catherine smiles, her cheeks flushed, happy at his early return. Ezekiel crawls across the table toward him, eager to sit in his father's lap. Nathaniel gathers the boy in his arms, balancing those small feet on the tops of his legs. He dares to look into Ezekiel's face. Red cheeks, delicate lips, eyes big enough to swallow him, all of his love gathered in one place. The boy is no longer scared of his father; Nathaniel no longer sees his own fear reflected back at him in the boy's features. It is as though a dark veil has lifted; now they can see each other without shame. Sarah takes a seat at the other end of the table, head bowed in prayer. Nathaniel offers a blessing for the food, for his family, for the town of Cana. When he finishes, Sarah's amen comes louder than his own. The apple did not fall far with this one. Here is Whitfield's austerity staring back at him. Not so hard to see why the two of them have found it difficult to relate. He must learn to be patient with her, this girl who now thinks she is the one adult in the house. Once her mother is happy again, returned to herself, the girl will no doubt follow. She has taken on too much responsibility, poor Sarah, after being spoiled for so many years.

They eat in silence. A comfortable silence, it seems to him, though Sarah's granite stare returns each time he looks in her direction. Catherine continues to work at the embroidery, something bright and cheery, perhaps a scene of garden flowers to hang about the crib. Though he eats only one or two bites of the pottage, it is filling, such is the size of his appetite these days. He eats these bites for Sarah, in gratitude for her hard work. He spoons a few small bites to Ezekiel, careful not to spill.

"And how has today been, family?" he says at last, hardly believing the ease of his words. By the sudden change in Sarah's expression, he can see he is not alone in his incredulity.

Catherine smiles, though it is not an entirely natural smile. "It has been an interesting day."

Sarah clears away their bowls, though Ezekiel has not finished his bite. Ezekiel swats at his sister as she takes the spoon.

"Interesting?" Whitfield says, laughing, for this is the first time Catherine has ever described her day at the house as such. He is happy to see her active again. Before he began to return home earlier each day, he would find her curled on one side of the bed, deep inside a troubled sleep. No matter how he tried to console her, no matter how tightly he held her against him, he could not seem to wake her from the nightmare.

"We'd a visitor today," Catherine says.

"Oh?" Taking up her enigmatic tone.

"Yea." Catherine looks at him with sharp eyes. "Can you guess?"

"Mercy?" The name of the midwife who occasionally brings them cuts of venison for Ezekiel's blood health.

"No."

"Could it have been Deborah?"

"I should hope not." Catherine's turn to laugh.

"Then I cannot guess."

"Anne Lyman."

Nathaniel's skin grows cold. What a terror, to have walked right into this trap just when he had believed he was safe. He must be cautious to let his smile fade naturally, before it becomes an open-mouthed gape.

"She wishes us to call upon them next Friday." Catherine places her embroidery upon the table: a scene of the garden, their garden, the garden he built for her in a happier time. There is some unstated question on those lips that, pressed tightly together once more, seem ever so subtly to accuse him. He feels she is waiting for some confirmation from him. The thought of Anne relaying something that might arouse Catherine's suspicions.

"The woman is certainly odd, though I do find her charming," Catherine continues, a little too offhandedly. "I've never until to-day really considered her. I suppose, now I think on it, I have never really considered Arthur either. Why do you suppose a man like that really comes to a place like this? Most of our flock were poor when you met them. They had very little to lose, myself included."

"I suppose the Word of God is not sufficient cause?" Fortunately, Nathaniel is skilled at keeping his face free of emotion.

"Of course, Nathaniel," Catherine says, her voice equally devoid of emotion. They have studied him too well, his family. "It is only that one might find the Word of God in any place. No, I think it must be something else."

That she does not utter her next thought doesn't mean he can't hear it: Arthur came to Cana for the same reason I did. Love, is it not?

"I don't believe Friday will be suitable," Nathaniel says. "I may be in Stockbridge."

"Well, dear, I've already promised her." Catherine returns to her stump work.

"Why would you do such a thing?" At the sound of his father's distress, Ezekiel begins to squirm.

"I should hardly think it merits such great concern. She seemed insistent, and I didn't much feel like being discourteous to a neighbor I hardly know outside of church."

He feels Sarah's eyes upon him, studying him. What could have happened while he was away? What have these two seen?

"I must plan my days properly. A single interruption may ruin me for weeks."

"I have always respected your plans, Nathaniel, but what about mine? Am I to sit in this house forever waiting upon your return?"

"I have been here when I am able. I have made the effort."

"You make it sound as though returning to your family is all effort. I am only asking for one night. I would like to know her better since you are so close with Arthur. You brought them here, did you not? They are seen by many as strangers, and I believe it is our Christian duty to usher them into the fold."

Nathaniel flinches at the name. "I don't know Arthur that well. Not so much as I once thought."

"Is there some trouble between you? Is that why you'll not go?" He cannot detect anything at all by her tone; perhaps his guilt has led him to conjure his family's suspicions, yet it seems to him the lack of anything at all might be the greatest proof of suspicion. "Is this the real reason you spend more time at home?"

He must offer some truth in this lie to avoid detection. "No, there's no trouble. It is only that he has been a bit of a distraction to me. He is always asking for favors, and I can't be seen choosing favorites within my flock."

"Well, he's a busy and important man. We owe him a great deal for helping us with Ezekiel."

Sarah pauses in her cleaning. "We don't really know how he would have fared, though, with the typhoid. He arrived after Abigail's death, when things were already much improved in our town. It seems to me he has not been properly tested. We do not really know the Lymans, do we?"

"What a frightful thing to say, child," Catherine says. Ezekiel, now fitful in the midst of these arguments, reaches for his mother. She carries him to her side and smothers the top of his head with kisses. "What's gotten into you, Sarah?"

"I'm afraid I must retire to my study," Nathaniel says, standing, already halfway out of the kitchen. "I've more reading to do before the service tomorrow." Another lie.

Without waiting for an answer from his family, he trudges up the stairs to his study. He closes the door behind him, careful not to slam it. The room feels unfamiliar in the new dark. In shadow, his face assumes its true form, first as a mask of sorrow at the loss of his will, then one of joy at the thought of growing closer to Arthur again, of being powerless to stop their meeting, at the mercy of their wives. The moon is a pale sickle on his desk; he has forgotten to bring a candle. Even the simplest of lies he cannot sufficiently provide for.

Arthur Lyman paces his study. Soon they will have need to light the sconces, finish up whatever preparations Anne has in mind before the Whitfields arrive this evening. He presses his fingers to the velvet cream buttons of his coat. An extravagance, certain, but Anne had all but asked him to wear it. She had burst into his study wearing her black and gold silk gown, its pattern so resembling lace work, the wide dome of her skirts all the more dramatic for her tiny waist. She had asked him, in a voice jolly with light mockery, what he might wear to match her glory. Her smile was infectious; he was happy, safe within the sphere of approval her beauty had always met in the city.

Arthur's fingers move between the buttons to the shirt beneath, smoothing the fabric. He checks his breeches for signs of wear. He stands before the looking glass and searches his face and neck for stubble. Behind him stretch the leather spines of his medical books, his volumes of botany, philosophy. Upon the desk at his back sit stacks of foolscap. Such is the appearance of a learned fop; he resists the urge to laugh at himself. In truth, though, Arthur looks handsome even with the pomp, and though all week long he had forced the thought of Friday out of his mind, he had risen early each day this week to tend to his ablutions with extra fuss, aware in some part of his mind that Nathaniel would soon be looking.

Downstairs, he finds Anne setting the hall table. Martha retrieves a stack of their good china from the corner cupboard, carrying it with some effort to her mother, a nervous frown upon her face. She will be a beauty like Anne. A troubled beauty, one who cannot help but fret like her mother. A light dusting of powder upon her blond hair. She wears one of her rare Boston dresses, of cream silk with a pearl stomacher, so light it could be made of cloud.

"Beautiful, child," he says.

She stares at him, startled by the compliment. He does not often give compliments; it is not in his nature to do so; something prevents him from doing the very thing that he knows will bring these women happiness. Tonight, however, his tongue has been loosed; he feels freer than he has in many months.

"Thank you, Father," Martha says at last, fidgeting with one of his buttons. "And you are quite the gentleman. It's been far too long since we've seen you properly dressed. Just because we live in the wilderness does not mean you must look like any old bumpkin."

"I must admit it feels odd," he says, taking her hand in his, pressing her fingers to his lips an automatic gesture he hardly takes notice of. "Though not at all unpleasant."

"I am glad to see you so happy, Father, though I don't believe you've ever shown it quite this way." Martha removes her hand, blushing. "It is as though we never left."

"Yea, Daughter. For tonight."

"Of course." The shadow of her mother's frown already threatening her quivering mouth. "Though perhaps there will be more of these nights once the two families grow very close."

"Let us think of tonight, child, and be content."

In the kitchen, he finds every surface crammed with serving dishes: roast turkey dressed with veal, stewed red cabbage, pickled black currants. They have saved their rations all week, eating little for supper, and here is Anne's magnificent result. He pauses before the spread, stomach protesting with an audible roar. He dips one finger in the boiled apple pudding, another in the onion soup, savoring, wearing a mischievous schoolboy smile in case he is caught.

The other rooms are similarly spiced: the festive garlands, the dried flowers Anne has placed in the corners of the rooms. When he meets her beside the dining table, he offers a peck on the cheek. She ducks, flustered in her haste to set the table, but he catches a smile.

"After a thorough inspection, my dear, I must say this is your finest work yet."

"I had thought this night was a grand idea." Anne searches about the room. "Suddenly I feel as though I've forgotten something, some crucial detail right under my nose. I cannot shake the feeling. I've lived with it all day, this dread."

"Do you not remember? You are always this way before a dinner."

"What if it's the biggest detail of them all? You don't think they're coming out of charity, do you? I had thought Catherine was pleased with the invitation, but then I said something about your traveling to Stockbridge when Ezekiel was sick, and I noticed some agitation in her, yes, the same agitation on your face right now. Is it something I should have left undisturbed?"

Arthur coughs into his sleeve, disguising his concern. "Nothing to disturb. The reverend and I are still quite close. You always fret."

"We are too worldly, I fear. Have you said anything untoward? Or perhaps he didn't tell her about your visit."

Another cough, then, "Likely the poor woman didn't want to be reminded of that time. You didn't see her when she came to the house. She hadn't slept for days."

"I suppose you're right, dear," Anne says. "Though it will never be quite the same as in the city."

"We must move on." He pulls her in for an embrace. "We have moved on."

"Have we, Arthur?" Something curious in her voice. Still, she answers to his touch. "I can't be certain either of us has changed. I fear I would give this new life up just to throw another of our parties one last time. A terrible thing to say, I know. I'm terribly ungrateful."

"Don't worry yourself, Anne. We gave up that life for a reason."

"But you do want it, don't you? You still want some of those old things?" Anne falls back against him, releasing herself to him.

"I didn't want to lose you," he says. His words are true, though they are the secondary reason for his bringing them all to Cana. She must have begun to suspect the primary reason. "I don't want to lose you."

"Would you help me with the trunk?" she says, breaking the spell, moving past him to the other side of the table. "It's in Martha's chamber near her bed."

"Do you think it appropriate?"

"We've discussed this," Anne says. "Catherine doesn't mind. Our minister should have a bit of fun."

Arthur pictures Nathaniel in costume. He has only ever seen him in a gown or a shirt or, on one enthralling occasion, wearing nothing. Anne has created a space where new modes of living might exist. After all, he thinks, mounting the stairs to his daughter's chamber, it would seem as though their wives wish for the two of them to grow closer once more; perhaps, in some odd way, God has planned for this, a kind of tacit agreement between all parties even if nothing is ever known for certain, even if there are only hints and doubts. And Nathaniel has agreed to all of it. Certainly that is the most important part. Nathaniel has agreed to come to the house even after their pact.

He carries the trunk down the stairs. Only after he has deposited it in the parlor does he think of the curtain. The tableau would be better with a curtain. He rushes to his chamber, searching for an old bedsheet. He finds some blue linen he can drape across one corner of the parlor, from the mantelpiece to the sconce opposite. Once returned to the hall, he snuffs out the fire in the sconce, and just as the smoke has begun to clear, he turns, fabric in hand, to see Anne leading Catherine and Ezekiel through the doorway.

The child's skin is all blush in the low light. Ezekiel has grown miraculously larger in the time since Arthur last saw him, his legs powerful now, sturdy enough to walk across the room with confidence. Arthur crouches, spreading his arms wide. Ezekiel rushes to him. As he toddles faster, the boy stumbles and falls, striking his elbow upon the hard floor. Ezekiel cries out in pain. The sound is so dreadful to Arthur; he is so wrapped up in the boy's well-being that he does not wait for Catherine to console the child. He rushes to Ezekiel and takes him in his arms, snuggling him against his chest. Desperate kisses upon the boy's cheeks, desperate soul-quenching kisses, how he had missed them.

"My sweet one," he says. It is the name he used for Ezekiel when the three of them were alone in the clearing. There had been three times, three times when Nathaniel allowed him to visit the boy there. And each time the boy had reached for him instinctively as he does now. "My sweet one, are you hurt?"

Arthur does not see Catherine's expression at first. He does not see anything but the boy and his pain, this desire to ensure the child never feels another second of it. Only once he sees the boy is fine does Catherine's face appear before him, lips parted in something like amusement, perhaps even shock.

"Always the physician," she says, her eyes not yet meeting his. "I should think if you reacted this way to every scrape and tumble in our town, you'd never find a moment's peace." Ah, here they are: those sharp all-knowing eyes. Arthur must look away. "I fear I may also be guilty of taking advantage of this excess compassion of yours. I called upon you when Ezekiel was not truly sick, and when his father returned the next day, all was right. I feel foolish about it, I do. I hope you can forgive me."

"I am always happy to be of help," Arthur says, careful now. "I cannot tolerate suffering of any kind."

"What a sensitive man," Catherine says. "I should find it unbearable to think as you do."

"It is not thought which governs that part of me, Mrs. Whitfield."

"Well, I am glad my little Ezekiel is not an exception. I should hate to think you preferred him to other children. It would not look right, the minister's son receiving special treatment. I suppose your traveling to Stockbridge on behalf of this little one was nothing extraordinary after all. I must confess, when Anne told me, I was quite surprised."

He searches her eyes for signs of sympathy or ire. He finds he cannot read her, not yet. But there can be no doubt she is in search of something. Whatever he says must be measured.

"Yea, Mrs. Whitfield, I would have done it for anyone in this town, though I was glad to do it for you."

"He seems to have taken to you from the first. Usually, he is uncomfortable around strangers."

The boy's grip tightens. Catherine edges close. It is clear she wants Ezekiel to cry out for her, but he does not. He and Arthur might as well be the only ones in this room. As she waits, a fire kindles beneath her expression; he can see it now. She knows.

Only at the approach of Nathaniel, who has appeared without warning at the edge of the room, does the boy turn from Arthur—almost as though, his blood recalling nights spent in the forest meadow, everyone save his two fathers has receded into the gathering darkness. Sarah stands beside Nathaniel in the doorway. Here are two more who know, Arthur thinks suddenly, as the pair advances. He is drawn at once to the handsome red coat with gold buttons and gold trim, so ornate it almost looks amusing on the minister, yet the cut is fine, perfectly suited to his slim frame. Sarah wears a

simple light-gray cotton dress to match her mother's, a scarlet ribbon tied round her waist. Her eyes are ringed with a worry far beyond her years, though there is something resigned in her look,
something that tells him she has known for quite some time, though
he cannot imagine when or how she discovered it.

Arthur pries Ezekiel from his neck and sets him down gently
upon the floor. The boy clings to his leg, pressing his face
against it, drying his tears upon the fabric. And here are another
two who know, this boy and I. We two pairs stand opposite one
another, a perfect symmetry for the stage, while Catherine and
my wife, now entering upstage, stand distant from each other,
though they are paired in ways they do not yet know, by a link they
are only beginning to understand. And here am I, curtain curled
round my fist, waiting, as though the performance has not already
begun.

Sarah cannot but admire Martha's chamber. Though it is nearly
identical to her own, small touches add color and meaning—drama,
really—to the space. There, above the doorway, hangs a nautical
spear, hardly fitting for a girl yet wonderfully exciting to one with a
fanciful mind. Over there, a bit of bobbin lace wrapped idly round
one of the bedposts, as though in the middle of the night one might
wish to caress its delicate surface. And just to Sarah's right, a chest of
drawers has been painted with the tendrils and little white buds of a
flower she has neither seen nor named. Martha leads Sarah to the bed,
patting a space for her.

"So you are the one to teach me to read," Martha says, yawning. Sarah can't help but gape at the red mouth, the pink tongue so delicate it might belong to a cat.

"It seems so," Sarah says, taking a seat beside her, noting the soft material beneath the mattress, wool or cotton in place of the plain itchy straw Sarah sleeps upon each night. "If that is what your mother wishes."

"My mother wishes me to learn nothing. Had we continued living in Boston, she might have had her wish."

"Do girls never learn to read in Boston?"

"They do if they want to." Martha studies the petite hands resting in her lap almost as though they do not belong to her. "But here in this town, there are so many rules. One must do so many things. Today I worked in the Griggses' fields for the harvest. Of course, the Griggs brothers were kind enough to spare me from anything but bagging, but I fear my hands may be spoiled now. I miss Boston."

Hard to imagine ten-year-old Martha can vividly remember her time in Boston. Nevertheless, Sarah understands how a mother's story can live on in her daughter. Even if she wanted to, Sarah can never forget that the birth of Cana, at least in part, resulted from a spark of passion between her mother and father, a forbidden kiss, that intimate but public moment that must have shocked all who saw it.

Before this glimpse of Martha's life in Boston, Sarah had never truly considered that the rest of the world might not operate in the same fashion for all women, that there might be other possibilities available to her elsewhere. Yet Martha's old life, a life without learning, a life in which one merely sits about in parlors wearing pretty dresses, such a life would no doubt prove deeply unpleasant to Sarah. Even as her back aches from the labor she must do in Cana, she is happy for the distraction work provides, the way work orders her life so the evil she senses creeping toward her family from the edge of the forest feels less tangible, if only for a moment. But might there exist, elsewhere in the world, a society where she could become the Sarah who is not merely her father's daughter, one where she might fashion her own rules? Yet such thinking could prove dangerous, more akin to her father's rebellious ways than it might first appear.

"Perhaps certain rules protect us from our worst instincts," Sarah says, wondering, as the words leave her, whether it was the Lymans' permissiveness, their general lack of moral sternness, that might have contributed to her father's corruption.

"Too many rules make one a bore," Martha says.

"And did your father have many rules for you when you were growing up?" Sarah does her best to make the question sound casual.

"He might have tried from time to time." Martha lies back on the bed, powdered ringlets fanning out behind her, quite pretty enough to pet. "Though if he did try, I never knew. Mother ran everything in Boston. Now it is the other way around, and none of us likes it, including Father."

"Why?"

"Father has only ever been happy when he listens to Mother. But she followed him here, and now he must lead, and it is so very unnatural. I shall never marry."

"Don't say that," Sarah says, though the words could have come from her own lips.

"I cannot lie to the minister's daughter."

"It is early yet." Sarah softens her tone. "You are young." Perhaps she has judged Martha too quickly. There might be room for reformation in her yet. After all, they are both the daughters of confused, selfish men; they have not been given the best models.

"Oh Sarah," Martha says, spreading her arms wide and closing her eyes. "You wish to judge me. Please do not take me seriously. I am a foolish girl. That is what they all say. In the schoolhouse, Mr. Shephard always uses me as an example."

Martha sits upright, taking Sarah's hands in hers, pressing them. Tears fill her eyes, threatening to spill onto her pillowy cheeks. "Will you teach me, Sarah? I look at you and I see such a godly woman. You are godly, and good, and right in all of your ways. You are the minister's daughter! I can't bear another second of their judgment. Even the younger children mock me. They say I am not of the Elect, and I fear they are right. I do not wish to be separated from my family forever, to burn eternally in the fiery pit."

"I am not who you think I am," Sarah says, startled by her own admission, which has been drawn out, in part, by her pity. She envies and pities the innocence she sees before her, the trust Martha has in others. All Sarah can do now is see two faces to every adult.

"I do not always know the right way," Sarah says. "I pray for guidance, but I, like you, never know if I am right. It was much simpler before. Now I am very confused."

"Before what?"

Sarah must think quickly. "Before I knew more of the world."

"You speak in riddles, Sarah. I suppose it is because you are wise beyond your years."

"I am a fool. I am just as lost as any sheep without a shepherd."

"How is it possible? The minister's daughter does not hear the voice of God more clearly? If that is the case, someone like me will most surely be damned. Oh Sarah, please tell me it isn't true. Tell me you can help me."

"You are looking to a human for help," Sarah says, "when what you truly require is God."

"I have tried." Martha shakes her head. "I have tried, but it is so difficult speaking to God. It is like speaking into the mouth of a cave. You've a father whose very voice channels the Word of God. You can hear Him, can you not?"

"Sometimes," Sarah admits. "Sometimes I can hear Him and see His visions. But other times, especially of late, I cannot do either."

"Teach me your ways, Sarah. I try to listen to your father every Sabbath service, but I grow so bored I forget what he has said by the end of it. I am sure it is all very nice, but if you were to tell me these same truths, I think I should believe them more easily. You've really something special about you. Don't shake your head. It's true. There is some magic to you. You could be a perfect natural on the stage, commanding the attention of a great audience."

"You are absurd, Martha." Sarah cannot help but smile at the girl's silliness.

"Then you will save me from myself?"

"I fear we both need saving."

"Then it will be easier, will it not, if we work together? Mother says all anyone ever speaks of in the square is an awakening. How I would love to be changed in the instant."

Is that the answer? Sarah wonders. If an awakening were to arrive in Cana, the town might be cleansed of her father's sin, they might all be saved. Perhaps the visions God has sent Sarah have been leading her to this truth the entire time; she must simply wait to discover their ultimate meaning.

A knock, jolting Sarah from her thoughts. Anne, beautiful in her black and gold dress, stands framed in the doorway, a vision of opulence.

"It is exactly as I'd hoped," Anne says, clapping. "Tonight you have become an honorary Lyman, Sarah."

Nathaniel arrives at the table long before the others, eager to find his place. Far too few candles in this hall, though he is grateful for the sense of seclusion this grants him, as though he is already safe and solitary at the end of a long night. The hall windows have all had their curtains pulled back, the moonless expanse an inexhaustible black closing in upon a huddle of light. It is as though everything in this house is but a dream, a flickering possibility that will snap into absurdity the moment he wakes.

In the parlor, they had been speaking of the awakening in Northampton. Anne had brought it up even as she seemed to feel sorry for mentioning it at all. He prides himself on ignoring the gossip in this town, on leading his flock without comparing himself to the deeds of other ministers in other towns. For the past year, he has ignored the excited whisper of the word "miracle," which has begun to spread about this continent far too often, for there are far too many claims that turn out, on closer inspection, to be mere whims, hallucinatory religious experiences brought on by an excess of emotion. One must be cautious, he had argued, his voice thunderous in the small parlor, as though standing before the pulpit. Give these awakenings time, and only then shall we see if they bear the fruit of the Spirit. He had noted their eyes as he said this, the way they all avoided his gaze. Of course, his words must have sounded false, the petty bitterness of a jealous minister who, once, many years ago, had so captivated with his own miracle, the saving of hundreds of souls.

But Anne had surprised him. Just when he thought he might have ruined the evening, she rushed to his rescue with a statement so surprising, so insightful.

"You are right, minister," she said. "We must not forget the events in Salem, after all, which took place not some forty years ago, and not so very far from where we now live. The people of Salem believed they knew how to weigh right from wrong, good from evil, who was a saint and who a witch. Now the magistrates in our great province admit they were wrong. They apologize for killing those poor women, but these apologies do little good. It is too late for those murdered women. We would not want, at some distant date, to wake up here in Cana and realize we have committed a horrible atrocity within our own flock. Yea, it is far better to remain cautious, as you are, Reverend Whitfield."

He had truly seen Anne then. Not on account of her beauty or the artful way she said those words, but for the fact that she had searched his soul and found the soft spot there, the deep uncertainty he could never quite put behind him, and she had soothed him. Though

Arthur had given his reasons for marrying Anne, it was only in that moment that Nathaniel fully understood why she was so valuable to her husband.

"Yea, Anne," he said. "Our emotions must be governed by reason, by thoughtful prayer." At this, he risked a glance at Arthur, whose eyes he had felt upon him the entire time. "When we give way to our unchecked senses too freely, we risk making fools of ourselves—or worse, harming others."

Waiting at the table now, Nathaniel can hear voices as the others enter the hall. Anne arrives with Martha and Sarah from the stairway while Catherine, Ezekiel, and Arthur arrive from the parlor, smiles upon each of their faces. He had been loath to leave them alone, but nothing had happened. For a moment, he forgets to fear love and its many permutations.

Arthur is larger than ever in his too-tight coat, one that must have been a perfect fit in his bachelor days, yet even so, it is pleasing to the eye. And there beneath the sleeve of his coat is the vein Nathaniel has traced with his finger, a purple ribbon running along the back of Arthur's right hand, always so plump. A vein, he knows, which travels through the forearm, growing wider, a river, and if he were to remove the man's clothes, he would find a deep crescent scar upon the arm where Arthur in his youth had fallen upon his father's scythe. When Arthur's father had learned of his boy's mistake, he told him to dress the wound himself, for the boy had been warned against sharp objects, he deserved his fate, so the boy had bled more than he should have that day, collapsing upon the grass until he awoke in a pool of his own blood. Arthur had told Nathaniel this late at night after they had coupled, and Nathaniel recognized within this story the story of his own cruel childhood, one he was not yet prepared to share. "I did not then know of tourniquets," Arthur said, laughing it off. "I suppose that was my first lesson as a man of medicine. Perhaps I should thank my father for it." Arthur's face as he said this is the same Nathaniel sees before him now, proud and direct, yet wise, with a commanding jawline offset by disarmingly sensitive eyes, like the ruins of a formidable empire now gentled by scholarly curiosity. Nathaniel remembers how that face gazed upon him from above as Arthur pressed him, as he felt weighted, for the first time in his life, by another man's bulk—a pleasant entrapment, one he hadn't known he needed until it was there.

Arthur's eyes meet Nathaniel's as he takes his seat at the other end of the table, a flash of the old recognition. Catherine, Sarah, and Anne return from the kitchen with heaped dishes, so much food he can hardly imagine it is meant only for them.

"Eat as much as you can," Anne says.

"Temperance in all things." Nathaniel lifts his plate. "But if you insist."

Waterman's Arms
Hull, Province of Georgia,
November 16, 1765.

Sister,

I write to you from the Waterman's Arms, a modest tavern frequented by the millworkers of Hull, of which I may now count myself a solid member. I take my seat at the rear of the room, for there are no private rooms in this place, and I certainly do not pass as a gentleman who could afford one. I am not certain I pass for a man at all; your brother has grown quite thin and pale; he might slip through a narrow crack in the wall as easily as a ghost. If it were not for this duster I wear, which appears to swell my flesh to double size, I might be seen as a woman, which, you must know, would not trouble me in the slightest.

I have only one friend in this town. His name is Samuel Dent, a sawyer and owner of the mill. His wife, Aphra.

Still young, both of them, residing in a proper two-room house. They have generously offered me board, and I have agreed to it, since earlier I slept where I could, often with only the slim walls of a hutch to keep out the elements.

Once again, I have found a place to call home. Strange as it sounds, I have not until this moment allowed myself to think on possessing such a place in the world, after running so far from the last place I could call by this name. Perhaps that is the reason I write to you now after so many years. I dreamt of your cooking only yesterday when, returning from the forest with a heaping of mushrooms, I assisted Aphra in making a stew. I remembered how you sat me at the worktable as a child and fed me from your spoon, how I could hear your sounds always throughout the house, of cooking and cleaning and praying. How glorious was that noise, and how sad it made me to think I might never hear it again.

At night, I hear only silence from their chamber. I include this detail because once, when Samuel injured his shoulder, I made a salve for him as Arthur might do, one composed of whatever was at hand—white grapes, juniper berries, mint—and as I pressed the paste into the wound, I felt him looking at me, studying me, as though he only just realized I was a person with a past, in possession of a full life. Since I do not speak words aloud at all, it must be easy for people to think I am not one of them; it is certainly easy for them to think they may utter anything they wish in my presence with no reason to fear my babbling to another soul about it.

So I have always been a receptacle of secrets since the day I first knew who my other father truly was. In fact, I have only ever seen that look of Samuel's in the eyes of the two men who called themselves my fathers. I know you feel as though this union of theirs operated as a corruption upon my soul, that it was the reason for my muteness. But through the years, I have come to realize that it had quite the opposite effect in me, and the love and goodness I witnessed in their eyes was the love and goodness of Christ Himself, a love which could never cleave itself from us no matter what society thought of it. It is only society's judgments, and Father's fears of those judgments, which I have begun to suspect has brought about my mute state. I do not know what will come of this look I saw in Samuel Dent's eyes. I was shocked to find it here, on the frontier, in this wilderness. Perhaps there are, indeed, many more men like my fathers, and only I can see them for who or what they are because I've the eyes to see it. I may never know the answers to these questions.

You may ask yourself why it is I am writing to you from such an unruly place. The answer is simple and perhaps disappointing. I have found it unbearable to continue living alone. I arrived here ready to forget that I am lost, the lost Whitfield. Nobody. I am a person whose past has been sealed away.

Do you recall our last happy time together, all of us as a family? I myself can hardly remember it. Perhaps it is only an illusion; perhaps that which I believe to be real is a phantom, and it was only I who was happy: I, the child once beloved by all. Perhaps not even that much is true. It could be you have always hated me, Sister. It could be you toss these letters into the fire, content never to speak to me again. I cannot bear such a thought. I will think on it no longer. Write to me, dear Sister, so I may banish it from my mind. I have been awaiting your response since my first letter to you in the new year. I travel to this tavern daily in the hope that one sweet morning you will return to me, if only in words. You have always been so gifted with words, Sarah. You have always been the most brilliant Whitfield of us all.

I understand the weight of history now, Sister. When I left you—when I abandoned you and Mother—I did not yet understand it. I was simply trying to save my life from ruin. I could not do what they asked of me. I could not commit an unforgivable act to save our family, for there would have been nothing left of the family to save if I had gone through with it. You no doubt view this as selfish. I do not blame you. What I have done to you is unforgivable. Just now, in writing this letter, I was angry you had not answered me. But I was not fair. It is unfair of me to ask you to write me after all that has happened, yet I find I cannot live without hearing from you, Sister. I imagine this is how you felt when you discovered I would not speak. Once again, it is not fair that I ask for something I did not give you. Yet still I ask you. I need you. Mine is a selfish need. It is best if you toss this letter in the fire.

Even so, I remain

forever yours,
Nobody

II

─────

COVENANT

1734

1.

Fall

The shore of his mother's palm, her warmth as she leads him along the banks to their spot by the river. On the other bank, women sing in a strange language. French, his mother tells him. The French who have claimed a patchwork command over this vast continent. She has learned a few words to greet them. He swallows her words, carries them in the back of his throat until one day, without warning, they erupt from his mouth. Bonjour! Bonne journée! The sound is bright, light on his tongue. His mother laughs. The women say something sweet and playful in their language, a rise in the sounds of their words like the flight of a dove. They wear simple gray dresses with no caps, arms bare, stained copper by the sun; where fabric meets skin holds magic, gathering his eyes there to feast: sleeves fluttering, the revelation of pale skin beneath. Their hair falls freely to their temples and cheeks, pasted like vines.

His mother shakes out their sheets with a sudden flourish, flashing them up to meet the sun. He helps her carry the heavy wet sheets to the undergrowth, where they stretch them upon bare twigs for drying.

"Who are those women, Mother?"

"Those women are nobody, Ezekiel. Nobody important to us here in Cana."

Beneath the canopy, in the tunnel they have made for themselves, they settle into the undergrowth, their backs to the dewy grass, a white sky now in place of blue. His mother stretches her arms behind her head, yawning, her mouth the long *O* of his alphabet primer. He watches her eyes grow heavy. Somewhere beyond their sky, the women begin to move off, their words soft, sweet against his ears, falling like the quiet buzzing of fireflies at dusk.

When he wakes, it is past noon, the sun already slung behind the pines. He knows its course now, knows how it watches over them with regularity, a burning clockface he has been told never to look at directly. He presses out of the tunnel. The women are long gone, the muddy tracks along the bank the only evidence they had been here. He has learned not to be shocked by appearances and disappearances. He and his mother have seen many people on these banks. She has told him that this continent houses people different from themselves, that these wanderers may be in search of a home like their family once was.

"But who are those women?" he asks each time he sees another group.

"Those women are nobody, Ezekiel. Nobody important to us here in Cana. They will find their own home soon enough."

He thinks of the women walking for days on end, with no horses—he has never seen laundresses on horses—singing hymns in another language, eyes wandering the landscape in search of a sign. Nobodies. Free to do as they like, to find a home as they like. The thought is terrifying and exciting. It is as though he were floating above them right now, safe beside the home he and his mother have built yet somehow out there with those strangers, too, directing their steps as the sun directs his day. Go, go! Follow the sound of rushing water. Follow it deep into the valley.

He returns to his mother's side and tries to shake her awake. She does not move. Only her eyelids begin to twitch. He shakes her again, harder this time. She moans but does not awaken. Not new, this little game of theirs. Only it is not a game. Something has hold of his mother, the same something that keeps her in bed all day. He cannot predict the hour it will take her from him. He does not know why it comes or why she submits to it or why he cannot see this something when it arrives. If he could watch out for it, even if it were mere shadow—but the something that takes his mother carries no form; it seems to live inside her; there is nothing he can do to prevent its grabbing hold of her. He is helpless before it, and even as he prays each day to be given the sight to see it—whatever devil it may be—he does not really believe it will ever appear, for the demon belongs only to her, and this makes him feel even more helpless and alone.

He gives up. Stands again. A family of geese has arrived on the other shore, stamping about in the tracks the women left behind. He draws close to the water, shields his eyes to watch them. The sun hot and burning on his neck. There, nearby, on the branch of an oak: a simple shift of fine white linen. The breeze inflates the sleeves, threatening to knock the shift into the mud. The river is fast-moving and deeper than usual. It is the *S* that cuts through the eastern part of their town, dividing the fields. Once, his father walked him the length of the river's span through Cana, listing each new sight. "These are but shadows," his father said. "We walk in shadows, child. One day, when we have reached those glorious shores of Heaven, we shall see not honeyed light but light made of honey, not mist like blue satin but satin itself, not birdsong but the song of creation itself. So long as you seek out the right kind of beauty, you will possess inside of you the power to comprehend salvation."

Ezekiel has been training himself to seek out only the right kind of beauty. His sense of the beautiful is often at odds with his father's command. Yesterday he had spotted a bit of yellow ribbon from one of his sister's dresses caught in her chest of drawers. Touching the fabric, so soft and pliant, he felt as though it were beauty crafted solely for his hands. He suspects his father does not want him to take notice of such things, that there is something wrong in what he notices, but he could no more ignore it than he could forsake the air he breathes.

The shift flashes in the wind. Below it, geese hunt the grassy banks for food, their long necks folding upon themselves in one easy fluid motion, the water beside them moving in tandem, so all about Ezekiel there is ease, surrender. He steps closer to the shore, shoes sinking into mud. He kicks them off. He removes his stockings and places them inside his shoes, tossing them somewhere behind him. He rolls up his breeches. When he steps into the water, icy tongues lick his feet, his calves. He is freed once more. At four, he must wear adult clothes. Gone is the gown he wore before this age; now he must wear his worms, the name he gives to the breeches that seem to swallow him whole, impeding his movement, his freedom. "Worms!" his father had shouted from the pulpit, Ezekiel watching from the pew directly below, in awe of this sudden stranger with his father's face who shouted and pleaded with the flock to feel, for a moment, the fiery flames of Hell. Where their worm dieth not and the fire is not quenched. "And if thy foot offend thee, cut it off; it is better for thee to enter halt into life than having two feet to be cast into Hell, into the fire that never shall be quenched." Ezekiel had heard the word echoing in his head after that. *Worms! Worms!* When he placed his legs inside a pair of breeches for the first time, he thought of worms digging their way up from Hell to meet him. Sometimes he grows angry that his father is allowed to wear the gown he wants to wear. He asked his father once why it is he continues to wear the gown, and his father told him that one day he, too, would wear the gown once more, when he finally becomes the minister he is destined to become. It is this idea and this alone, of wearing a gown again, that attracts Ezekiel to the ministry.

As the water swells round his thighs, Ezekiel considers how it would feel to cut off his feet. To cut off the hand that so desperately wishes to touch the shift on the opposite bank. How to cut off skin from the body—every inch of it—skin that desires nothing more than to be held in the loose fabric of childhood. What would be left after all of the cutting? Would there be a person after that?

The water pulls him deeper. Though his heels sink into the mud. The sun cooks the back of his neck, its reflection in the water bright, blinding. He closes his eyes, the water now lapping his shoulders, his chin. He breathes through his nose. When next he opens his eyes, the shore is still far away, but it is too late to turn back. He checks to see if his mother is asleep and, yes, she remains buried beneath the sheet, oblivious. He steps deeper into the water, unsure now, but there is no going back; his balance has already tipped toward that other shore; any moment he will sink under. He is tired, tired like his mother. The shift flashes white, a flag offering surrender, peace, Heaven. He lets himself go to float toward it.

When Catherine awakens, dusk fills the air. Where there had once been no life in her limbs, there is now an abundance of energy. She scrambles to her feet, knocking the clean sheet to the dirt, rendering useless the one thing she had been able to offer the day. Sarah, the real woman of the house now, will no doubt wonder what has happened to her. She had not told a soul where she was going this afternoon, had used up the sudden willpower she detected in herself with immediate action, as if to prove she could still be Catherine. But there is something else. There had been something else. Why is it she must now move with haste to the bank? There had been the women, yes, and—

She searches all about her, looking for any signs of Ezekiel, her heart suddenly outsize for her chest. He is nowhere, her boy. Lost. She calls out to him, her voice no longer her own, the desperate sound of an animal caught in a predator's jaws. Geese honk angrily in response. She returns to the undergrowth and searches every inch for him. There are no signs, no clues. Nothing he has left behind aside from a confused set of muddy tracks. For a moment she is angry with him for being so careless, then she reminds herself that it is not his fault, that he is a curious boy. Her vision escapes her. She cannot see. The shadows have begun to creep in, and soon it will be dark, too dark to find him. She calls out again, this time with something beyond desperation, a hint of resignation she does not wish to hear, for it should not be possible for a mother to give up so easily, to lose hope, to sink into despair, but she is such a mother, she knows, because for as long as she can remember here in Cana she has felt that a punishment is due or perhaps that one has been slowly enacting itself upon her.

Catherine sinks to her knees on the muddy bank. Had she the energy to pray, she would offer up one final prayer: that the Lord spare her child and take her in his place. When next her eyes meet the opposite bank, however, what she sees is a flash of pale light, almost like a rising moon, somewhere within the line of trees. Perhaps whoever is in those trees will know where her son has gone, will tell her where to look. She glances behind her once more, then enters the water, realizing, too late, that she has not removed her shoes. She feels them sink into the mud, eagerly abandoning her feet. With each step, she sinks deeper, half fearing she will land upon bone or a tender bit of flesh, something to tell her the son she loves is under the water. When she emerges on the opposite bank, her legs are coated in mud; she shivers from the cold. She must look like a madwoman, but her feet propel her toward the stranger in the trees, the person who seems to be hiding from her now. As her feet meet the other bank, it is not so much the shape of him or his movements that tell her this is her son, a stranger now, so much larger than he ever seemed to be, so much older, though certainly his shape and the movement of his limbs are more familiar than her own; rather, it is his restlessness, his untamable nature, that announces his presence, the same nature living inside herself; only in him its expression takes the form of a wandering spirit, a desire to venture forth into wilderness, whereas in her it brings forth heaviness, surrender, submission to the bed's tide. A blessing, to move outward rather than inward, to push forward rather than to retreat inside.

"My boy," she says, stretching out her hands, sobs rising to her chest. "I thought I had lost you."

She presses him to her, coating him in mud, kissing the top of his head. He is warm despite the coolness of the evening, despite the fact that he, too, has been coated in the river's mud. In the bit of world beyond his shoulder, she can see his shirt and breeches hanging upon a limb, discarded, and it is only once she sees this that she realizes he is wearing a woman's large shift, the fabric falling to his toes.

"What is this, child?"

"I came across, Mother. Father said I should seek beauty."

"Did one of those French women bring you here?"

"No, Mother," Ezekiel says, eyes filling at the sound of his mother's fear, her anger. "I wanted to wear it."

"What is this about your father?"

"He said I should find shadows of Heaven."

"But this shift is ugly. Someone didn't want it. It is not for you to wear."

"Why?"

"Because it's not fitting for a boy to wear. Your father did not mean that kind of beauty. You must take it off at once."

"Why?"

"What were you thinking, child?" She cannot breathe; the sobs grip her throat. "You could have drowned."

"Are we in Heaven yet, Mother? Father said I would find the heavenly shore if I sought beauty."

Catherine's hand moves before she can think. A slap, one that sounds just like her mother's. His face is so surprised that he doesn't cry at first. It is Catherine who is the first to cry. She holds him tightly, begging forgiveness through her touch, for she no longer possesses the words to ask it.

Nathaniel stands beside his daughter, watching the road grow dark from the parlor window. At fourteen, Sarah has risen to his shoulders, a woman now, with features already hardened into grim determination, as though set on not becoming her mother. The two women share the same mouth, however: petulant, a hint of extravagance where one would not expect it, the same blasphemous scripture-spouting mouth that had so enraptured him in Hingham. The sight of it now, as he turns to her, quickens his pulse, as though her mother has already returned. Rarely does he see a smile on those lips; instead, he detects this frown of suspicion, never more so in Sarah than in this moment when her mother and brother have gone missing.

"I should be out with the others." He faces the room for the first time in an hour.

"We've enough people searching," Robert Inverness says, placing an arm upon the mantelpiece. Nathaniel had remembered to remove

Catherine's extravagant clock at the last minute, just before the Invernesses arrived, though now he feels he might have made a mistake, perhaps the clock has the power to draw Catherine back to him. "You must be here when they return."

If not the clock, then perhaps some magic in looking away. To trust in the Lord rather than the eyes, and when next Nathaniel turns back to the view of the road, they will be standing there, safe.

Deborah Inverness sits upon the divan with a piece of unfinished embroidery in her lap. The sight pains him, for he had seen Catherine sitting there just last evening, a bit of yellow stump work in her hands, what would soon become a jonquil in a garden scene. They had passed the night together pleasantly. He had read from the gospels, and she had been comforted by Christ's words. *With men it is impossible, but not with God: for with God all things are possible.* "We must believe it," she had said. "We must believe anything is possible." And in her look, he had known that she still believed in him despite everything; even in his state of sinfulness he was loved. She had offered him her smile, however faint.

"Catherine has always been skilled at needlework," Deborah says. "Though none would know it. How long has it been since we last visited the Whitfields, husband?"

"A thousand years on Earth is as a day in Heaven," Robert says, taking a pinch of snuff from the pouch at his belt.

"And to find ourselves here on such an occasion," Deborah says. "It should not have come to this, reverend."

"Oh, leave the man alone," Robert says, sniffing loudly. "You of all people, Deborah——"

"When Catherine and the boy return"——Deborah continues,

unfazed—"and they shall return soon enough, reverend, I've no doubt of it, we must make an effort to see one another more often."

Not enough time has passed to search the window again, but Nathaniel can't bear to turn around. His eyes have nowhere to go, so he fixes them on his useless feet.

"If it were left up to Catherine, I'm afraid only Anne Lyman would ever lay eyes on her. Catherine possesses far too many gifts of the Spirit to hoard them all to herself."

"Leave it, Deborah," Robert warns.

"I don't mean to be hard on anyone. But you must know, reverend, how it is certain people speak of our mission. They have sought an awakening for quite some time now, yet it seems all anyone wishes to do in this town is continue sleeping, your wife being the principal example."

Nathaniel's face assumes the mask it knows so well. He squares his shoulders. He'll not stoop as Deborah hurls her rocks.

"The flock follows the lead of their shepherd," Deborah adds. "That is what it is in their nature to do."

"You are right, Deborah," Nathaniel says. "I'm afraid I make a sorry minister these days."

Sarah bursts into sudden movement beside him. She tosses another log into the fire, prodding it with the rod, a burst of embers scattering upon the hearth. Robert offers to help, but she dismisses him with the wave of a hand.

"Not right to talk like this in front of the girl," Robert says.

"I'm not a girl," Sarah says, eyes on the flames.

"A rare woman indeed," Deborah says. "Woman of the house at fourteen."

No more of this talk. Nathaniel wants to kick the Invernesses out onto the street, such is his desire for solitude until Catherine and the boy return. He hadn't wanted to tell a soul when he'd first discovered their absence, but Sarah had insisted they include others in the search. It hadn't been clear when Catherine left with the boy, or why, for Sarah had been tending the garden and Nathaniel calling upon Mr. Shephard, the schoolmaster, to discuss Ezekiel's learning, which has been alarmingly slow; most boys by the age of four have already learned to memorize Bible verses, for it is seen as a sign of corruption if the child does not take naturally to the Word. Nathaniel has been tutoring the boy in private, hoping to stimulate Ezekiel's interest with his Shadows of Divine Things, but even these seem to sit curiously in the boy's mind. He had been planning to offer another of his lessons to Ezekiel just before he discovered his boy was missing.

At first, Nathaniel had thought their absence nothing more than another of Catherine's whims, but Sarah's concern ate at him until finally he came to fear the worst. He wants no one in this room as he faces this possibility. Or no—he does wish for one person, the only person who could help him feel less alone in this moment, but to call upon him now would rouse even greater suspicion, for Arthur would take one look at Nathaniel and know at once what was troubling him. Arthur wouldn't be able to prevent himself from crying out, from rushing to Nathaniel's side and embracing him before the others. It would be as though they were alone, for in Arthur's eclipsed view, they would be. Nathaniel cannot escape the fact of Arthur's love no matter how many times he's tried.

He returns to his post by the window. No movement. The trees across the road have turned to shadow, only the hint of their bare limbs visible against the new dark. He feels Sarah draw close.

"Will they be safe, Father?" she says. He's touched by the sound of her voice, childlike, trusting. Her head settles upon his shoulder.

"They will be safe, Sarah," he says. Is it a lie to believe something only because you cannot imagine its opposite?

Dark now. He hasn't looked at a clockface for many hours. Can it be? The sound of footsteps. Slow, yet clear. He would know them anywhere.

Catherine submits to him, this stranger with her husband's features. He holds her feet in his hands as he kneels before her, caressing them, loosening the cold-clenched muscles. He has closed the two of them in his study, a steaming bowl of fire-warmed water between them while Sarah and the Invernesses tend to Ezekiel's sunburn. They must have called for Arthur by now. Catherine cannot help but feel she is being hidden away in order to spare Arthur the sight of her, yet as she gazes upon the nape of Nathaniel's neck as he bends lower to wash her feet in the manner Christ instructed His disciples, she senses absolutely this man's devotion to her.

"I thought I had lost you."

"Don't be silly, husband," she says, though her words, issuing from a throat hoarse from crying, cannot but sound serious. "It was a foolish mistake. Anyone could have made it. The day was hot, and the wind pleasant."

"We could have lost the boy." Nathaniel's fingers dig into the arches of her heels, the flesh tender and pained there. Light from a nearby candle swoons with his labored breath. "He requires more guidance. I should start taking him with me to the meetinghouse."

"He is too young." She closes her eyes. The room recedes, soft cotton rising up to meet her skin. She breathes in the scent of lavender and rosemary, herbs he has added to the water.

"Perhaps you are right. Perhaps it's best if Ezekiel is away from both of us. He may fare better living at one of the other missions."

Catherine doesn't hear the words at first. She sits up, feet slipping from his hands. "What is your meaning, husband?"

"Neither of us is entirely fit . . ."

"Ah, that," Catherine says. Rarely have they spoken of each other's weaknesses aloud, but it is here in the room with them all the same. Right above her husband's shoulder, pressed into the pages of a book on philosophy—letters. She had been curious after she discovered Sarah snooping in this very room; what she found herself, after searching, was evidence of a benefactor in London who alluded to certain temptations, certain ways of looking.

Nathaniel guides her feet back to the water. "God may not be merciful next time." He dips a rag in; slowly and carefully he runs it across the bridge of her foot. He wrings the rag out so every last drop, now clouded with mud, returns to the bowl. "We must consider what's best for him."

"You'll not take my only remaining joy from me." Catherine

stirs, the brackish water spilling over the edges of the bowl, nearly extinguishing the candle. "Not after everything I've endured."

"He could have died, Catherine. Both of you could have died. I cannot lose either of you."

"You should have thought of that earlier. It was you who brought him into . . . into that." The words are stale now. Every now and then, they must recite this liturgy in order to retain the arrangement that makes their flawed lives possible. Today, however, with both her and the boy's lives on trial, she must plead her case using all of the evidence against Nathaniel, reveal more of what she knows. Though she is tired, sick with worry, she must break her vow of silence. Nathaniel was right; she had almost lost her son today, and she'll not lose him now. "Sarah told me all about the forest, Nathaniel. I challenged her after I discovered the letters from Edwin. She said she heard Arthur use the word 'family.' All this time, and my own daughter thought I had been keeping this secret from her, a secret you don't even know how to hide."

Shock. She has shocked him.

"Did you think Anne and I hadn't spoken of it in private? You've no real idea what this has done to both of our families. But I am your family, Nathaniel. We are. The family you left behind. You cannot send us all off to some distant mission and forget about us."

"I—"

"And Sarah will hardly speak to me these days, for I've now done the very thing she accused me of doing all those years. I asked her to remain quiet, to join you and me in this secret. It is a poison which will one day ruin her as it has ruined me."

"Don't say those words, Catherine. I'll not let it happen."

"So many promises."

She studies his face. A heroic act, looking directly at his pain.

"You're right, Catherine," he says after a long pause. "We might both of us change for a while, but what if, after all of our promises, we end up here all over again? And in all of that wasted time, Ezekiel will have been learning from us, watching us, becoming us. He'll have been drinking that same poison. Perhaps he even remembers those trips to the forest, I cannot be certain. But I know he must be spared from us."

"From *us*?" Catherine nearly spits the word. "You cannot possibly mean to compare your affliction to mine. I fell asleep, Nathaniel. I didn't wake up in another man's bed."

How can she have said these words aloud? But he had pushed her; he had threatened to take away her one reason for living.

His grip tightens, too tight. "Does the Bible not say all sins are equal in the eyes of God?" he pleads. She has never seen him so desperate for her approval. The sight warms her to him, even as her anger grows.

"Ah, there is that blasphemy of yours, preacher." Catherine struggles out of his grip, but before she can escape, here he is with the towel. She resents his kindness after her cruel words.

"Please, Catherine," he says, meeting her eyes for the first time since she arrived, mud caked, at the doorstep with their son in a tattered dress. "Please do not say it is all my doing. Spare me that. We must pray our children do not suffer as we do."

"To suffer is to be blessed," Catherine says. "I've heard you preach it many times."

"How can you call this blessed?" Nathaniel stands. She had forgotten how tall he can be. How grand when he rises to meet the sermon's peak. "Do not leave me again, Catherine. Do not leave me alone in this place."

She's not seen this stranger in many years. Here he is again, her Nathaniel. "I am too tired for leaving," she says.

She has shocked him a second time. He had underestimated her; he hadn't considered the possibility that she would actually leave him, this woman who once readily traded one life for another.

"Yea, I considered it, husband. I considered moving to Boston with Anne. We discussed it one day. All afternoon we discussed it. But what would we have found there? More judgment, the same old hatred. I'd not be able to withstand life under such conditions. I'm hardly alive as it is."

Nathaniel starts. He wants to rush to her, comfort her, but something holds him back. "What must I do, Catherine? I'll do anything to keep you."

"I ask only that you not take my son from me. I shall not wish to live if you take him."

"I understand," Nathaniel says. "I do. But are we not selfish? Are we not placing him at a disadvantage by holding him so close to sin? Sarah will find her own way; Sarah has always been strong, but our boy—haven't you seen it? Haven't you seen he's different from the other children? For years I hoped I was imagining it, that he wasn't stained as I am, but I can no longer deny it. Mr. Shephard told me just today that his mind is a sieve. He holds no knowledge of the Bible. His soul rebels against the very Word of God, Catherine. There can be only one reason for it."

Nathaniel falls once more to his knees. The sight of him in this low light, a supplicant, thaws the remainder of her cold heart. She had seen his face when she walked in the house. Unmistakable, his relief. He'd not even scolded her, not once. Not even as Ezekiel, dressed as one of those French women, red from the sun, began to cry while Sarah and the others held him.

"He is your son, that is certain," she says. "But those people also belong to you. The flock is yours to lead. You brought them to this place. You brought all of them here on a promise, the promise of a better, holier life. Though I cannot claim to understand the nature of your affliction, I know you are the same man. You are the same man who loosed my tongue."

She pauses to catch her breath. The candle gutters, low now. Between sudden swipes of darkness, his eyes glow with tears.

"But you cannot send them away, these sheep who would be lost without their shepherd, any more than you can banish your own son from his father and mother. To lose that love would be far crueler than whatever it is he might learn from our sinfulness. He'll learn it elsewhere besides. Do you think the world outside Cana any less sinful? Do you not remember your father, Nathaniel, and my own mother? Anything is preferable to that kind of life."

Nathaniel takes her hands in his, kissing them. "Arthur once said much the same."

Catherine casts her gaze heavenward, a failed attempt to hide her pain.

"I'll change," he says. "I must."

"Let us not lie to each other anymore," she says. "If all sins are equal, let us not add this to the pile."

"You should have heard Deborah in the parlor today. They blame me. They think I'm the reason no awakening has come to Cana, and they're right."

"They left loveless lives in search of a bigger love, Christ's love. Invite them into that love again, and not one of them—including our dear boy—shall ever wish to leave."

"I thought I knew how to love them, how to love all of them, but then—I thought by coming to this continent I'd avoid the question of what my heart wanted altogether, but now here I am, a lost sheep leading other lost sheep. I don't know how to return to things as they once were, not now that I've felt this."

Though his confession pains her, she feels closer to him than ever. This is honest; he is trusting. She turns to the window. The forest is a black nothing, the moon hidden behind the pines. In the reflection, Nathaniel with head bowed at her feet, the light radiant on his gaunt cheeks.

Whatever she might say next has the power to change their fate. She could end his pain right now. With one swift sentence, she could destroy this man kneeling before her in all of his nakedness. She could tell him it is not Ezekiel who must be sent away but Arthur. That is the simplest solution, is it not? Though he's an excellent physician, there are others like him; the church already mistrusts the Lymans; perhaps they never belonged here in the first place. She might lose Anne, yes, but she might win a real husband. Yet even as she considers this possibility, even as she prepares to say the words, she knows the real Nathaniel, the one she loves, is the one she has witnessed today in this study. Even if Arthur was gone, Nathaniel would still be who he is.

Haven't I felt such a love before? she thinks, and with this thought, an unexpected sweetness suffuses the room, the scent of something cooking below. Wave upon wave her thoughts crash against her. She was to be pitied, young Catherine of Hingham, a child waiting for the smallest sign he would return, cloaked in silence, leaving her parents' world behind before she ever left it. She had had no choice, not in any true sense. Even if Arthur were to leave, Nathaniel would follow.

Silence. She cannot look at him. The sweet smell drifting through the floorboards. Even as I know he will cease to exist, I want him to suffer. I want him to suffer because it is not I who has inspired such a love. Wave upon wave. She will drown if she continues. Truth, which had been so freeing only a moment before, now threatens to drag her under. Can she live with it, this horrible truth: that she is not the one.

Still she cannot bear to look at him. Into that silence, a knock. Faint. Then another, louder this time. Catherine stands. How long is one to wait before opening the door on the most fateful scene of one's marriage? Slowly, carefully, she turns the knob. Anne. Beautiful Anne, thinking she's come to save her. Anne holding a tray of biscuits.

"I thought you might like something sweet."

The boy remembers. Unmistakable. Though it has been several years since the three of them met in private, Arthur can see in the boy's eyes a recognition of his other father. And in that recognition, Arthur can see, faint yet persistent, the pattern of his own features.

"How do you feel, child?" Carefully, he presses Ezekiel's bare shoulders. "Does it hurt when I do this?"

"No, sir."

Arthur has been left to survey the boy's body for injuries: the dip of his belly, a rounded shadow there; the red marks of the sun, crescent moons on his thighs, his arms; the line on his neck where hair has begun to inch farther down—each boundary, each mark, each a beauty to behold, for Arthur hasn't laid eyes upon his growing boy in quite some time. How he had wanted to bathe him, to care for him. The boy averts his eyes, shy at being studied so carefully.

"You may call me by my Christian name, Ezekiel," Arthur says. "Do you not remember it?"

"Arthur," Ezekiel says. "Your name is Arthur Lyman."

How sweet the sound! "Your memory appears to be in working order." Arthur spins the boy round to check for bruising. "Now tell me, Ezekiel Whitfield, why it is you decided to cross such a dangerous river."

Ezekiel points to the discarded shift at his feet. "No worms."

"Worms? Oh, you mean your breeches? Every good boy must wear breeches."

Ezekiel tucks his chin into his chest.

"Why so sad?"

"Mother hit me."

"Mother hit you?"

"She struck me."

"Why did she strike you?"

"I asked why."

"Your mother was very tired and confused," Arthur says. "She's sick, Ezekiel. You must understand that she is sick. She didn't mean to hurt you."

"Is it a demon in her?"

Arthur crouches, eye to eye with Ezekiel. "Would you like to know a secret?"

The boy nods. "Yea, sir."

"Arthur."

"Yea, Arthur."

Arthur smiles. This will be the boy's first lesson in science. "Though it may be right to believe in demons and spirits as the Bible says," he says, glancing over his shoulder to ensure no one is listening, "I don't believe them to be the cause of most of our problems."

Arthur can see he's confused the boy.

"What I mean to say is there's no demon in her. Your mother simply needs more attention, more care. Do you think you can give that to her?"

"Yea."

"Do you think you can wear your worms for her? It'll make her happy to see you acting a grown boy."

Ezekiel hesitates a moment, then nods. A good boy.

"And your father? Do you think you might comfort him? Your father's life isn't easy. He must watch over the souls of everyone in this town, including yours and mine."

Ezekiel closes his eyes. "Father scares me."

"Why?"

"Because I'm poor at learning. Mr. Shephard says so."

"Why do you think that is?"

"There's something wrong in me."

Arthur presses his fingers to the boy's brow, gently coaxing his eyes open. "There's nothing wrong in you, child. You are made in God's image."

"Then why does Father stare at me so?"

Arthur tilts the boy's chin up. "He wants the best for you. He worries because he cares."

Ezekiel shakes his head. "But is there a demon in me? Sister says I met one in the forest. She wants me to remember so my soul can be saved. She asks if I signed my name in the Red Book, but I can't remember."

It is Arthur's turn to close his eyes. The memory of the forest is precious; it sustains him, and to think the boy may not remember. "You remember nothing, child?"

Ezekiel sighs. An adult sigh. A world-weary sigh. "I don't know."

The boy will soon cry. Too much is being asked of him. We all want him to remember, Arthur thinks. We want him to remember for very different reasons. He must sense no answer will satisfy the adults. One of us, perhaps more than one of us, will be ruined.

Nathaniel couldn't believe it when Catherine opened the door. He had been kneeling, a beggar before his wife. Humbled, brought lower than ever before by his declaration of love. He had been willing to give up everything to keep her. Though he would only be giving up an abstract love—he and Arthur had never broken their pact—it had been allowed to exist because he had never fully admitted to its continued existence until a few moments ago, either to himself or to Catherine. Now that Nathaniel has admitted it, he must do something about it. Moments before the knock, he had felt whatever Catherine might say would decide things once and for all. He would either put Arthur behind him or—but there can be no "or." He knows what she must say, the only thing she can say. So why had he felt differently before the knock? Why had he felt they were about to cross over to someplace new, someplace far from everything they have ever known?

"I thought you might like something sweet," Anne said.

But Catherine didn't seem to hear it. He wondered if Anne had been listening on the other side of the door.

"I made some tea as well," Anne says now, resting a hand on the corner of his desk.

"Thank you, dear," Catherine says. "You're a blessing."

"I had to hear it from Goody Munn. Oh, if you two could have seen her face. She was so pleased to tell me. Those gossips love nothing more than a good scandal."

"Goody Munn means well," Nathaniel says.

"Everyone means well," Anne says. "That's the problem."

The two women exchange glances. Nathaniel pretends not to notice.

"Well, you go tell Goody Munn I'm still here." Catherine chooses one of the biscuits from the pile.

"The shock will kill her," Anne says.

"Nothing will kill that woman," Catherine says. "The mean ones never die early."

Anne laughs, a burst of sunlight on this dim stage.

Nathaniel looks away. He feels as though he's the one intruding on their private conversation.

"Well, now that I know you're in one piece . . ." Anne makes her way to the door. She casts a quick glance at Nathaniel, the first since she entered the room. "You are in one piece, Catherine?"

Catherine nods. A signal, he thinks, to let Anne know it is fine to leave her alone with him.

"No matter how bad it seems . . . ," Anne says.

Catherine rushes to her. The women embrace. "I promise," Catherine says.

The back of his eyes itch. He hides his face in the bookshelf and waits for the women to finish their goodbyes. Catherine returns to his side. She offers him the plate of biscuits. He takes one. He hadn't known how hungry he was, how long since he last ate. Catherine stares at him with something like amazement.

"She's harmless," Catherine says.

"Of course. She's a good friend to you."

"That afternoon when Anne and I first spoke openly of everything, I told her to leave Cana without me. She's enough money, with or without Arthur. And she's not a minister's wife. The rules aren't the same."

Nathaniel takes another biscuit, grateful for something to do. What can he say to this?

"She wouldn't consider it. She said she wouldn't leave without me. She said even if Arthur left she would find ways to visit. I could come stay with them. But nothing has changed. We're all still here in Cana."

He wants to say, Maybe it's easier to leave things as they are than to make a decision. He wants to plead with her to stop this conversation before they reach a place of no return. After today, it seems absurd that she has the energy to continue, to keep pushing them toward some inexorable fate. She must have been storing up the words all these years, waiting for the right moment to arrive, and now that it is here—

"You said you would change, Nathaniel." She places a hand upon his arm.

Far easier to leave things as they are. That is what he has always done. He must teach Catherine that freezing in place is the best way, for both of them. He can see Arthur, he can dream, he can't bear to lose him, he can't bear to lose either of them. He must find the words to convince her. More demanding than any sermon, what he must say, more personal, far more raw, all the more difficult to express.

"I'll go back to the way I used to be. I've felt things before, and I've resisted them. The thing to do is to freeze before anything else is said."

"The way you used to be. Oh Nathaniel, has it been as bad as that, being married to me?"

"Not for a second. I cherish the years we've had together."

"Somehow I believe you," she says. "This house has seen its share of happiness."

"It has, dear. We have."

Catherine smiles. "But I'm already frozen. I've been frozen since the day Arthur arrived in Cana, though I hadn't known why. I can't bear to leave things as they are. In this one evening, I've felt closer to you than ever before. I see the man behind the minister. Perhaps this is the first time I've ever fully laid eyes on him."

Lips pressed to her fingers, he won't let her go.

"Something must change, Nathaniel. I'll only grow worse. I fear today is but a premonition."

"Our boy might have been killed today."

"And he is more like you than you know. I can see it now. You're just a child, Nathaniel. Helpless, as he is. Take pity on him. Take pity on us all."

2.

Winter

Arthur leaves town before dawn. In his medicine case he packs a wide assortment of herbs, a few potions, seeds he has collected over the years. He borrows one of the Griggses' horses, a sturdy chestnut gelding he can ride hard so as to make it to the village before sundown. He wears a greatcoat and a duster, a hat to keep out the cold, leather gloves, and in his pockets, he carries the hardtack Anne prepared for him. Even so, as he moves along the ridge outside of town, as the sun begins to crest over the hills, breath steaming before him, the cold has already slipped into the deepest pockets of his clothing. He cannot stop shivering. He's not left Cana in many years. When he offers it one backward glance, he's surprised to see how tiny the town looks from this angle, as though it might melt into the soft winter air. How insignificant compared to where he is going, the place where Nathaniel needs him.

Priscilla Griggs stands at the edge of her yard, watching her gelding leave with the physician astride it. The sun rises over the eastern hills, and there is Arthur, a shade, shrinking to a black dot at the edge of the horizon. The wind carries the scent of ash and pine and cold soil warmed by fire, a burning just beyond vision. She stands, transfixed until the dot disappears. She is cold, certain, but there is something else pricking her skin, and all throughout the morning as she tends to breakfast, she begins to feel faint, too cold and hot at once.

"I'll lie down for a spell," she tells Judah.

"Today is harvest day," he says.

"I'll be but a moment, Judah."

She makes her way to the bed. She reaches for the Bible. Before she can open its pages, the trembling has begun. Her skin feels as though it will burst, and soon her arms thrash about of their own accord. A scalding hand reaches inside her, digging beneath her ribs. No longer Priscilla. She is no one. Nothing. She is everything and nothing. God, the universe. Her vision leaves, eyes rolling to black.

Below, her children have just thrown off their bedclothes, unaware that their mother has been altered forever.

Thou shalt have olive trees throughout all thy coasts . . .

Thou shalt have olive trees . . .

The trees with their olive-finger leaves and twisted roots, an all-root tree Ezekiel had seen once in an engraving on his father's desk now blooming in his fancy to a pale dusty green, beyond everyone and everything, on a distant shore that waits only for him. The verse Mr. Shephard has asked him to memorize drops somewhere behind the image, yes, like an olive troubled by wind. The walls of the schoolroom, pressed tightly to these huddled benches; the fireplace with its hot caliginous gloom; the pupils beside him sitting in their worms; the red-faced fat man with his lips pressed tightly in displeasure—all recede as the ocean tide gathers round him, carrying him into the warm sea. Color, light, green within green. Now the world is composed of shores once more, but they've grown more distant, harder to reach, less constant. He must travel farther each day from the shores of his mother and sister, far from the house, up the road with its angry winter trees threatening to hook into his skin, to this schoolroom asking him to leave the shores behind and focus only on the Word, the impossible Word opening in his mind to become something else, something behind Word, the Word made flesh: a landscape of color and light and touch.

"Yea, Ezekiel, but what is the rest of the verse?" Mr. Shephard slaps the back of Ezekiel's head two times, then two more when he does not flinch, so the schoolroom returns, the olive trees vanish, and all is Word and gloom. Mr. Shephard's lips glisten with spit. The children laugh quietly, nervously.

"Thou shalt have olive trees . . ."

"And?"

"Thou shalt have olive trees throughout all thy coasts . . ."

"We've heard that part. Where's the rest, Ezekiel? Are you not the minister's son? I should hope this is not the promise of a minister-to-be."

If Sister were here, she would put an end to Mr. Shephard's ire; she would help him with the Word, but she is too old for school now; she must work as a woman works. He is to be the next minister. He is to be his father one day, the father who is not here.

Mr. Shephard places the hornbook in Ezekiel's hands and there, within the decorative border he forces himself to ignore, swim words he cannot yet read in their entirety. The wood is heavy in his small hands.

A boy beside him stirs. "I can say it," the boy says. Gideon. Gideon has been nice to him. Gideon has kind wood-colored eyes and cheeks that puff out when he talks.

"I've asked our young Whitfield," Mr. Shephard says. "You must wait your turn, Gideon."

An ember pops. Two more. Ezekiel cannot think. The words do not form meaning. The silence is terrible. Ezekiel looks about but there is no shore, none perhaps save Gideon, who smiles sadly into his lap.

But then something else is there on Gideon's face. A light playing upon it, a light that is not from the fire and not from the window but from some other place. A light rendering all other light insubstantial.

Gideon has begun to thrash. Now there is only the terror of the boy's flailing limbs, his head knocking hard against the bench as he falls to the floor, his cries no longer that of a young boy but rather some wild animal Ezekiel's never encountered, one that must live far west of here, the kind he's seen printed on maps of the unknown territories: chimeric monsters with triple heads, dragons perched atop the highest peaks, waiting with clenched claws. The children push back in one mass, afraid of touching the boy, afraid of the blood now spilling upon the boards. Ezekiel crammed between the bodies, unable to move. He can't see Gideon but he can hear the thuds as the boy continues thrashing, as he cries out to God in a strangled voice: "Lord, Lord, I am yours, Lord!"

Ezekiel remembers. From this moment on, for all of his days, he'll never again forget the verse. *Thou shalt have olive trees throughout all thy coasts, but thou shalt not anoint thyself with the oil; for thine olive shall cast his fruit.*

Arthur does not pause beside the cottages. He knows the reverend will be in one of the longhouses; he prefers them to the cabins. Kaunameek is small, yet the circle of thatched dwellings, gathered as they are about a central well, presents an obstacle, for none seems more likely to house the object of his concern. In his haste he had not paused to consider what his reception might be. He expected Nathaniel to greet him, to be waiting for him, for Arthur had been thinking only of Nathaniel the entire journey.

As he waits beside the next longhouse and a young Mohican passes him by with nary a look, Arthur can see he had not given this enough thought. He had answered Reverend Colman's letter without hesitation. He hadn't even considered consulting Anne until after he'd sent his reply. When Nathaniel left Cana a few months back, Arthur had tried to dream up a thousand ways he might join the minister on his trip to New York and the surrounding missions, but no easy excuse had come to mind. Now—miracle of miracles!—he has been invited here to this mission. He had assumed Nathaniel played no small part in the invitation, yet now that he stands alone, helpless, since he is worse than a novice at the Mohican language, Arthur is not so certain the minister desires his company at all.

He waits a moment more, then enters the longhouse. Thick black smoke stings his eyes. He blinks rapidly until his vision returns. The room is empty save for a few women working at the fire. He's already preparing to leave when he sees a sign, a stack of books in the far corner of the longhouse that can only belong to Nathaniel. He glances cautiously at the women, but they ignore him. When he arrives in the corner, he sees the bedclothes have been carefully folded, the books neatly stacked. The women say something in their language, then leave. He's not sure what to do, so he reaches for the bedclothes. His fingers hesitate only a moment before gripping the fabric and pressing his nose there, but the scent he craves will not rise to meet him; the smoke has obscured it. He thinks he detects it but then it is gone, gone so quickly he cannot be sure it was ever there, so he must content himself with pressing his face to the blankets. This reflex is like some new science he is discovering by himself, his only tools the nose pressed close, the probing hands. It is not love he is discovering, or it is not only love but something older, ancient, hidden away, asking him to take hold of it without restraint.

When Arthur returns to himself, he is glad to see that no one has entered. He takes up the topmost book, a volume of Mather's funeral sermons, and leafs through the pages idly. He does not see the pages as pages but as surfaces upon which Nathaniel has transmitted his touch. Midway through the book, he's startled to discover something pressed inside. A flower. Not just any flower, but the flower that had come to populate his dreams; so often had he pictured it lying at their feet. Arthur cautiously traces its crimson petals. So he had wanted to remember. So he had brought it with him. Arthur closes the book, careful lest he lose the minister's place.

Sarah is the first to grasp what happened in the schoolroom. Martha had been accompanying her home from the Lyman house, happy to have finished the Gospel of John that afternoon, thanks to her friend's unwavering insistence, when the pair came upon a group of children gathered at one end of the square. With the harsh angle of the setting sun, Sarah couldn't see that her brother was among them, so small was he. She assumed the children were up to mischief as usual.

"Leave them to it," Martha said. "They're harmless."

"They shouldn't be out so late."

"They'll be little adults soon enough."

As the pair drew closer, however, Sarah saw that the children were not mischievous; they were more serious than she'd ever seen them. Red eyes. Tears on their cheeks. On her brother's cheeks. Here he was with them.

"What can have happened?" Martha said. "This is frightening, Sarah."

They soon learned that the boy, Gideon Jacobsen, had been led home by Mr. Shephard, there to discuss with his family what had happened. The children did not yet use the word "awakening," but Sarah couldn't help but repeat the word in her head as she listened to their account, and when she looked into Ezekiel's eyes, which could not lie, she knew the miracle she'd been anticipating, the miracle she'd all but given up on, had finally come about.

"My dear, what did I tell you?" Martha said. "It was no accident I was so slow with the final verses. You were meant to hear this, Sarah. Do you not remember your dream?"

Sarah had witnessed the vision only a week before: through the bedroom window crawled hundreds of white ants, bits of lunar incandescence; when she reached out to touch one of them, the body of the ant popped beneath her finger with a blind flash, and all throughout her fingers and arms she felt the caress of some invisible hand. She hadn't known what any of it meant at the time. Like many of her visions, she stored it somewhere for future Sarah to one day decipher, though admittedly she had begun to doubt these visions; she had begun to believe her father when he told her women were not meant for such things. "But it must mean something," Martha had said. "You're meant for great things, I know it."

Hundreds of souls illuminated, hundreds awakened. As Sarah listened to the children speak of this boy's cries, of his complete bodily and spiritual surrender to the Lord, she allowed herself to consider that there might be something to Martha's words.

"So it is happening," Martha whispered. "And with your father gone."

Sarah calmed them, these frantic children, reciting some verses for comfort, and when they were calmed, she saw they were different, the childishness she had always perceived in them vanished, just as her childishness had vanished with the death of her friend Abigail Jacobsen, Gideon Jacobsen's sister. The incident today confirmed with outward signs that Gideon had been delivered unto eternal life rather than physical death like his sister; death could never reach him now. She saw the children were eager and willing to do the Lord's work. If she prayed right, if she asked for guidance, she could deliver these children into the hands of God, too, for it was clear that, with her father gone—yes, with her father so far away—she could become a leader among the children.

"I was right to see it in you," Martha said, clapping her hands. "I may be blind to many things, Sarah, but I am not blind to your power. Perhaps I shall be saved from the pit after all."

"Don't be a fool," Sarah said, but in her thoughts, she was already weighing the truth of her friend's words. Though Martha was indeed sheltered, though this child of drama hadn't detected a single whiff of the parental tragedy unfolding in her own house, Sarah had come to believe she possessed at least one rare talent, one that had drawn them closer in spite of Sarah's discomfort with the Lymans. Martha saw the best in people. She saw what they could become.

Sarah and the children agreed to meet the next day at Gideon's house to discuss what happened and to read the gospels for inspiration. Martha would join them.

"They shall write of you one day," Martha said. "The greatest Whitfield."

Now, having sent Martha away, Sarah leads her brother home, holding his hand lest he trip on the uneven surface of the road.

"Why are you crying?" she says.

Ezekiel says nothing.

Though it is nearly dark, she can spot a bank of snow clouds above the roof of their house. She thinks, briefly, of her father, and wonders if he's safe and warm in some praying town, what he might be doing, if he'd be proud of her for taking charge in his absence. As soon as the image of Arthur appears, however, she puts him out of her mind.

"You must answer adults when they speak to you, Brother," Sarah says, tugging him closer. "I've noticed this habit in you of remaining quiet. Mother's instruction must not always be taken so literally, else we'd all be in the bed."

Ezekiel sniffles loudly. As they pass the glow of their neighbors' windows, his tear-wetted cheeks glisten. She folds her dress sleeve in her palm, wipes his nose for him.

"What you're feeling must be strange, but it is good. You must believe it is good, Ezekiel."

Ezekiel shakes his head.

The wind is cold, but Sarah doesn't move them toward the house. She doesn't want their mother to coddle him, for then he might absorb nothing of today's miracle. Yet even as she holds him in the cold a minute longer, she can't help but sympathize with her mother's indulgence; she can't help but feel sorry for him, this helpless being; how did she ever believe someone so innocent could sign his name in the Red Book; how could he be anything but perfect, this lamb who wouldn't hurt a soul?

"It is good, Brother," she says, kissing his brow. "We must believe it is good."

Ezekiel shrinks from his sister's touch. Nothing had been good today. Something in Ezekiel had not allowed him to receive God's blessing. God had passed over him in favor of Gideon. Ezekiel's mind hadn't been able to move into the cold, empty Word Mr. Shephard required of him. He remembers his father's words: "You must be strong, Ezekiel. Life will be harder for you. I cannot explain why, but it will be harder." Ezekiel hadn't understood. He still doesn't understand. Where is his father now to tell him everything is indeed good? He cannot answer his sister. He cannot speak.

"Will you say nothing?" Sarah says. "It is good. You were there for an awakening, perhaps the first in this town. Do you not feel changed by it, as the other children were? You must bear witness. You must testify to it, so that others around the world may come to believe."

He had not been able to resist the beauty of the olive trees. He had not denied himself, for in his heart he did not find the Word beautiful. Gideon's eyes, the featherlight hairs resting upon the nape of his neck—these were beautiful, these were glorious to behold, not his face contorted and crying out, not the lashing arms, not the blood. He would have liked to pet Gideon, to tell him everything is fine. Gideon smiling up at him with his warm eyes.

The snow has begun to fall, its heavy flakes clinging to his riding cloak and tricorne hat by the time Nathaniel returns to Kaunameek. He had been driven into the mountain by an urge for escape, a premonition that something was chasing him. He wanted to be free of his worries for a few hours, and the arduousness of the ascent more than accomplished his goal, so that, returning to the village, seeing its cheerful fires set against the falling snow, he feels he has returned to himself, and the premonition that plagued him, whatever it was that had been chasing him, must have been the one eaten by the giant beast of the mountain, a great coiled snake according to Mohican legend.

He's barely off his horse when an out-of-breath Thomas Alcom appears.

"I hope you're not cross with me, reverend," Thomas says, smiling tentatively. "We hadn't known he was coming so soon. We gave him David Brainerd's old quarters. I thought he might like a rest after his journey."

So that was what had been worrying Nathaniel. He had known Arthur was coming for him today. No one sent him a letter, yet he'd known all the same.

"Thank you, Thomas. Is the cabin warm?"

"We made him a good fire."

Nathaniel wastes no time getting to the cabin. The weather has set in for the evening, snow already upon the ground. Even with his coat bundled tightly, he can feel the wind slipping inside, searching out his weakest spots; since he's grown thinner these past few months, the cold finds him easier; he must admit he's not prepared for what the season might bring. The curtains are closed tightly; he cannot see inside, so he makes his way to the door and knocks. He can hear a bit of shuffling inside, but no voice. He waits, then knocks again, louder. After a great deal more shuffling, the door opens.

At first, the fire is so bright he can't understand what he's seeing. The figure in the doorway is large and imposing, but the man moves so quickly toward Whitfield, ushering him out of the cold, patting down his sleeves, dusting off his hat, that by touch and gesture Whitfield knows it is Arthur. His only reaction can be one of delight, though he can see from Arthur's face that worry is his friend's foremost expression. He can feel by the man's hands upon him— removing his coat, smoothing his shirt, rolling up his sleeves to survey his skinny arms—that the sight of his altered body, which had not seemed so drastic before this moment, must be difficult to take in all at once. He feels a sudden pang of guilt at not having written his friend, of placing him at such a distance that they have become strangers once more.

"Let me look at you," Arthur says, backing away to appraise him.

"How did you get here?"

"You've no muscle, no meat." Arthur turns to the open medicine case upon the desk. "What have you been eating? Be honest."

"Succotash mostly."

"You must have some meat. Ask Thomas if they can bring you some venison tomorrow. Open your mouth and hold out your tongue."

Arthur removes the cork from one of his vials. Whitfield allows him to place some pungent root upon his tongue.

"I cannot ask them for venison. This is a harsh season. They need it for their own people."

"Why are you not eating? Tell me, truly."

"I've been busy. Tomorrow you'll see how busy."

"Let me help you." Arthur removes Whitfield's coat and hat, unbuttoning his shirt.

Whitfield turns his back to the man, facing the fire.

"I am a physician," Arthur chides. "I must be able to see you."

When all of Nathaniel's clothes are removed, Arthur can't help but emit a gasp. He sees first the protruding shoulder blades, then the narrow waist, the stark parallels of the sacrum. He places his hand upon Nathaniel's back.

"Do you mind?"

Nathaniel shakes his head. He pushes against the hand. "I don't know what to do."

Arthur grips Nathaniel's shoulders and carefully turns him round to face him. Nathaniel will not meet his eyes. Pitch-black hair traveling from chest to navel. Out of modesty, Arthur does not look any lower, not yet. He palpates the flesh round Nathaniel's chest, then presses two fingers to the man's neck to check his pulse. He may be weakened, but Nathaniel's heart beats steadily, rapidly, the blood flows easily. Arthur can smell the man's breath, surprisingly sweet yet mixed with a faint coppery earth that weakens his legs.

So be it. Let him die having lived. There can be no end to his examination.

He examines the minister's thighs, his calves, then asks him to take a seat so he may examine the rest of him.

Nathaniel does as he's commanded, but not before he retrieves a blanket from the bed to wrap about his middle. He stretches out his feet, and to his surprise, Arthur drops to his knees. "Easier this way," he says. Arthur's hands have changed their course, now kneading his heels, moving up his ankles, relieving his tension almost at once. Nathaniel has already begun to make a tent of the blanket, and though he should be embarrassed at the admission it makes, instead he feels proud. He looks at Arthur, whose eyes have traveled to his. He nods.

Arthur can hardly believe his luck, though he doesn't waste time. He buries his face in the blanket, pressing his cheek there.

They've never gotten to this, he and Arthur; Nathaniel has never allowed himself to commit to the full act, to the word that has haunted him since he first heard it as a young man. The gentleman who took him in as a boarder in London, Edwin Sharpe, had warned him with a grin that indeed there were some who wished to perform such abominations. He arches his back, pressing himself against Arthur's fingers. The word, "abomination," redefines itself with each second that passes, so it seems to lose all meaning, for what they are doing now is more than a word; he feels neither the violation nor the humiliation that had seemed bound to its meaning only a moment before. It seems to him now, as he relaxes for Arthur, that everything has led him to this point, that everything is as it should be. This is His flesh; this is His blood boiling and bound before the moment the spear pierces His side. This is what it means to receive His communion.

Only half a mile from where Sarah stands in her yard with a pouch full of eggs, a man emerges from the public house wearing a duster lined with many pockets. In one of them is a golden fob, his signature piece, sure to attract a crowd. To one of the young boys who come round to deliver a fresh supply of firewood, this man hands a carefully transcribed notice.

EXOTIC GOODS FROM AFAR

PROCURED AT GREAT EXPENSE AND RISK OF SELF

ONE FOB OF PARTICULAR CHARM

A TRULY STRANGE TALE FOR ANY

WHO WISH TO HEAR IT AND BE AWED

What was young Nathaniel like?" Arthur turns on his side to face his love, who has closed his eyes for the first time all night. "I am trying to picture him. Was he always so serious? We might not have even been friends. I might have taken one look at you and decided it best to leave you where I found you. Can you imagine?"

"Yours is a complicated question." Nathaniel pushes himself up to sit comfortably in the bed. Light has begun to enter the cabin: blinding white, as though a sheet has been draped across the window. Wooden ceiling beams creak with the weight of snow, and a profound quiet has settled in the village. Likely no one will come calling upon them anytime soon.

"I was happy when my mother was alive," Nathaniel says, surprised at his openness. "She was a woman who loved books. She taught me how to read, how to make my way through all of those imposing words. She'd sit beside me for hours and wait for a moment when she might explain something to me which I found difficult to grasp. I've a strong recollection of her bending close to the page whenever she searched for one of her explanations, as though she were peering into the world of the book and asking its inhabitants what they saw there. She made me believe that the words were merely a veil. The real thing lived beneath, hidden from us all this time. In that way I was not unlike Ezekiel."

"He is imaginative, our boy?" Arthur places a hand upon Nathaniel's arm. He is too eager, too honest about his love for Ezekiel, but he cannot help it. He's waited so long to speak openly with this man.

"I fear he might never learn as I did. I outgrew it, of course. I learned to take a practical view of words. They are tools, just like anything else, and we must respect them. There is no getting around their usage. A man who can command his words can command hundreds of men. He can lead them to God."

"As you did." Arthur remembers watching Nathaniel as he stood upon that scaffold in Boston, the sound of his words ringing out: an honest sound. But more than words, it was the way he used his hands, the tilt of his head as he recited scripture, the soft gestures suggesting a depth few men possess.

"Yea, I learned. But the boy is so quiet. He is so raw, so tender. I see my younger self in him, and I worry I cannot help him grow stronger, I cannot help him because of whatever it is that's inside of me. Catherine tells me to leave it alone, to stop my worrying, but sometimes I think the best thing for Ezekiel is to send him far, far away from us."

"Have you ever thought it might not be such a bad thing, his being like you?"

A pause. The silence thickens. Then, with a pat on Arthur's hand, Nathaniel says, "No, I never once thought that."

"Well, it might be worth considering." Arthur sits up to face the minister. "I would very much like to meet young Nathaniel, the boy who sits with his mother all day and dreams. He sounds delightful. I've a book right here if you'd like to reenact it with me."

Arthur reaches for the Bible on the desk. The page is already open to the verse. "I've been reading about David and Jonathan," he says, placing the book between them. "Here. Would you read this verse here, young Nathaniel?"

Nathaniel frowns, but in his eyes is a sly glimmer. He laughs quietly, then begins, following Arthur's finger as it moves across the page. "I am distressed for thee, my brother Jonathan: very pleasant hast thou been unto me: thy love to me was wonderful, passing the love of women."

"And what do you see just beyond those words, young Nathaniel? What do the inhabitants of that world whisper to you when you peer closely?"

"Nothing more than is said." Nathaniel closes the book. "You take far too many liberties, Arthur. Do not search that holy book for mirrors of ourselves. That is unwise and sinful. What we have done—what we are, whatever this is—it is something altogether different, and we shall have to live with it. Don't you think I've tried to find it? Don't you think I've searched every verse for evidence of someone with my affliction? It is not there, or at least it is not there in the way we might hope for it. No, it is better to face ourselves with at least some semblance of honesty. I do not want to cheapen things, Arthur, and we will cheapen them if we try to be something else. What we are doing in this room belongs only to us. We have just invented it. Never before has another man done what I have done or felt what I have felt. It may sound ridiculous, but it must be true. God did not create this. It is not natural. It is not divine. It is nothing but what it is, here in this bed."

"But there are signs of it, in Greece." Arthur says. "In other cultures, in other times. Did you not come across this in your education?"

"You are bending God's words to suit your purpose. Bending history itself to justify your sins. Ignoring whatever is inconvenient and true. This is exactly what I have sought to tame in Sarah."

Arthur wraps a blanket around himself. The room is cold, the fire dwindled to a spark. He rises from the bed and makes his way to the hearth, pausing there. "I take it someone else taught you that fine lesson," he says. "And what a fine lesson it is. So you say you must tame us all. We must be made to look like you, in your image. Angry, embittered, lonely—never more than a child, really. It is a nice little trick. A fine use of those words you hold so dear. I fell for it for quite a while. I agreed to your conditions, thinking I was the one who was wrong. I stopped seeing you and Ezekiel. I stopped expecting things. And now here you are, all the same, naked in my bed. Tell me, reverend: Which of us has been properly tamed?"

"I am sorry, Arthur," Nathaniel says. "I am trying to be honest with you."

"You've never told me about your father." Arthur crouches, adding another log to the fire. Something has emboldened him. It is not so much that he feels he can lay claim to this man's history but rather that he has already laid claim to his whole life; what they have done together has placed them well beyond Nathaniel's reservations, and whatever else the man is holding back will soon reveal itself. Nathaniel has already lost the battle. Arthur can see that. Now, like a greedy victor, he wants all of the spoils at once. He wants to know everything about this man who is now his.

"Fine, Arthur. But there's not much to tell. He was a bookbinder. We lived in a town called Chester on the River Dee. He was in every way an entirely dishonest man. When my mother died, I learned he was illiterate. He had me write to her relatives and demand money. I was young, around Ezekiel's age, when I learned how to lie through letters. I pretended to be my father. I suppose my poor mother had been asked to do the same when she was alive, and it would have worked out for both of them had she not succumbed to her illness."

"And how did he run his business after your mother was gone? Surely he didn't ask a child to write as a grown man of letters to all of his customers?"

"That is exactly what he did." Nathaniel sighs. He's not spoken of his father for many years. Sitting in this snowbound cabin in a tiny village an ocean away from England, he feels as though his childhood is far from him, more distant than ever, yet at the same time, as an aching pulse spirals through him from where he had taken a man into himself for the first time, he senses also the familiarity of his fraudulent life, the one his father taught him from a very young age.

"It was quite an education. There were many famous editions to be bound. Milton, Donne, Shakespeare. My father wished to express his finest appreciation for these works when corresponding with his collectors in London, though, of course, he had no appreciation at all; books were merely a means to money. He more than once told me he thought men who stared at bits of wood all day were nothing but fools. Though I did not understand everything in these great books and had hardly lived long enough to sympathize with many of the feelings expressed therein, I remembered the tone my mother used when offering her explanations, and I learned how to lie on my father's behalf. I also learned a great deal from the writers themselves. The first thing I learned was that my father was the one who was the fool. These works contained ideas of infinite value. If there's one thing I'm grateful for in my childhood, it's that I doubt I would have read these men so carefully had my father not been acting gaoler the entire time. Together we crafted this mask. It is a mask I have been using ever since. Many of my contemporaries have been educated at Harvard, and no doubt they find it useful and even necessary to discover these rarefied truths in abstraction. My classroom was not theirs. It fell to me to learn from these writers for the sole sake of putting bread on the table. I no longer knew what it was to read books for the pure pleasure of learning their ideas. I read them only for coin, for survival. The thing which my mother had gifted me, this love of words, had been prostituted to my father's avarice. I was the reason we ate and the reason we slept under a roof every night."

Arthur returns to the bed, taking a seat next to Nathaniel. Cautiously, he moves his hand close to the minister's knee. "Yet it may be that your education made you the famous minister you are today. You take a practical end at all times. When you discovered these wonderful ideas, you wanted others to know them, so you spoke out as loudly as you could, wandering the continent in search of those who would listen. When you found you had led hundreds of souls to the Lord, you wondered first where you could put them, and you found a place where we could all live as equals. It seems to me you have only taken the good traits from your parents and have tossed out the rest."

"If only the story were that simple, Arthur," Nathaniel says, closing the gap between them, taking Arthur's hand into his own. "Are you certain you wish to hear this? I've not told another soul this next part. I fear it may be shocking."

"You still think you have the power to shock, minister?" Arthur says, kissing the man's lips. When next he leans back to survey the minister's face, he is happy to see a smile there.

"One of my father's clients was a man named Edwin Sharpe. A very wealthy man who had attached himself to the ideas of the Reformation. He was a Protestant and proud of it, though the books he wished to be bound were not always religious ones. To answer your question, yea, there were Greeks in his collection, and I read them." Nathaniel pauses, offering another smile, this one impish. Arthur can almost see young Nathaniel now. "Edwin was one of Father's most intelligent clients. I saw this in the way he responded to my letters. Fairly quickly, he discovered my father was not the man he purported to be. Rather, it was his son whose mind he admired, and far beyond any pleasure he had received in having his favorite books expertly bound, it was his correspondences with me which brought him his principal satisfaction. Soon Edwin began to write directly to me, hinting that he knew of the fraud and did not judge it. And because my father could not read, and I had learned to lie when reading aloud these letters, I began to write back to Edwin in my own voice. I was lonely, and here was a man who loved books and ideas as much as I did. He was the closest thing to a friend or a father in those days."

"I wish I'd had an Edwin," Arthur says. "All I had were local idiots and a father who would rather see me bleed to death than forget one of his life lessons." Arthur holds up his arm. The scar is still there. Without thinking, Nathaniel traces it with his finger.

"So you see," Arthur adds, "we both of us received our gifts from pain. How very Christian."

"I believe we receive them most readily through our own sufferings. Not the suffering inflicted by others."

"Where is the line?"

Nathaniel does not know how to answer this. Sighing once more, he continues. "It was not long before Edwin paid us a visit. He knew of our address through our correspondences. Though I never asked for it, he caused quite a scene with my father. He told him he knew everything, that the man was a fraud and that he would tell all of London about it if my father did not meet his conditions."

"How did he look? Were you surprised by any of his features?"

"Where is your mind?" Nathaniel laughs.

"Well?"

"He was a handsome man. Much older, at least I thought so at the time. He must have been around forty. Standing beside my father, he looked like one of those ancient Greek statues, strong and well-built with long, lavish curls. He wasted no time in telling my father his conditions: I was to be educated in London at one of the best Protestant schools, and I was to board with him. He would do everything in his power to ensure I grew up a gentleman. My father protested at once, not because he would miss me, but because he knew a business opportunity when he saw one. To counter, Edwin promised him a handsome monthly allowance for the years I would lodge with him. All Father would have to do would be to spend it. As I stood between these two men, surprised to find myself so desired after many years of hard use, I did not then understand why Edwin was taking such great pains on my behalf. Years later, after I had stayed with him for some time, I came to understand it was because he saw something of himself in me. He wanted to give his younger self another chance at life, a different kind of life. There must have been a great deal of vanity in the act, but it was the only love he could give me, and it was sufficient."

"How lucky for you."

"At the time I thought it providential. Now I am not so sure it was not infernal. The story has not yet played out."

"You are here, are you not? A famous preacher in the New World."

Nathaniel's eyes settle upon the Bible. "Yea. I am here. A famous preacher in the New World. Sitting naked on this bed with another naked man."

Arthur grabs hold of the bedsheets and tosses them aside. "Now you are naked," he says, admiring the view of his love's body. "We must be accurate."

"My father agreed, of course, once the price was right. What followed were the best years of my life when all I was asked to do was learn, when I was no longer forced to prostitute my learning for others. Edwin's gabled manor never brought me back a childhood, but it did offer me safe harbor during the remaining years of my young manhood. Edwin ushered me into a much larger world. He taught me to conduct myself properly, to ensure no one could find fault in my behavior. I added another mask to my collection, yea, but this one fit better, for I was no longer pretending to be my father, I was pretending to be myself."

"Or your mother."

"Stop it with your nonsense."

"I am trying to be honest with you," Arthur says, imitating the reverend's voice.

Nathaniel stares down at his body, at the small mound of loose skin his stomach makes, a mound so troublesome to him after he lost weight, something he wished to cast off like an unnecessary garment, now in Arthur's presence made, if not beautiful, at the very least no longer ugly. Arthur had said he liked all of it, all of the flaws which in his eyes were but details, the things which made Nathaniel. Hard to believe such a thing could be true, but the idea spurs him on.

"Edwin kept me sheltered from the many men who called upon him. I was given my own wing of the house and a room next to Edwin's grand library. You cannot imagine my excitement when first I glimpsed the line of books extending from ground to ceiling in almost infinite measure. I met Edwin only for supper. The days were peaceful, and I always looked forward to telling him what it was I had learned that day. I loved hearing his ideas on every subject of study, no longer encumbered by long waits between our letters but here in this place together, exchanging ideas at a rapid pace. On a few occasions he would invite another man to join us, usually a missionary or a schoolmaster. I was to dazzle this man with my education, for Edwin paid a great deal to the Protestant school I attended and I was their prized pupil. I did not always enjoy these dinners, for this was the only occasion Edwin ever reminded me I was his charity. To these men he boasted how he had found me amongst the rabble, how my education fit in nicely with what many philosophers were discovering about the human spirit. I was his blank slate, his proof that, given the right environment, humanity would prevail. One such guest at our table was the missionary Reverend Mathew Colman, whom you may have heard of."

"Ah, I am beginning to see the line. He's the man who wrote to me about your health. I thought you knew it or else I wouldn't have dreamt of coming."

"I had no idea you would join me here. He must have taken note when we passed by your old practice in Boston. I couldn't resist saying something about how essential you are in Cana."

"He was worried about your health."

"He has always worried. I'm not certain he has ever considered me healthy."

"Go on."

"Colman was very taken with me from the first. He spoke of educating the Indians, even the Africans, for he envisioned a world where all peoples flocked to our Reformation. He warned us against the French and Spanish who sought to corrupt the ignorant peoples of the New World with their popish ways, for if Catholicism had its way in the world, God would surely send plague and pestilence and ruin to this new continent."

"As your physician, I feel I must inform you that He already has, in the form of smallpox. The English as well as the French and Spanish and many other such peoples helped spread it."

"Thomas has said as much," Nathaniel says, a little wearily. "He says we have brought with us not only sickness but many sinful habits. I always thought the price was fair, that their souls must be saved at all costs, but now I seem to know very little. Can I even bring myself to step foot outside this cabin to greet those in Kaunameek once more? Cana is even more doubtful."

"Whatever sins we have imparted here, I do not think our coupling is one of them," Arthur says, serious at first. Then, following the logic of the thought: "If our condition spread like a disease, Cana would be a town full of sodomites. So far as I can tell, that is not the case. A pity, really. I believe it would have solved many of our problems."

"You go too far, Arthur."

"I cannot help but go far with you so near."

It is Nathaniel's turn to stand. He wraps the bedsheets around him, tiptoeing his way across the cold floor to the window. He opens the curtains to nothing but an oppressive whiteness. Aside from the distant mountain, he cannot see anything he recognizes in this alien territory.

"When Colman told me it was my mission to tame the wilderness, I believed him. Who wouldn't wish to be told they were meant for great things, that there was a spiritual battle being waged in the New World and I one of its greatest living warriors? He saw my potential. He praised me even more than Edwin did. I did not yet know if I wished to be a minister. I was still learning so much each day. I did not wish to relinquish my newfound freedom so quickly, only to live in a wilderness where books could not be so easily acquired. Nevertheless, I was flattered. I was also relieved, for someone had already drafted a future for me. My next mask."

"How old were you then, so I can picture it? I want to picture that look of indecisiveness on your face."

"You might be the only other person who has seen that look since then. I was sixteen. Old enough for college if I wanted it."

"I am beginning to see him now, our young Nathaniel Whitfield. He is very serious."

"One night, out of curiosity, I crept out of my chamber to see what Edwin's guests got up to in the drawing room. At least once a month he invited a gathering of gentlemen to join him in his manor, and on each of these occasions I had been asked to remain in my wing of the house. Desirous to please my benefactor in all ways, and grateful for his shelter, I had never questioned his rule. Now that I saw myself as a great figure, however, now that Colman had let me know it, I grew bolder. The doors of the drawing room were locked, but there was a keyhole."

"In many such stories, the eye is drawn to the keyhole."

"So it was. When I finally peered inside, what I saw was more shocking than anything I have ever seen before or since."

"More shocking than last night?"

"Much more so. It was my first time seeing such a thing. I did not yet understand what it was I was seeing. Within the room were dozens of enraptured men, some with heads cast to the sky, some with heads bowed low. Some lounged about in a torpor, entangled in a pile. I saw what looked to be a woman's silk gown with bare furred legs sprouting from the skirt. The woman, who was in truth a man dressed as a woman, pretended to give birth to a false child, a small wooden baby which had been drizzled in blood. The father stood beside her, clutching her hand, kissing it, encouraging this mother to push harder. Two men dressed as midwives attended the wooden block as they would a real infant. It had the air of a natural birth and was treated with gravity and great dignity."

Arthur closes his eyes, picturing it. The two men are silent for a long while. "So there are other men who wish for such a thing?" he says at last.

Nathaniel laughs. It is a cruel sound, though it had not been intended as such. He can see the look of betrayal on Arthur's face. "You wish to dress as a woman and birth a block of wood? You wish to have me stand beside you, holding your hand as you do it?"

"No," Arthur says. "Don't be so literal. I simply meant I understand their desire for such ceremony. If they feel as I do . . ."

"Wait until you hear the rest."

"Continue then."

"I saw two men at the other end of the room standing in matching bridal gowns, the fingers of their hands interlaced, gazing into each other's eyes. There was a minister to marry them, dressed in a black gown and white collar. To my shock, he held a Bible in his hands and was intent on reciting scripture from it. As I looked about the room, searching for Edwin, I saw fornication all around, bodies moving in lust. Most shocking of all, I saw a man lying beneath another man who began to use his mouth as a privy. I had never imagined such a thing. My first thought, oddly enough, was how Edwin kept the room so clean and tidy and so sweet-smelling after such use."

Arthur wants to laugh, too; he wants to tell Nathaniel this is nothing compared to the wharves, where he has seen one man drink from several such fountains, but he can see how serious the story has made his minister. He is still an innocent, this man. He is still young Nathaniel.

"The man, upon further inspection—the one who drank so greedily—was, in fact, Edwin."

"This is quite the story."

"I'll not lie. I grew excited upon witnessing such debauchery. After kneeling at the keyhole for quite some time, I rushed to my chamber and placed a chair against the door. Falling upon my knees once more, I tugged at myself, picturing what I had just seen, until I finished upon the floor."

Arthur draws nearer. Nathaniel feels the man press against him, the swelling. A hand reaches into the bedclothes, cool against his skin. "I am picturing it, young Nathaniel."

"Then I did something I would never have thought to do had I not seen something like it in the drawing room. I bent low to the floor, examining the mess I had made, and I pressed my nose into it. It was as though I were some Russian babushka kissing the dusty floor of the chapel in worship. I was horrified at myself, at how quickly and without thought I had succumbed to my lust. I suppose I wanted to rub my nose in it, to force myself to see what I had done in my desperation."

"It excites you now, remembering." Arthur grabs hold of Nathaniel, moving his fingers lightly along his length.

Nathaniel grows dizzy. He closes his eyes to the blinding whiteness outside. "Molly," he says. "That was the word I called myself that day in my chamber. I am a bugger and a molly and I reside in a molly house."

"Ah, that word," Arthur says, recalling the stories he'd heard from the men at the wharves, stories of London residences where at a certain hour of night, in certain locked rooms, men came together like in Edwin's drawing room.

"When I emerged from my stupor, I wondered what it was in me that had first responded to Edwin's letters, whether I had known somehow that he and I were alike in this way. How had I known it with you, Arthur?"

"There are signals, hints," Arthur says, running his fingers through the trail of dark hair on Nathaniel's belly, resting his palm against the man's beating heart.

"You seem to know a great deal about this," Nathaniel says, flushing at the thought of Arthur with other men. "Were there many others before me?"

"I'll ask you the same question."

Nathaniel does not hesitate. "No."

Arthur responds in kind. "Yea, there were other men. In Boston. But none who remained. None whom I would remain with in this room."

Nathaniel falls against Arthur's shoulder. "What were our signals? What did you first see in me?"

"When first you looked over the crowd in Summer Street, I saw your eyes land upon mine. I felt them linger. The passion which had struck you, the love of God—it passed into me. It pierced me at once. I could not look away."

"I didn't see you then, not really," Nathaniel says. "I saw you only after you came forward to declare that God had touched you. You seemed happy. Happier than anyone else I had met in a very long time. Somehow, I knew this happiness was not temporary, that this joy would remain with you and I would become more joyous in your presence."

"Have I made you happier?"

"Much happier, in some ways. The minister whom you first met was already beginning to lose his mask. I feared at any moment God would abandon me, for I knew my thoughts were sinful, I wished for more than had been given unto me, and this wish was selfish. When first I spoke with you, however, I discovered a well of limitless faith. You made me believe the dream of Cana could survive whatever rottenness was inside me. You made me believe once again that God had chosen me to lead the flock."

"I still believe it."

"And for the first few months of your stay in Cana, I did not think of you as anything more than a dear friend. I did not imagine this room."

"Not once?"

"No. But something changed when I was in your workroom, when you pressed the salve into my wound. I suppose I felt weak then, vulnerable, a little foolish for injuring myself. You made me feel powerful again. I do not know if it is something in your profession or if it is something within you, but you let me know—by your touch, by your care—that my weaknesses were beautiful, that they carried their own strengths."

"You made me feel the same, minister."

"Do you remember what you said to me then, in your workroom?"

"Something foolish, I'm sure."

"Quite the opposite. You told me I was closer to Christ than ever before since I had driven a nail into my hand. You said wounds allowed love to enter the body more freely."

Arthur scoffs. "The Great Metaphysician. I was wiser then. I am a fool now."

"Certain you were right about the wounds. My first real encounter with God befell me directly after I witnessed that scene in Edwin's drawing room. I had been studying so very much, learning from brilliant men who explained the Word of God to me, yet I had always felt removed from it, closed off, perhaps because of the fraud I had already committed against words in my father's house. When I was kneeling on my chamber floor, however, I felt the full weight of this tragic life, all of my sinfulness and weakness—all of the world's evils—I felt all of this bearing down upon me, and I cried out in a language only God could hear, for it did not live within words but rather in some long-smothered cell within my heart, one which must have been closed off since before I could remember. God's answer was immediate and unconditional. He let me know I am loved."

"And how did you come to forget this love over time?"

"I suppose I came to believe in my mask. For a while, this mask was all I needed. Saving all those souls only furthered that belief. I was their shepherd, I was to lead my sheep to glory, and I was prepared to sacrifice my personal desires, my doubts, in order to accomplish all that has been accomplished in Cana. I was proud of that accomplishment, truly proud. Proud, and completely devoid of God's love. Abandoned."

"We all have moments of doubt."

"But meeting you opened the wound once more, for I knew then I wanted more, much more. When first we coupled in the meeting-house, I felt that weight pressing down upon me once more, the full weight of this tragic life. I was fastened to the rack. I could sense God's presence in the sanctuary. He was there with us. He is here with us now. I cannot explain it."

"Then why did you run from me? Why did you push me away?"

"I pushed you away for the same reason I pushed Edwin away. Each night following my discovery, I read from my Bible until my eyes grew tired. I prayed for hours and hours, never sleeping. I had never been so devoted to God. It was ecstasy, knowing I was resist-ing the pull of some temptation I desired with my entire being."

"The push and the pull. Feast and famine. You are a true Chris-tian."

"Without it, I fear I might not be Christian at all."

"So this is why I am here," Arthur says, bitterly. "This is why you let me stay last night. Tomorrow you will send me on my way, ban-ished until the next time you need me to stab you with my sword so you can beg God's forgiveness."

"It is not so simple, Arthur."

"Indeed it is, minister. Do you not see you have been worshipping a false idol? Denying all of us who love you—and there are a great many of us who do love you—just so you can torture yourself into religious ecstasy. If this is what an awakening truly is, I am not sure I want it."

Nathaniel forces himself to look at Arthur. The man has said something profound, that is certain. This morning, as he sits beside the man he loves, he can almost picture it: a life in which Arthur's happiness, his pure faith, could be his; a life forged from the strength of their bond, one lived in honesty rather than lies.

"But how could I be a Christian without sacrifice?" he says. "Christ commands us to take up the cross and follow Him. Those words are not mere decoration."

"Your mistake is in believing you may choose your sacrifice," Arthur says. "Even Christ questioned His father's orders. Even He did not go to the cross without reservations. It is your pride which makes you think you can control the method and delivery of God's grace. It is your pride which prevents you from accepting the gift of unconditional love."

Nathaniel grows quiet. Arthur fears he has said too much too quickly, all of these thoughts he has wanted to share with this man for so long.

"Do you want to hear the rest of the story?" Nathaniel says.

"Please, reverend. Continue."

Nathaniel closes his eyes. "Edwin confronted me one night. He asked me if I had seen something in his house, for he had noticed a change in my behavior, a new zealousness. When he asked me this, I grew bold, certain I was armed with the Holy Spirit. I asked him if the others at the school, the ones who accepted all of his money for the cause of Protestantism, if they knew what went on behind those drawing room doors. Without blinking, he told me there were always rumors, but he was known as a kind man, a bene-factor to many young men like me, and whatever his faults might be, he was seen as an honorable Christian. The others were more than willing to turn a blind eye. I then asked him if he had planned all along to induct me into his molly house, to which he responded he had not wished for anything but the best for me, and if I wanted to enter those doors, I was welcome, but if I wished to seek shelter elsewhere, he would provide the money for it. He said he knew from the first there was something of himself in me, and he had merely wanted to save me some trouble in life by placing me in a house where I could be safe from the rest of the world. I denied it, of course, but he saw through me. His eyes peered into my soul. I felt, in that moment, as if I were wrestling with the Devil himself."

"I see no reason to think him an evil man," Arthur says carefully. "It sounds to me as though he only wished to help you."

"You are right, Arthur. I have come to see it that way, at least as far as I can gather."

"I wish there were such houses here in the New World."

"I imagine there are. Before I met Edwin, I did not see the world double. Now, behind every façade, I imagine I can see the secret life beneath it, just waiting for someone to open its doors."

"I take it you accepted Edwin's offer of escape?"

"Yea. He arranged a meeting with Reverend Colman, who traveled frequently to the continent to oversee several Indian missions. Only a few months later, I boarded a ship bound for Boston. Once in the hold, Colman delivered a warning to me I have never forgotten. He said it only once, but once was sufficient. He said he saw great promise in me, but he would never forget from which house I had come to him. 'Do not ever betray me,' he said. 'Edwin Sharpe does a great many things for our church, but his sin should not be yours.' Edwin had assured him I was no molly. I, too, promised him I was not."

"And now you are here."

"Now here I am. And what of my promise to him? What of mine to Catherine and yours to Anne?"

"I do not think of it as betrayal." Arthur's voice has grown quiet now, a whisper. "I cannot bring myself to think of something so glorious as betrayal. We learn, we receive revelation. I believe this is one such revelation."

"I do not know, Arthur. I feel such despair. Sometimes I cannot breathe."

"Allow me to share it with you. Allow our families to share it together."

"I want us to remain in this moment, in this room, with the snow blocking our path and the fire always blazing. I wish to be prevented from my life."

"Perhaps if we remain honest with each other . . . If our families are both honest even though we do not share it with the rest of Cana . . ."

Arthur finds he cannot complete the thought. If he says any of it aloud, none of it will be real. The unspoken possibility is all they have, mystery begging to become miracle. For how could they, the Whitfields and the Lymans, live these two lives, one amongst themselves and one amongst the flock?

"Before I left Cana for here," Arthur says, "the flock was acting very odd. There was some agitation in them, almost the same agitation I felt being away from you. I know it sounds foolish, but some part of me believed that by coming to you, by aiding you in this mission, I might cure them as well. I do not think it good for Cana when we are not together."

"How can that be? God does not reward what we are doing. He has prevented an awakening all these years because of it."

"How do you know?"

"Something is preventing the awakening, and it is only a matter of time before Colman begins to question why."

"That day you saved hundreds of souls," Arthur says, drawing out his words slowly. "What was it you felt? What was different?"

Nathaniel smiles at the memory. "I had met Catherine. I was to return to her at the end of my itinerancy. That morning, I remember thinking happily how we would soon live together in one place, in one house."

Arthur smiles. "And what were you thinking just now?"

A small crowd has gathered in the square. Mary Ninnens shivers in her greatcoat beside her sister Charlotte, who has wrapped herself in two cloaks. Beside them stand Chastity Overton and her husband, Levi, whose stern expression has not budged all morning since first he heard of his wife's plan to join the others for this exhibition. "These spongers come and go," he had said to her. "They want nothing more than to take your money for some bit of dross."

Priscilla, equally bundled, waddles forward now, drawing closer to the white cross at the square's center. She reaches one gloved hand toward it, bowing her head in reverence. Since her awakening, she has moved more deliberately; she has felt as though she were wading through water, though the resistance she encounters only further energizes her, for she knows the Devil wishes to see her lose her faith. At any moment she feels she might ignite in flames. She is conscious the others are watching her; they are perplexed by her behavior, for none yet know of the miracle taking place within her. She has told no one, not even her husband. Even so, she cannot help but press her hand to the surface of the cross. She holds it there, willing the Lord speak to her once more.

Goody Munn and her husband, Josiah, wait beside the barber's, watching the crowd at a distance, cautious, ever cautious, lest they be seen by the others as overeager. From here, the people are as tiny as a cloud of blackbirds, their new prints in the snow stretching from all directions, evidence they have all come out to see the salesman. They could be traced back to their houses. They could not deny it. Goody Munn is glad the minister is not here to witness the spectacle, for though the flock is not exactly forbidden from meeting these salesmen who occasionally travel through their province, lodging in the widows' public house from time to time, there exists a natural distrust of them, borne of the knowledge that these men could come from any place, could have been anyone at any time, could be lying about who they are. Most of all, as Josiah has pointed out to Goody Munn time and time again, they can always lie about their wares. A trinket or a charm said to be from the coast of Africa could turn out to be some Englishwoman's old castaway.

Deborah and Robert Inverness, equally cautious, wait beside the stalls, gawking as the drunkard Hiram paces the stairs of the public house. No doubt this is more exciting than most of his days, Deborah thinks. It seems the crowd gathered about him is in a guardedly festive mood, ready to join in his merriment when the right moment arrives. Perhaps they will even take a nip at the bar after all of the commotion. As Deborah narrows her eyes at him, she wonders privately what it was that had caused her to remain on this side of drink. For many years, those years when she had tended her children's graves, she had been tempted, sorely tempted. Yet something had prevented her. Perhaps, had the minister not shown up when he did, she would have ended up the same as Hiram. This brief moment of charity leaves as quickly as it enters her head, for now that Robert has chosen to remark upon the ungainly sight of the man, she remembers that he is not to be pitied, that he has had every opportunity for redemption, for this is Cana, not some desolate frontier town, and, after all, there are some who are simply too weak to resist the bottle.

"I should say it is wise of us to survey this spectacle," Robert says. "For if the time comes when we should be called upon to recount this folly, we shall be able to provide a full account. Lucky it is we heard from the schoolmaster of some poor child, one of those dirty Beall children no doubt, passing around these pamphlets. 'Procured at great expense and risk of self'? I should think so! Thievery be a hard and risky enterprise."

Deborah turns to her husband. "Have you heard anything more from Mr. Shephard about that Jacobsen boy, Gideon? I am not inclined to believe it anything more than a fit. I did not see any signs of Christ within that child. When his sister died, he did not handle it well. He grew sullen and did not use it as an opportunity for godly growth, as some have."

"As you have, my dear," Robert says.

"Well?"

"Well what?"

"Mr. Shephard. Is it a real awakening or not?"

"Only time will tell." Robert smooths the hair at his temples. "But if there are no more awakenings, I am inclined to consider Gideon's episode a fluke, a childish tantrum. Say, what has gotten into Priscilla?"

"That woman has always wanted attention," Deborah says, watching as Priscilla moves her hand along the cross's edges.

"Well, she shall have her fill of it when she pricks her fingers on that rotten wood. The minister should have tended to it years ago."

"He should have tended to quite a few things." An arched eyebrow. "He has been far too busy tending the Lymans."

"Speaking of," Robert says, nodding to the opposite end of the square, where Anne Lyman and her daughter have appeared.

Anne and Martha cannot help but seem worldly in their cloaks, both of them bright red and fitted with a collar of fine gold chenille stitchwork. Martha, wobbly in her clogs, clings to her mother's elbow; she is more beautiful than ever, a few honeyed strands peeking from beneath her cap. Nearby, never far these days, is August Griggs, the oldest Griggs boy whose intentions toward Martha are widely known. He is a handsome boy with a high brow of some distinction, Robert thinks, though he will never be educated to match it. The only one in this town destined for a fine education is the minister's son, Ezekiel, who will end up at Harvard or Yale, though recently there has been some doubt, since Mr. Shephard told the Invernesses in private that the boy does not gravitate naturally toward the Word.

"Where do you think Arthur might be?" Deborah says.

"I heard he borrowed one of the Griggses' horses. To tend to the minister, of course."

"Ah, then we have our answer."

"Quiet, dear, the salesman has arrived."

The public house entrance, its doors now flung open to the cold, holds within it the figure of a tall man in a worn gray duster and a tricorne hat of felted beaver fur. His face bears the scars of a weary traveler, perhaps a seaman. If he is impressive, it is only on account of his carriage, the squaring of his shoulders, the way his eyes move placidly over the crowd as though he expects nothing. Every soul in the square turns toward him, so now, dispersed though they are, it is clear the town is here to see him. Priscilla Griggs removes her hand from the cross. August joins her, gently pulling her away, for he does not know why his mother is acting so oddly; he does not want a scene in front of the others.

"Ladies and gentlemen," the salesman says, his voice naturally equipped to carry across the square. The man opens his duster, revealing dozens of small pockets stuffed with wares. "If you will follow me inside, I shall tell you a story, one best heard before a warm hearth, which has been prepared by our generous hosts, the Anderson widows."

No one moves. It is one thing to gawk, but it is another to be invited inside, to accept this stranger's invitation. Everyone who has come here today has felt some agitation of late. For Chastity, her restlessness has taken the form of an ache in the pit of her stomach accompanied by a vague sense of burning within her chest. For Mary Ninnens, it has been dreams, sensuous dreams, sometimes of towering sweetmeats, sometimes of hands caressing her body from all sides. Her sister has found herself longing for the old comforts of their family home back in England. All those gathered here today have felt they are alone in these sensations. They have all heard of the awakening overtaking much of New England, how it has altered once-somber Sabbath services: hands raised and legs quaking, declarations of God's visions, God's voice, His presence felt personally, intimately, passionately, in a way that had been not so much forbidden but hidden, locked inside their bodies, with no easy path of escape save that of vice or degradation. They are waiting for the Lord to gather them up, to prevent them from losing what little they know of themselves. For every one of them, Reverend Whitfield had at one point shown them how to take these feelings and place them within a religious way of thinking; he had been able to do this, they felt, because he was a man of extraordinary passion—you could see it in his eyes; you could hear it in the story of how he married Catherine, how he took her in his arms and kissed her before the congregation—yet now, with his increasing absence, they feel the old restlessness returning, the old passions stirring, and they must be awakened once more.

"I promise my story will not be a long one," the salesman says. Without waiting for an answer, he turns from the crowd and slowly makes his way back inside.

Chastity Overton is the first to join him, dragging Levi along with her. Mary and Charlotte Ninnens follow, pleased to find shelter from the cold, for they are older now and no longer possess the constitution for outdoors. One by one, each person enters the public house with the exception of two couples. The Munns return to the street from whence they came, while the Invernesses wait beside the public house's large central window, grateful no one but the sales-man can see them peering inside, for all heads are turned toward the man standing before the hearth. They soon hear footsteps crunch-ing through the snow behind them. They turn to see Sarah and Eze-kiel walking across the square. Sarah appears to be searching out the reason for all of these tracks, her expression quizzical, yes, but also filled with something else, something new.

"This is no place for the minister's daughter," Deborah says, wav-ing Sarah over to her. "We are only here to observe. You may wait with us here if you must."

As the pair approaches, Ezekiel struggles to keep up, heroic in his efforts, his face scrunched up against the cold. He is growing quickly, that one, though his features are not exactly his father's, or not merely his father's. There is some other element in them. Once again, Deborah tries to place what she has seen today, to match like with like. As the boy struggles up the steps, the hood of his coat fall-ing upon his shoulders so his face dazzles in the sunlight, she comes to it. The same jawline she had just seen on Martha, the same frosty eyes, distant and rather haughty, as though they descended from generations of bored royalty, yet mixed with the warmth and open-ness of youth. Nothing so scandalous as an affair occurs to Debo-rah, for on closer inspection he also possesses hints of his father's sharp features, yet she cannot deny there is some miraculous simi-larity, something that declares itself even in the face of impossibil-ity. It is as though the Lord were rendering something conspicuous about the boy so one will look longer, harder, until the mystery of His existence reveals itself. Deborah cannot look away.

"What are you doing out in this weather, children?" Robert says.

Sarah holds her cap against the wind. "Have you not heard?"

"Of what, girl?"

Sarah bristles at the word "girl." She is a woman now. She has been chosen by God to help lead the awakening. As she reaches the top step, pausing beside the Invernesses, she holds her chin high. "An awakening has begun."

"The Jacobsen boy?" Deborah keeps her eyes trained on Ezekiel. "Why, that is nothing. He does not take the Word seriously. We must wait for further proof."

Ezekiel looks up at this woman whose hard gaze he had felt upon him from across the square. Her eyes pierce him. What is she searching for? What has she found in him?

"Gideon is the first to be awakened," Sarah says. "And he'll not be the last. I've had a vision. Something is happening in Cana. A miracle."

"I'm not sure, Sarah, if it is right in a woman—"

"I have seen God's will." Sarah meets the woman's eyes, daring her to contradict these words. "He wishes me to lead the children into a greater understanding."

"The other children are not here, Sarah," Robert says.

"I am on my way to call upon Gideon and the others. I only stopped to see what you were doing here."

"Then might I suggest you continue walking?" Deborah says.

Sarah ignores this. "What's happening in there?" She peers through the frosted window to the crowd gathered before the fire. "I saw many of our neighbors enter these doors."

"A salesman," Robert says, full of mock seriousness. "Come from far away."

"This is what they do when my father's not here?" Sarah steps closer to peer between the lights. "While their children are witnessing glory, they're blinded by trinkets. I am sure they make a fine golden calf wherever this salesman is from."

"Best not to enter, Sarah," Robert says. "It wouldn't look right."

"You can't tell the girl anything," Deborah says, already making her way down the steps. "Come along, Robert. It seems we're not needed."

Ezekiel takes his sister's hand, eager to follow her into the heat. He can feel her arm trembling, the fire there. He had heard her words. He had been told them before. The golden calf, from the story of Moses and the Ten Commandments. He pictures his father as Moses, the commandments dropping from his hands to crack upon the ground, scattering fragments. The image scatters with them. In its stead are pressed bodies and heat from the fire. Ezekiel cannot see beyond the bodies surrounding him. He remembers the schoolroom, how he had peered through the limbs to see Gideon writhing upon the floor, head pounding against the boards, the blood there. He had had no shore then. His sister had not been there. But she's here with him now. He closes his eyes and breathes in the smell of rich game and a wet mustiness he cannot place, his palm clamped to hers. His sister bends low, close to his ear.

"Wait here, Ezekiel," she says, leading him to a table by the entrance. "It may not be safe."

His sister leaves him. The shore recedes, the tide rising. So many eyes. He feels them all around. Yesterday it had been in the schoolroom, Mr. Shephard's eyes. Today it is Deborah Inverness. Eyes belonging to those who wish to find fault. In front, the salesman mounts a chair, his weathered face visible above the crowd. Constance and Humility Anderson stand upon the hearth on either side of the man. The firelight has rendered Humility's scar more visible, a jagged *J* down one side of her jaw. Ezekiel can't look away, not until the man claps his hands together for quiet. When the salesman's hands move apart, a golden fob drops by a chain he has surreptitiously wrapped around the index finger of his left hand. The watch is beautiful. As it spins, flashing, Ezekiel can see the elaborately etched design of a rose upon its case. He has seen only one other object like it, the clock in his own parlor.

"Time stopped when the owner's lover tried to stab him in the heart," the man shouts, pulling the fob up by its chain and wrapping it into coils, a satisfied snake on his dirty palm.

"What use have we with a dead man's fob?" Levi Overton says, shaking his head. Chastity quiets him.

"Ah," the salesman says, his tone calm, practiced. "You see, that man is not dead. I have met that man, and he had quite a pretty story to tell. If you'll allow me to tell it, sir, ye shall learn the full truth."

Levi shakes his head again. "Lies," he mutters.

"Let us listen to what he has to say," Charlotte Ninnens whispers, clutching Mary's arm. "And once we do, we will make up our minds."

Silence. The man clears his throat, then spreads his arms wide. Ezekiel climbs upon the nearest chair, the wood sticky and damp. From here, he can see the man's eyes upon him. Another pair of eyes. Appraising. His sister now stands in the center of the crowd, unnoticed.

"The man who owned this watch fell madly in love with a woman who was not to be trusted." The salesman smiles mysteriously. "In fact, she was betrothed to another man. She wished to own more than one man. When the man discovered her duplicity and was prepared to tell her husband-to-be the truth, she crept into his lodgings at night, dagger in hand, and stood over him while he was sleeping. Now, it just so happened the man was wearing his jacket, for he had fallen asleep in an anxious stupor over his situation, and in the pocket on the spot above his heart rested nothing else but—"

"That fob?" Hiram says, looking about to see if he'd guessed correctly.

"A smart man," the salesman says, placing a hand above his heart.

"A drunk!" Levi says.

"There is no law saying I cannot be both," Hiram says.

"How do we know you're not lying?" Humility says, resting one arm upon the mantelpiece to lean aggressively in the salesman's direction. The scar seems to grow twice its size in the flickering light.

"I have proof." The salesman's eyes narrow.

"My sister and I allowed you to stay with us," Constance says. "We do not house thieves."

"I didn't want him here in the first place," Humility says.

"Of course he's lying," August Griggs says, a head taller than anyone else in the room. "What else did you expect? Come along, Martha. This is no place for a young woman."

August offers Martha his arm. She has come all this way; she had begged her mother to let them go, for they have seen nothing interesting in this town for years; she is fourteen, old enough to visit the public house, and now that a moment has arrived when they can pretend to live as they once did, she must go. But she cannot say no to a man who might one day offer escape. She hesitates a moment, looking to her mother for approval, who nods sadly. The two walk toward the entrance. Ezekiel wants to run to Martha, but she does not see him. Only angry eyes see him. To all goodness he is invisible.

"I have proof!" the salesman yells, clapping his hands. "I have proof, ladies and gentlemen." He opens his duster and the coat beneath. He unbuttons the top of his shirt, and there, above his heart, is a perfect moon-shaped scar roughly the size of the fob.

"How horrid!" Mary Ninnens cries, though secretly her restlessness is satisfied, if only for a moment, by the sight of something so perverse.

"This is where she tried to stab me. This is the spot, ladies and gentlemen." The salesman is breathless now. "But her plan failed. This fob protected me. And it has protected me time and time again on all of my travels. Now I know nothing bad can happen in a nice Christian town like this one, but believe it or not, ladies and gentlemen, there are those who wish to take all of this beauty and peace away from you. There are those who wish you only harm. There are those who are not satisfied until they have everything you've got and more. That woman—the horrible vixen—she wanted to snare every good man she could, yet this watch kept me safe. Fool Death, this fob will. He'll pass you by, thinking Time's already finished with you."

At these last words, the salesman presses the fob's latch release. Even from where Ezekiel stands, perched on the edge of the chair, he can see the hands of the watch frozen at midnight.

"Why, the watch doesn't even work!" Levi shouts.

"It doesn't work in the conventional sense," the salesman says. "But it does work against all evil set upon you. No one ever need feel frightened again, wearing this watch. And it has other powers, too. People will respect you when you wear this watch. That's why all of you fine people came to listen to my speech even when you didn't trust me. Wearing this watch is what did it. So who will it be? Who will purchase this watch today? I carry many other wares, but this watch is special, and I've decided today is the day to pass it on to its next owner. Who is the right person here for this watch? Come, have a closer look if you'd like."

No one in the crowd moves. Then, with sudden celerity, Anne Lyman makes her way to the front. Admiring the fob's design, almost like a fine bit of crewelwork, she is reminded of Catherine's clock. What were the words she had said when she first saw it? It shall bring me great pleasure to think of time in such a way. And it had brought her great pleasure. She wants to possess this bit of beauty, something she can hold rather than imagine, something to remind her with more frequency that her time is valuable, but more than that, she wants protection against the very people in this room, against those who would judge her. She stares into the man's eyes, wanting to trust him, knowing she cannot, the limits of her faith struggling to meet this moment.

"I see clearly you're the one, fine lady," the salesman says. "I see it in your eyes."

"A fine pile she must still have," Charlotte whispers. "Hidden away in Boston."

Anne moves closer to the man. She thrusts out her palm. With great solemnity, the man uncoils the golden chain and lifts the watch above her head, almost as though he would bless her with it.

Sarah, silent all this time, steps forward. She finds her place beside Anne. "The truth is, you likely dropped this fob in water. When you realized it was broken, rather than fix it, as any decent man would do, you decided to make up a story. It really is quite clever of you."

The salesman takes a step back. "And who are you, girl, to say such a thing?"

Sarah does not answer. The word has stuck in her mind again. Her father had told her women cannot preach the Word of God, but God has told her otherwise, so she must not be all girl; she must be more than this. Yet the way this stranger has addressed her—he has made her feel weak, unfit. It is the way others see her. It is a truth she cannot escape.

Mary Ninnens answers for her. "She is the minister's daughter."

"I don't care who she is," the salesman says. "This young girl called me a liar."

Sarah finds her voice. "Many people here today have already suggested you are a liar," she says. "I am merely adding my name to the list."

"Yea, but none of these fine people spoke with such judgment. I see it now. Ah, yes, I see it. You remind me of that horrible woman— that vixen. Perhaps you are her, disguised once more. Tell me, young girl: Do you carry a dagger beneath that coat? I must warn you it will not work, not so long as I hold this fob. Oh, women such as yourself are the bane of this life!"

God has given her strength. She must believe it. She wills herself to take her rightful place. She steps onto the hearth, facing the crowd. She does not look at the salesman. Constance moves aside to make room, joining her sister.

Anne closes her palm, lowering her head in shame. The moment has passed. There will be no beautiful things for her so long as she lives in Cana.

"I am not so greatly concerned by the presence of a liar," Sarah says, raising her voice. She has never spoken aloud in such a way. She is surprised to find it comes naturally, that God has given her this. "The world is full of such liars. Outside this town, I'm sure they are everywhere."

She takes a deep breath, preparing herself. The Holy Spirit fills her lungs. He has shown her the way. "I am sure some of them even live in this nice Christian town."

"Nothing but an Anne Hutchinson, ladies and gentlemen," the salesman says. "I hate to say it, but I must speak the truth."

There is that name again. Sarah wants to rip the rest of the man's shirt away, to humiliate him, expose him. Instead, she wills her face to grow calm, mirroring the calm she has seen in her father's features time and time again. The fire in her breast gathers words, words channeling anger into righteousness.

Ezekiel watches his sister from the back of the room. He has never seen her look so fearsome. He remembers those Sabbath services when he would look up from his pew to his father on the towering pulpit and feel nothing but fear. He had learned to love his father in spite of this fear. This mask he now sees upon his sister's face is what he is supposed to one day wear, a face he cannot imagine wearing, for he cannot bring himself to love the Word as Word; he cannot control his feelings in such a way. No, better to lie in bed with his mother than to go out into the world wearing such a mask, cut off from all love, from all shores, wearing clothes that do not fit and living a life he loathes. For the first time in his short life, he begins to question the god who has created such impossible conditions. When his sister's angry eyes meet his, he looks away.

"What I am concerned with," Sarah continues, "is that all of you have not only invited a liar into this town, feeding and lodging him, but you have invited his false idols to join us as well. You have lusted after the golden fob he carries, this charm which if it does possess any powers no doubt receives them from Satan himself."

Sarah doesn't know if she can continue. The eyes of the flock are upon her, weary and afraid. Who is she to say these words? She closes her eyes.

"Perhaps you'll not believe me when I say you have been trafficking with one who is like the Dark Man in our forest." She pictures the clearing, the light from the lantern, the crimson flowers. She remembers how she felt then: betrayed, appalled that such duplicity could live under her roof. She has wanted to say this to her own father, she has wanted to put an end to all of the lying, but she has been too afraid to do it. Always, he has managed to tower over her with his title and his sex, but now she is the one standing before the flock; she is the one God has chosen to lead the awakening in his absence. "By humoring this salesman's words, you have all but signed your bloody names in his Red Book."

She has never felt such a rush of power. This is what it must be like, she thinks, to ascend the pulpit. Without pause, she rips the fob from the man's grip, dangling it by its chain before the crowd. She forces herself to see the fob as an ugly, cursed object.

"This fine ornament is but a snare for those of you enticed and bound by the carnal world. You heard how the man wished to sell it. He promised you that Death would not come to you if you should carry this talisman as luck. This man promised you what God alone may promise us. He promised you everlasting life, and you believed him."

"I did not believe it," Anne whispers. "I did not truly believe it." Her eyes plead with Sarah to stop, to spare her, but Sarah does not see her.

"While your children are being awakened—yea, awakened— like Gideon Jacobsen and, as God has shown me, many more to come—while they are awakening, you are lusting after false idols. You must pray to God you will be spared His judgment."

Sarah's anger, her passion, all of her restlessness find release through her speech. With each word he hears, Ezekiel feels his throat tighten, the syllables gathering there, blocking his own words. He had loved the sight of the watch. He had wanted to possess it, like Anne. If he could, he would plead with his sister to cease her talking, but he cannot speak.

Priscilla Griggs is the first to cry out. It is as though some invisible being has gripped her arms and begun to shake her, such is the intensity of her movements.

"I have been awakened!" she shouts. "I was lying in my bed when it happened, when the Lord touched me. Oh Lord, forgive me for saying nothing. Forgive me, for I was afraid! Oh, how quickly we sin again. Please forgive me, Lord!"

Like a fast-spreading fire, others join her. Mary Ninnens falls to the floor with a startling crash. James Beall and his wife, Hannah, begin to cry out, sinking to their knees before the hearth as though it were an altar.

"The fault is mine!" James cries. "It is all my fault. I allowed my sons to spread this filth about the town. In all of my sinfulness I let them share this liar's message. Lord, please forgive me!"

Others follow. Sarah can hardly believe it, the speed with which the Lord has worked His miracle. She watches as one by one the flock falls to their knees. She offers her own prayer of thanks to Him. There can be no room for doubt any longer.

The only person who does not cry out, who does not sink to his knees, is Ezekiel. Once again, the Word has missed him. He finds a spot in the corner of the room where he can hide. His sister is no shore. She is an angry tide. He must find safety elsewhere. He thinks of his mother's bed, her rosewater scent, the heat of her.

The salesman flees the room, fearful of attack. Sarah addresses the widows beside her. "Do you see? Do you see what the Lord hath done here, how He hath cleansed this place of sin?"

Humility cannot look at this girl with her wild eyes. This can only mean trouble. Less business. This can only mean change, and change is the last thing she wants. Her sister will speak for her, as always. Her sister will embrace the change. Once more they will be cast into unknown territory, thanks to another Whitfield inviting more chaos into their lives, when all they need is each other.

"I see it," Constance says, wrapping an arm around the girl. "I see it, Sarah. This is just the beginning."

Catherine is alone in her bed, half asleep, when she hears a loud clattering below. She can see by the sunlight that it is already midafternoon. Though she wants to leave the bed, she cannot. Perhaps tomorrow she will be able to stay on her feet for more than an hour. Perhaps when Nathaniel returns, she will be herself again. She rolls onto her side, a triumph of movement. At least she can do this. She can do this one small thing.

More sounds below. The kitchen door opening. If she raises up a little, propping her hand just so, she will be able to see what is happening outside the window. She brushes the curtain back with her free hand and peers over the sill. There, beside the garden, stands her little girl, no, a woman now. She has never seen Sarah look so alive, so vibrant, her face as red as a hawthorn berry. She will turn out quite pretty, her daughter. It is a relief to know Sarah has no interest in the foolish boys here, though Catherine does worry after her, as any mother would. Where will she find a good man? Is there even such a thing, knowing what she now knows? Perhaps it is enough to find a man who is mostly kind, as Nathaniel is. Yes, it is better than what happens with some women. The only problem comes with loving them. It would be easier if she did not love Nathaniel with her whole heart.

It takes her awhile to see the clock in Sarah's hands. Her precious heirloom. Looking up at the window, Sarah raises the clock above her head and, with great ceremony, smashes it upon the ground. Then, grabbing a nearby spade, she begins breaking the clock into pieces. Little bits fly across the garden: a cherub's arm, a wing, a severed head.

That is my garden, Catherine wants to shout. He gave it to me. But she hasn't the energy for it. She shouldn't care so much, but she does.

"No more lies!" Sarah shouts, wiping her brow with the back of her hand. "No more lies in this house, Mother. You have lied to us. You have hidden Father's sin. Something new is happening. Something new, and wonderful! God has chosen me. Me! There is an awakening, Mother. Rise from your bed. You must awaken."

Catherine discovers she has the energy to cry. There is life enough yet to mourn the loss of beauty.

3.

Late Winter

At first, Ezekiel's mother is the only one to appreciate his newfound silence. He had never been one to cry too often or to speak up, but now that he is mute, he is her protector; he watches over her sleep; he ensures the wooden floors are floured and the cotton properly stacked in the entry sideboard. He sits with her for hours on the bed, looking out with her upon the garden.

"Your father built it for me," she says. "He made it so I could see love in every room. Borage, spearmint, sorrel. All the flavors I loved when I carried you inside me. That is why you are special, Ezekiel. You have been made from those things which I loved and which he gave me. I ate them every day you were with me."

Ezekiel looks out upon the mounds of snow that have buried the rooms of the garden. He tries to remember how it looked in spring: bright green stalks rising up through the snow, giant flowers of all colors.

"Isn't it marvelous, Ezekiel?"

He nods.

She runs her fingers through his hair. "You are like me." She presses her brow to his. "You understand the virtue of silence. Those other fools do not."

The snow has made the outside match the inside. When he listens, when he stands beside the garden, it is as though his ears have been sheathed in wool. He closes his eyes. A tide pulses beneath the silence if he listens long and hard enough. The sound is a great comfort, especially as more men enter the house each day, as his father ushers them to his study now that he has returned, sitting with them for long hours and talking animatedly with loud booming voices about the awakening overtaking their town.

"You must be my ears," Catherine says. "You must tell me what they are saying."

Ezekiel presses his ear to the cool wood of his father's study door, listening. One man's voice rises above the rest, a musical baritone that tells Ezekiel the man is a minister like his father, a voice he cannot imagine ever using. He cannot make out all of the words, but he hears the man repeating the names of people he has known all his life, now inflected with a strange foreignness, an exotic flavor, for they are no longer the people they once were: Priscilla Griggs, Charlotte and Mary Ninnens, Levi Overton. Gideon Jacobson, too, of course, the first of the children to be altered. He does not hear his own name.

One day, the man with the musical voice leaves the study before Ezekiel can escape. Ezekiel hears the scuffling of feet, then the door opening, but he cannot make his way down the stairs quickly enough. He feels the eyes upon his back. Reluctantly, he turns to the man.

"Mathew Colman," the man says. "I've seen you in the garden, child."

The man is large, with a gut so hefty the buttons of his dark gray coat strain against it. He is older than Ezekiel's father, though Ezekiel cannot tell by how much at first, for all ages run together after a certain point, and if it weren't for the long gray hairs curled at the ends, Ezekiel might not see that he is truly old.

"Your father has told me you won't speak anymore," the man says. "We shall see if we can change that. Of course, it is natural for the spirit to rebel at first. Often there is great promise in a man when he is odd. You'll soon outgrow it, I assure you."

Ezekiel nods. He has grown very talented at nodding meaningfully. It is the one thing that will satisfy adults, at least for a while, until they grow used to his silence.

"Your father was fairly quiet when I first met him. I've known him a long time, since before he came to this continent. A man quickly finds his way under the right tutelage. If God wishes me to live long enough, I suspect I will also tutor you in the ways of the ministry. How would you like that?"

Ezekiel stares at his feet. It really is a funny feeling to be standing midway upon the stairs, frozen in place as a stranger speaks of a future you cannot imagine.

"Your namesake was also struck dumb. God imparted to the prophet Ezekiel knowledge of the future, of the damnation that was to come to the Israelites for turning their backs on the Truth. Have you by any chance seen any visions, Ezekiel?"

Ezekiel does not move his head this time. It is his sister who sees visions, not he. She's the one to cry out at night. Fragments, impressions—these are what Ezekiel sees. Not a thing far off and waiting in the distant cold.

The man takes the stairs two at a time. When he reaches Ezekiel, he wraps a large arm around his shoulders. Ezekiel wonders if the stairs will hold them both. With the added weight, each of their steps to the bottom makes a loud creaking noise. He thinks of his mother listening alone in her bedchamber. They pause in the entry, the sideboard china still clattering.

"We shall play a game," the man says. "You won't have to say a word, Ezekiel. You'll simply nod your head yes or no."

Ezekiel holds his head still, afraid of what's to come. It is a sin to lie, he knows. It is a worse sin to lie to a minister.

The man coughs. A wet cough, full of phlegm. The man's sounds are far too loud in this house. Ezekiel has failed his mother terribly.

"Is your mother really very sick?"

Ezekiel does not know how to answer. He has heard she is sick, but to him she is perfect. He is to protect her, to ensure nothing harmful will ever reach her. He shakes his head no.

"Does she ever leave the bed?"

No.

"Does she ever say anything of the awakening?"

Yea.

"What does she say of it?"

. . .

"I apologize. Does she say she is happy there is an awakening?"

No.

"And your sister: Does she say she is happy there is an awakening in Cana?"

Yea.

"Does she say she knows the Word of God better than the men in this town?"

Ezekiel stares at his feet again, thinking, trying to remember. Sarah had said something about how the men of this town hold her back, how they know nothing. But does that mean she knows the Word of God better than those men? She certainly knows it better than Ezekiel ever will. He nods his head yes.

"And is there anything your father has told you to keep secret?"

His father hadn't told him to keep a secret, no, but there must have been something about the forest, something involving not only his father but also Arthur Lyman. He feels the man's eyes upon him, pressing him. Ezekiel shakes his head no. It is not a lie, not really.

The man sighs. To Ezekiel it sounds almost as though he's disappointed.

"I need you to be my eyes, Ezekiel." Reverend Colman places a wide black hat upon his head, opening the entry door to the blurry white expanse of the road. "If we are to maintain what we have gained in this town—if there is to be a legacy to what your father has done here—we must be ever vigilant against the forces of evil which seek to ruin us. Your family is most certainly under attack. You must be strong. You must show great promise as well, child. You must find your voice once more. When next we speak, I'll expect more than a nod from you."

So he is to be not only his mother's ears but also this man's eyes. Losing a voice means you must take on other people's senses. He stands in the doorway, letting the cold in. He doesn't think to shut the door until bits of snow make their way inside. He watches the flakes quietly dissolve, then returns to his mother's bedside. He is happy to see her sitting upright. She's even run a comb through her hair and fixed the front of her undress. He wants to tell her he is sorry for the noise, but he sees in her eyes she has already forgiven him. She pats a space next to her, and he climbs up. Here it is again, the heavy scent of rosewater, so reassuring, like warm milk on an empty stomach.

"You're so cold, little one," she says, rubbing his arms, warming him. "Do you remember how I used to breathe clouds for you? A raft of clouds."

He nods, though he does not remember. He can picture it as though he does remember, which is just as good if not better. He's already learned his fancy is far superior to his memories, the world of his mind far more interesting and less disappointing than the world he must face outside.

"I heard every word that man said." Her voice is not her own, or not the one she uses with him. It is a hard voice. She pulls him closer. He is her shore. He can be her shore and she his. "Do not listen to him, Ezekiel. You are perfect as you are."

He closes his eyes, breathing in the scent of her.

He kisses her in the spot where his head had rested, on the crease of her elbow. She pulls him up to face her. There are tears in her eyes. He has not seen her really cry more than once or twice in his life. He begins to cry with her. The first sound he emits in a long time. A whimper, then a sob he swallows with a gulp.

"I know what we must do," she says. She wipes the tears away, first on her own face, then his. "We're going to dig up Mummy's old clock. Do you remember the one, Ezekiel? It used to sit upon our mantelpiece above the fire. You loved it so."

Ezekiel does remember the clock. In this one case, at least, memory is better than whatever his fancy could conjure. He has dreamt of this clock and missed it sorely, missed the impish cherubs surrounding the pearl dial. His friends. He used to imagine them roaming the house while he was asleep, performing their ministrations, mending bits of fabric here and there, flitting about with their shiny white wings, sprinkling faery dust meant to protect him from evil. When he had asked his sister about the clock, she told him it belonged to the Dark Man, that she had destroyed it in order to protect them. He had not understood it then, but he had chosen to believe her; he had felt guilty for pining after the clock, for wishing, in spite of what his sister said, that he could gaze upon it once more, touch it once more, before it disappeared forever. He might be willing to part with it if he could say goodbye to it.

"I want you to go out to the garden, Ezekiel," his mother says, excited now. "I want you to search through the snow for any pieces of the clock you might find. We shall assemble them here in this room as best we can."

He nods, excited now, eager to make her happy again. He moves quickly out of the room and down the stairs, careful with his quiet steps. Without thinking of a coat or gloves, he rushes through the kitchen to the garden, remembering his shoes at the last second. The air outside is colder than he remembered, but he does not care; the warmth comes to him just thinking how happy he'll soon make her. He falls to his knees, the frozen earth hard under his worms, and with both his hands, he begins clearing away the snow. There is so much of it, layer upon layer. The top layer is soft and fuzzy, pleasant even. Beneath that, the snow is like ice, harder packed the farther he digs. His hands go numb after a few seconds, and when he moves them out of the snow, they are a bright angry red. He digs again, meeting brittle stalks, tangled vines, dead leaves that crumble like old calfskin. Nowhere does he find any evidence of the clock. So much snow, too much of it, to form a clear inventory. He falls on his rump and scoots closer to an untouched patch. He begins to knock at it. When next he surveys his hands, they are bleeding; some stalk has snagged him. The blood has trailed through the snow, a bright red thread. He cannot feel his hands, but he does not stop. After he knows not how long, he finds part of a cherub, fortunately the top half with the head and its precious locks of hair, so detailed one can imagine the artist whittling carefully with his knife in some Italian woodshop with a little ochre fire behind him. He turns it over in his red hands, admiring it, and only after he has looked at it from all angles does he realize he's staining it with his blood. He submerges it in the snow again, cleaning it, but in doing so, he drops it once more and finds he must dig again inside the burning snow with these numb hands that are now curling from too much cold. He looks up at his mother's chamber. Fortunately for him, she's not peering out her window. After digging through the snow another minute, he finds the cherub, though it's still stained red with his blood. Now his whole body is cold, his legs numb. He hears his teeth chattering before he understands they must have been chattering for a long while. His vision, assaulted with so much glaring white, has begun to cloud. When he tilts his head back to look at the empty treetops, he sees a flashing bright yellow square overlaid upon it all. He closes his eyes. There is no darkness behind his lids, only more flashing bright yellow squares moving about, pulsing. He is dizzy. He tries to get to his feet but finds his feet cannot move, so he crawls out of the garden on his hands and knees, brushing aside more snow, always more snow, infinite snow. This is the last thing he thinks, the last thing he can remember, before he gives himself over to the shadows.

When he awakens, he's in his bed. A small crowd gathered near, though he can't make out who they are. The first person he recognizes is the man from the stairs, only now he's turning in the doorway with a look that distorts his features. The man leaves. Others leave with him before Ezekiel can get a good look. Only Sarah remains. She bends over him. She holds his hand.

"What were you thinking?" she says. Her face is distorted also; it has been distorted since the day at the public house when the salesman came. "You were to watch after Catherine, not follow her orders. You're old enough to know she's not in her right mind, Brother."

He does not answer her. His throat is closed off to words. The first thing he thinks to do is to check his hands. They are covered in dark gray fabric. Beneath this fabric, smeared on his skin, is some kind of unguent. He turns left then right, searching the room for the cherub. It is nowhere. He hopes his mother has it. At the very least he could have given her this.

"What's gotten into you?" Sarah brushes his hair from his eyes. "You must pray. You must ask God to forgive you your sins. Many of the other children are awakened now, Brother. We hold Bible studies in the public house. The Anderson widows were very impressed by my speech and have offered one of their cabins for our lessons. I'd very much like you to join us."

He turns away. He cannot bear her gaze any longer. He had been frightened by his sister's speech, by Gideon's tremors. He wants quiet, only quiet.

"Is it on account of the forest, Brother? Do you remember it?"

He closes his eyes. Still a faint yellow square but within that square now a flash of bright red, a carmine flower. There had been a man holding him, his father, and there had been another man there with a light. Was it real?

"If it is that, then I should think God would forgive you. It was not your fault, the world they brought you inside. You were far too young to know anything. God may still forgive you if you pray. You might still be awakened."

When next he opens his eyes, the sleeve of his sister's dress stretches down to meet his nose. A simple cotton sleeve, but beautiful. She brushes the hair from his eyes, the sleeve grazing him. He reaches out to touch it, but when his hand meets the fabric, he remembers the unguent. Tears sting his eyes.

"I've always tried to protect you, Brother. From the moment you were born, I made it my mission to keep you safe. But I don't know anymore, I fear I don't know anything at all about how to keep you safe. I merely saw the fire, but you touched it. They brought you into their secret, Arthur and Father. They brought you inside, and Mother allowed it."

Quiet now. The boards creaking above. Their father in his study. Ezekiel pictures his face in the lamplight, a smile upon his lips. He had been happy. Yes, his father had been happy as Ezekiel had never seen him before, while the man with his light—it must have been Arthur—while Arthur with his light smiled back.

"But this awakening, Ezekiel—it has the power to set things right. It may be just the thing. If it can spread, if I can help it to grow . . . Perhaps if it can spread to everyone, it will cleanse this house, too, and we'll all be saved."

Ezekiel doesn't wish to be awakened. He never wished to be the next minister in the family. She can have it; he's not suited for it; if only everyone would stop expecting it of him, he might be able to open his mouth once more and speak. If they hadn't named him after that Old Testament prophet. If they hadn't forced it on him. Worse than worms, his name. The one word that has bound him to the Word and therefore to a god who frightens him, this god who hovers above their lives, watching, detached, knowing everything before it happens. It is a lie, he thinks. I am not this person, this boy. I wish to be no one, to live in peace with the world as I see it.

"You'll soon be safe, Brother. God will soon find you."

Ezekiel has failed his mother. Now there are all sorts of people moving in and out of the house, making noise everywhere they go. He covers his head with the pillow. On the rare moments when he opens his eyes to the room, the light is too bright, the pounding in his head grows stronger, so strong he feels his skull will cave in. His only option is to remain still, so still his every muscle begins to ache from the strain.

He opens his eyes. A miracle: the sun gone and candles lit. Arthur Lyman is here. The man takes a seat on the side of the bed, drawing the bedclothes around Ezekiel's frame, tucking him in at the sides where they had come loose.

"I should have liked to care for you more often," Arthur says. His dark green eyes peer down at Ezekiel, bits of gold flashing in the candlelight. Ezekiel stares into them, seeking out tiny reflections of himself. "No good, seeing you only when you've been hurt."

Ezekiel tries to sit up, but Arthur gently urges him back down.

"Your father and I thought things would be different when we returned from the mission. My God, it's only been a month, and so much has changed."

Ezekiel's vision goes blurry. At first, he cannot tell why, but his eyes soon flood with tears. He cannot bear to see Arthur in so much pain. He cannot take it all in; the pain is overflowing; he will burst.

"Am I making you worse, telling you the truth? I fear I may be the cause of your illness. It was selfish of me to see you. But I saw how happy you were, with us, your fathers, there with your other family. I was not mistaken, was I?"

Ezekiel shakes his head. It is the most he can do.

Arthur beams. He takes Ezekiel's hand in his.

"Oh, you don't know how happy you've made me, Ezekiel. There was something good then." Arthur shakes his head. "What am I saying? What on earth am I saying to you?"

Ezekiel doesn't know what to do with his eyes, with the hand bound with this man's, any more than he knows what to do with what this man is telling him. He cannot make sense of it. He cannot seem to make sense of anything, his skull muddled and pounding.

"I'd almost forgotten why I came," Arthur says. He opens a medical case at his feet and pulls out several clanking brown bottles. "Something to calm your fever."

Ezekiel cranes his neck, opening his mouth to meet the lip of one of the bottles. Above the man's shoulder, the door is opening. It is Anne, peering into the room through the gap. Beneath her bright face, Ezekiel can see a slender piece of her dress, something brilliantly green, like the river's mossy banks. Ezekiel draws a sharp breath; it is so beautiful. As she comes nearer, the tension in his body eases.

"I dressed up just for you and your mother. I thought if no one else appreciated it, at least you would."

He nods. If he could reach out and stroke the fabric.

"I'm off to visit Catherine. She's concerned for your health, Ezekiel, only she mustn't get out of bed yet. She sends all her love."

Arthur and Anne leave the room together. The bit of brilliant green vanishes. Ezekiel sinks back into the bed. Where is his father? Where has he been? He's heard him around the house, talking in hushed voices with Reverend Colman and the others, but he's not seen him. He closes his eyes. The room is dark, but he needs it darker, still darker.

When next he wakes, his head is worse. Still worse is his dizziness. The room has begun to whirl about his bed. He fixes his gaze upon the chest of drawers. Soon the chest of drawers leaves him, floating away. He wants to cry out, but his throat is packed with straw. His hands numb. His legs. He feels cold, though he can see, as he turns on his side, that he has sweated through the night. The sun, blinding now, pierces the curtains. He is alone. There is no shore. He cannot reach his mother at the top of the stairs. He lies upon the edge of a cliff. Two paths emerge. One leads to cavernous hellfire, nothingness. The other climbs somewhere he cannot see. Easier to fall, to let himself go. A door opens. A single footstep. The door closes.

Sarah has tried to ignore her brother's illness, but now, as she gathers the ingredients for a stock, she cannot help but remember her friend Abigail Jacobsen on her sickbed, how in all those months of sickness Sarah had been prevented from comforting her childhood friend, for her parents had feared she and the other children would catch typhoid. She had always wondered, after Abigail's death, whether her absence had been the real reason for it.

Once the pot begins to boil, she returns to his door. She opens it a crack. Asleep. His face red, redder than it should be. Sweat on his brow. Hard-fought breathing. The more she watches, the more she cannot look away. She's surprised to feel a pang of guilt. If she had not destroyed the clock. If she had been here when her mother sent him out without a coat. But she had been far more concerned with the awakening than with her own family. She had thought the awakening would heal them all, but perhaps she had been wrong. Perhaps her father had been right, a woman was not fit to preach. She must think of something to cheer her brother.

She closes the door. A shadow at the top of the stairs. Her father. He has been watching, quietly watching. He retreats to his study without a word. She had wanted to prevent him from influencing her brother, from corrupting his soul. She had wanted him to retreat to the shadows. So why now, as he obeys her silent command, does she wish for nothing more than his descent? Why does she feel more than anything that her father is the only one who can comfort Ezekiel?

She mounts the stairs noisily so he'll know she's there. She stands outside his door, breathing slowly, calming herself. If she is to speak with him, she cannot let him see her anger; she must not let herself give way to emotion.

He had had the audacity to travel home from the mission with Arthur. She'd heard not one but two horses outside. She had run to greet him. Despite everything, she'd been excited to tell him of the awakening, to boast of her role within it. Yet when she saw Arthur with him, she knew whatever words she might say would be lost on such a person. Here he and Arthur sat upon their horses with such proud bearing, smiling senselessly, all while her mother was rotting in bed. Arthur had been the first to ask after the town, and when Sarah offered the news, she delivered it in a bloodless tone; she said that much had happened in their absence and that they would find the town changed. By that point, there had been more than two dozen awakened, and Sarah had already begun to hold her lessons in the widows' cabin. Within her tone, she meant to suggest they had had nothing to do with this awakening; it was hers, it belonged to her, she had found it, and she had been guided by God to bring it forth. She watched their faces fall. She saw the happiness leave. She was glad for it even as the sight of it pained her.

Reverend Colman is partly to blame for her now-diminished position within the awakening, for the minute he heard of the awakening, he swooped in with the other ministers of Boston to investigate. His pride has blinded him, Sarah can see, for after she had provided him an account of the salesman and all that had occurred within the public house, he did not commend her for her sermon, instead he commended her father for all his years of hard work. "I have lived to see another miracle," he said. "I was right to trust your father. Now they will all see it, those who had begun to doubt. They will see it, and they will know Reverend Colman's eye is a discerning one." Sarah had stared at him in disbelief, but his discerning eye had not seen her. He had not recognized her God-given authority, when it should be plain to anyone that she was the one who had accomplished so much, that she was the one to lead Cana into this glorious new era. "Perhaps we shall receive our monies for the next mission after all," Reverend Colman said. "No one will doubt us now. This is just the beginning."

Those last words haunt her. The same ones Constance Anderson

said to her after she delivered her first sermon. It was supposed to be
her beginning, not theirs. Now there are men all about the house,
men from the missions, so many that Sarah cannot hear herself
think. Her father has been asked to pen an account of Cana's awakening, and this is what he spends his days doing, locked in his study
when the men are not here.

She knocks. The sound of rustling papers, slow footsteps. The
door opens. Her father stands shyly to one side. She enters the gap,
meeting his hesitant eyes. The scent of tobacco; despite his long-
held belief that men should refrain from such habits, he has been
taking to snuff.

"Will you not see Ezekiel?" she says. "It's been several days."

"Soon," he says, distractedly. "Soon."

She enters the room entirely. She enters rooms entirely now. Her
father will not change that, not even with his forbidden scent of
tobacco.

"It's grown more serious since yesterday. Arthur has been here."
Sarah studies his face. He cannot hide it now. Something has changed;
something has made it impossible for him to hide. His nakedness
disturbs her.

He pretends to study the spines there crowding his bookshelf. "I
fear it won't do him any good, a visit from me." Though his words
are cold, he is not. Sarah detects a slight trembling in the hands at
his sides.

"How can that be true?"

"I've not been much help to him thus far, have I?" He looks at her,
eyes anguished. She hadn't anticipated his honesty, this stranger
baring his soul to her as if he were no longer her father nor she his

daughter. "You believe I've corrupted him, do you not? That he cannot speak because of me? That he burns with fever because of me?"

Sarah ignores his obvious plea for her pity. She must push forward if they are to save her brother. "I do not wish to worry you, Father, but we must pray for his recovery while there's still time. You must comfort him."

"Who am I? I am but a fraud, an illusion. Nothing I do will help the boy."

Now it is Sarah with her eyes on the bookshelf, on the spine where she'd first discovered the letters. So much time has passed, so much has happened. "You can't mean those words, Father. Please. He is your son."

What she does not say: I am your daughter. She cannot bring herself to plead on her behalf to another man who cannot see past his own nose.

"But you do believe it? That I am the cause of our misfortunes?"

"What does it matter what I believe?" She had meant to stay calm. She had meant to hide behind their joint mask, but he has dropped his, and she finds she must do the same. "I am a mere girl. I'm not fit to make such lofty judgments."

He retreats to his desk, resting a hand upon one corner, a sham bid for authority. "Don't you see you do not want this, Sarah? This thing you're chasing—it is a curse." He looks upon his piles of paper with something like contempt. "Everything I've ever done has been papered over in lies, these meaningless lies. My own father was a wretch like me, but at least he understood they were lies."

"This, from the man who is said to lead the awakening in Cana."

"You're angry it's not you? You wish for your great accomplishment to be spread about the land? To be talked about in Boston, in London? You would know better than I what happened here. You are the one who brought this on. You are the one to lead them."

She must disguise the elation she feels at his acknowledgment. "It is not vanity I seek."

He sinks to his chair, defeated. She has often wondered what he did in this room, how he must have looked as he pored over his books. She has imagined herself in his position. She has envied him. Now there is nothing left to envy.

"Accomplishments are what trap us," he says. "Expectations. We think we are fit for them, but they are the ones fitting us. They carry with them a life sentence, and if we deviate from that life—"

She meets his eyes. "That is easy to say when one already has them."

"And far easier when one does not."

"God has chosen me."

"So your mother told me. She said you declared it while dashing her clock to bits in my garden. You know how much she loved that clock."

"It must be said. People must know of it. You of all people should understand this."

"And the people who learn of it will hold you to it. You will be imprisoned. You will belong to them. It is not God you will belong to. God's voice is a much quieter voice, Daughter."

Daughter. She feels her face redden. "And who helped you to grasp such a revelation?"

Her father does not hesitate. She is ashamed to hear no shame in his voice. "Arthur."

"If the truth comes so readily to you, why do you not share it with the others? Why do you not declare it before our flock? Why are you writing a book full of lies?"

"That is a good question," he says, gripping the stack of papers. He tosses them irritably to the side. "Reverend Colman has asked me to write an account of your awakening, an awakening I was not here for. And I shall forge these letters as I always have—yea, I shall, because to do otherwise will only bring harm to us all. One starts out wanting to be pure, to do good, and soon enough . . . Sarah, I've no doubt this awakening was good at the start. It was good when you first saw it. It was good when I saved the five hundred souls, when I first founded Cana. It was certainly very good when I met your mother. But soon enough, the lying begins, the false feeling. I see very well how it is my fault you are like this. You have followed my example. It is too late for me, but it is not too late for you."

Sarah must not cry. She mustn't give in. "What would you have me do, Father? What choices have I?"

"I do not know, Sarah. I only know this life—the one I have lived—is not the one for you."

"It is you who'll receive honor for what I have done. You confess to me, in secret, that you are sorry for it—yet it will be your name on the book, your name people speak of, and if they ever learn it was I who was responsible for the awakening—why, as you've told me many times, they'll send me off to die like Anne Hutchinson. And you will let them. Do not write the book. Free us of your sins. Do not continue to make us your accomplices."

"You do not yet know their game, Sarah, how this world works. Do you know what they do to men like me? If they learn of me and Arthur, you and Ezekiel will have no future at all. Cana will be no more. You'll have nothing. This book is the only way."

"There is no future as it is," Sarah says. "You've made sure of that. You cannot say you are helpless before your passion. To be with Arthur was a choice, a choice which will cost you your family."

"Have you not made a choice in preaching as a woman? Was this not your passion?"

She hates him for these words. To drag her into his tangled lies, to suggest her calling as a preacher might be the same as his sin.

He turns to the window. Outside, night has begun to fall. "You're right," he says. "You're always right, Daughter. I can see what the others must have seen in you at the public house, the power of your conviction."

She prays her prayer silently to herself: Please, Lord, please, Lord, keep us safe. She cannot lose her faith, not in the moment when it is most important to have it. Though all paths indeed seem impossible, there must be a way to save at least her brother.

"There is a light now," she says. "One far more powerful than all of this darkness."

Her father is silent for a long while, watching the garden. "It is like listening to young Nathaniel." An odd choice of words. "Allow me to rest for a while, will you, Daughter?"

Sarah hesitates. Then, returning to the door, she obeys him one final time.

"There is no future in Cana," he says quietly. "Not for me."

"Then let there be a future for Ezekiel. Go and cheer him, Father. Do it for me."

Now there comes a time when he remembers them both—the shore and the darkness between each shore—and he longs for them both. A soul flickers to life in his chest.

"My son, I am here."

His father's hands upon him, cooling him.

"My son, I am sorry."

Ezekiel opens his mouth but nothing arrives.

Ezekiel cannot open his eyes for more than a minute, yet there is no relief even in the darkness behind his lids. Unnamed shapes suggest themselves first as faint red lines, then as flames seeking a dry host. His mouth is parched. Though the glass of water beside him is never empty, for his sister has made sure of that, he does not possess the strength to bring the glass to his lips. He wishes his mother were here to sit beside him and tend to him as she did when he was smaller; she has come only briefly, in the night, a fluttering dream in her white gown. To feel her hands upon his back; to hear her sing the songs of her old life, soft and deep dwelling and mournful. He wants to feel his father there beside her, the light and the darkness, those opposite shores healing him through their mysteries.

He opens his eyes. Sarah is here, watching him. She brings another candle to his bedside. Her worried face: Is he to die, he wonders, and what will it mean if he dies without having experienced an awakening? That would be the ultimate separation, the ultimate torture, to be severed forever from those he loves, cast into the eternal pit where the worm dieth not and the fire is not quenched.

"You'll be better soon, Brother. I've prayed for you, and God has let me know you'll be better soon."

He moans. He turns on his side, away from the bright flame. A piece of straw stabs him. No strength to move. He wants his sister to move for him, to know what he needs without his needing to say it, and for a brief instant, he is angry that she cannot read his thoughts, that she does not know him as his mother does.

"Is there anything you need, Ezekiel?"

. . .

"Just speak it, Brother. You can speak it."

. . .

"What would make you feel better? Is there anything which would make you feel better, Brother?"

Sleep, he thinks. Quiet and sleep in a place with no light. She leaves the room, closing the door quietly behind her.

Suddenly it is morning. His sister sits beside him, wringing a wet cloth into a bowl. Coils of steam rise from its surface. She places the cloth upon his brow. He can hardly feel it, though he knows it must be warm. His sister wears a green dress. A fresh pine color, he can almost smell it. His hand reaches for it. He takes a bit of its hem in his fingers. He can feel his sister's eyes upon him, the worry there. He does not look into her face, such is his fear of seeing himself worsened in her eyes.

"Wait a moment, Brother."

He closes his eyes. Red lines assault, forming impossible shapes, shapes his mind tries to make sense of but cannot. Fiery orange embers swim between the shapes. He does not want to see them, but he cannot unsee them. He cannot prevent his mind from working hard to make sense of them. He opens his eyes, seeking relief. Here is his sister. She is worried, but there is some new hope in her expression.

"I tried to find one to fit you," she says. "Mother usually has me give them to the other children once I outgrow them. But there was one—this one I kept."

She holds out a blue silk dress, the one with the lace-trimmed stomacher he had admired many times; when they were younger, she used to let him caress it, sometimes for hours at a time. She takes his hand in hers and presses it to the surface. He runs his fingers down the silk skirt, frayed now at the ends, and allows his fingertips to be tickled. He smiles. He sees his sister smile with him.

"Only a bit of fun," she says. "A bit of silliness. I can't imagine it will hurt this one time when you are sick."

All night he dreams of the dress. The soft silk. He is one of those Frenchwomen wandering the shore, careful with his hem.

"Mother, who is that?" a boy calls out from the opposite shore. It is Ezekiel. It is his old self, there with his mother.

"Oh, that is nobody, child. Nobody important to us here in Cana. They will find their home soon enough."

Nobody steps through the mud with bare feet. Nobody lifts the hem of the dress and nods to the boy with the wide, gaping eyes.

Has he died?

Has he died and this his punishment?

Forever dreaming and never being. Always on the edge of birth, always wishing to return to nothing and to be something at once. Nobody and a boy named Ezekiel, a voiceless prophet. One of them must die, he is sure of that. He has no idea how much time has passed, how many days since the dream. His only certainty is that one of them must die.

His sister helps him prop himself up. "Do you think you could fit into it, Brother? No one but Mother is home now. No one will see, then I'll put it away once you're better. We can't ever do it again."

He nods.

"Now, time to muster up some strength." She grips his forearms. It takes all his effort to stand, but he manages. She steadies him. He wobbles a bit, tumbles into her, but she props him back up. His legs feel as though they're made of shifting sand.

His sister tuts. "Now, you must hold your hands above your head."

He does as he's told, nearly toppling over. His sister's hand rushes to his hip, steadying him. With her other hand, she slips the dress over his head, tugging in spots where the fabric catches. She holds him still with one hand and continues smoothing the fabric with her other. The hem goes a little past his ankles, but the fit is good. When he looks at his body, he is covered in silky blue sky; he is floating in sky, free. He feels as though he can walk now, now that he is no longer tied to the earth. His sister takes his arm and leads him carefully out of the room. He is seeing the world anew, everything is new, the parlor belongs to a different family, for his vision is now trimmed with the sky cottoning his body, and he has never seen this room, or any room, while sky cottons his body. Even without the clock on the mantelpiece, the room is pleasant. It is like a second birth, this feeling. He cannot stop smiling. Though he is weak, he feels some of his strength returning with each step.

"Look at yourself," his sister says.

She leads him to the looking glass. In the empty space where the clock had been, he can see the stomacher dazzling upon his chest. He is not dreaming; he is awake now. His sister stands behind him, holding him to her. She pinches his cheeks. Two ripe cherries sing out upon his face.

"Only this one time," Sarah says.

He nods. He cannot look away.

SARAH WHITFIELD

Waterman's Arms

Hull, Province of Georgia,

April 15, 1766.

Sister,

Once more I find myself in the Waterman's Arms awaiting your letters. I know today will not be the day you
answer me, yet the habit of coming here, of waiting here,
has become a meditation, another benediction. Often, I
reach the tavern before the widow who owns it has time
to open its doors. We have come to an arrangement, she
and I. While she sleeps, I open the shutters and tidy up
whatever mess has been left in the night.

The widow and I have become quite close. She is an
old woman who has seen much, and she speaks to me
with a frankness, even a crudeness, which I admire a
great deal. Despite her station in life, she is not a sad
woman. She has confessed to me that she never loved her
late husband; he was a brute; he owned several slaves

whom he beat for no reason other than to satisfy his rage. There seemed to be no end to his cruelty, and though she has never spoken of it, I am sure he treated her much the same. The Anderson widows would be pleased to count her as a sister.

I am not certain why she confides in me so readily, though I have been exceedingly grateful for it. Companions are rare in this wilderness. *If ye was a real man, I might marry ye*, she said the other day. You cannot guess what extraordinary gladness those words wrought in my heart, Sister. *Ye look a fool in them clothes*, she said the first day she laid eyes on me. One day, when I came in early to clean up, I found a pile of worn dresses beside the bar, and I knew without asking who they were for. I wear them sometimes when no one is around.

Only this one time, you would say, and lock me away forever. I've the urge to crumple this letter, sweep it up with the rest of the filth in this place. Why do I dare commit these words to paper, Sister? It is only because I know you will not read them. I do not exist. I am an impossibility, born of an impossible union. A life with no name.

Samuel Dent, the sawyer, is nothing but a rake. Though he treated me with kindness at first and offered me his lodgings, his kindness was expended once he satisfied his lust. His wife, Aphra, was out to market. We were home, in their chamber. I was not shocked to discover such deception came easily to me, for though I had grown close with Aphra, the truly starving will do anything to satisfy their hunger.

When Aphra discovered us one afternoon thus engaged, Samuel beat her within an inch of death and I could not stop it. I hate myself for it. I know I am partially to blame. I must move on from this place; Samuel will not allow me to continue working at his mill, but I have reached the very edge of the frontier. I do not know what lies beyond this place. In my travels I have circled round the mountains to the north, hopeful the half-finished map I studied a few towns back will prove sound, that the forest will soon thin, the mountains soon dwindle to hills, and the dots with no names will be more than wine stains. Most maps of the region grow sparse the farther west of Georgia you look: large empty plains claimed by the French and Spanish after skirmishing, vast Indian territories where few white men have ventured.

But I am lonely, Sister, I am tired of running. I am full of such self-pity. It seems no matter what I do or where I go, I am reminded of Cana. *Ye are like unto that preacher,* the widow said just the other day. *What's his name? The famous one up north. Ye know. Them Boston preachers snuffed it out but everyone who was there that day saw it. They saw how it happened. The news has reached even this far place.* I shook my head. I lied to her for the first time. *Well, don't go acting on it if ye are. It's one thing to wear my dress, but it's another to—well, ye know.* I looked at her with terror.

So ye are one of those. Well, don't look so surprised. I've lived long enough to spot a thing or two. I'm not one to judge, not even a murderer. But ye should know people are talking. People are wondering what ye been up to, seeing as ye don't speak. I'm not one to judge, but ye should probably move on.

Yet I am here for now, and you are there, and I do not know if you and Mother are still alive, or if you think of me, or if you still care for me at all. Perhaps this is what I deserve. Perhaps I shall be banished from this town, cast into the wilderness once again. This may be my last letter, Sister. Nevertheless, I shall always be

your brother,
Nobody

III

LITURGY

1745

1.

Spring

The shore of this father, always near during the day. His other father, the one who has grown so distant, like the rumor of an island thousands of miles away, sees him only in the evenings, after he has returned from the building site smelling of sawdust and sap, his graying hair flecked with wood shavings, and his eyes, more wrinkled now at forty-five, half-closed, sleepy, barely seeing him. It is like this, Ezekiel has learned. The two fathers cannot be seen together, especially not with him. The two families barely meet now. Long gone are the dinners at the Lyman house. Each year they fade further; each year they all seem to grow older and less wise, yet despite this troubling fact, despite their diminished happiness, Ezekiel manages to find some joy during his days, for here is Arthur beside him with his bag of tools as they travel from house to house. Ezekiel observes him, foolscap and chalk always scribbling, always sketching, adding to their knowledge of the human body and its ailments.

Ezekiel is an excellent clerk and a diligent apprentice in medicine, though he has not yet performed any surgery. Until now, he has not been skilled at many things. Like all the other children in Cana, he had been asked to try out a great many professions: farming with the Griggses; cutting wood with the carpenters and millworkers; selling wares with the merchants who trade in Boston, traveling dozens of miles by horseback and carriage to enter the busy shops; tending to the metalwork at the blacksmith's, where he mostly just gaped before the roaring fire; he had even joined the women at the looms, at the gristmill, and at the sewing circles where they stitched bedclothes and blankets and dresses and shirts, his fingers traveling the length of a stray piece of fabric and imagining the feel of it against his skin. He had been useless. He had become invisible, a silent thing to be passed around from place to place until someone or something claimed him or he just disappeared altogether. Mr. Shephard had given up on him years ago. "A useless boy like yourself could have at least had the decency to become a scholar," the man said to him on a day when Ezekiel's mind had wandered from a bit of rhetoric to the purpling sky outside, to the rain waiting behind that color, rain he could already feel in the tinctured wind passing through the open window, its scent of wet earth and promise, of lush greenness. He had even been poor at God; he had not been awakened while so many of his friends who sat in the pews each Sabbath service gleamed up at his father with the full knowledge of their righteousness, of their place in Heaven. People in Cana no longer speak of his becoming a minister like his father. Since he does not speak, they do not speak of him. It has granted him some peace, to be left alone.

But now that Ezekiel has reached the age of fifteen, here is this man leading him to something he can do.

"Bring some paper with you, Ezekiel," Arthur had said on their first day working together. They had met at the Lyman house, and Anne had given him some tea and a bit of raspberry tart.

"It won't hurt him," Anne said, answering her husband's look.

Arthur took him up to his study and handed Ezekiel some foolscap and chalk. Ezekiel had to lick his fingers free of the sugar before he touched the paper.

"I'd been guessing when they would send you to me. I'd see you going about with the others, wondering when it'd be my turn. I'd begun to think you would never come, that we would never have the chance. I thought maybe he didn't want you to be here."

Ezekiel blushed. He could feel the chalk crumbling in his hand. He wanted to hide it.

"But now you're here, and you're at an age when you might find a profession for yourself. Let us see to it that you enjoy this one."

The first few weeks had been only sketches. Arthur had taken him round to several houses, the Ninnenses' most often, on account of Mary Ninnens's illness, which was mysterious and seemed to afflict only her right leg. She said there was a great pain. The leg had swollen to twice its normal size, its veins ready to burst. Arthur had bled it several times, though to very little relief. Ezekiel stood beside him and sketched a remarkably lifelike drawing of the leg. He approached it from many angles; he had a natural knack for composition; one could begin to see, as he continued sketching, the full extent of the leg's swelling at one glance, as though one possessed multiple pairs of eyes. Arthur would consult the drawing often, adding notations in places he felt appropriate. The drawings began to take on more significance than the leg itself. When they were alone in the study, Arthur would shake his head over the drawing, muttering to himself. The swelling went away by the third week, once Arthur discovered, with the help of Ezekiel's sketch, that Mary had a case of gout that could only be cured by a change in diet.

After those first weeks, Ezekiel hazarded his own notations. He began to add the little observations he heard Arthur muttering as they surveyed the flock's illnesses. He was so quick with his work that Arthur, looking up from his patient's body, would merely arch his neck, and Ezekiel would rush to his side with a fully comprehensive survey of the situation, as though Arthur's thoughts had materialized in an instant.

"You've saved me a great deal of time," Arthur said. "You're surprising, Ezekiel. You must possess many hidden talents."

Ezekiel has discovered that Arthur, for all of his plain efficiency and skill, also does things his own peculiar way. Each morning before making their rounds, Arthur brings them to the top of Sled's Hill, so named by the children who seek out its slopes in winter, and from that perch, they survey the town as it wakes from quiet slumber. The people in the square are so tiny, the smoke from their houses curling like questions. Looking down, Ezekiel feels he can breathe.

On this morning, the first real morning of spring, when one can feel the warmth of the sun needling past the cool wind, Arthur points to the far eastern plain where the new meetinghouse is being built. Ezekiel follows his finger and there, right before the half-finished building, is a tiny dot, barely perceptible, that he knows is his father. Beside the tiny dot is a larger one belonging to Reverend Colman. Ezekiel feels his heart grow heavy once again.

"They should be finished soon," Arthur says. "They'll build more houses for the new members once it is done, all along the road, down there."

Ezekiel pictures it: dozens more people moving about the roads, swarming the new meetinghouse like ants. The town has grown by at least two hundred in the last decade, since his father published his famous book on the awakening, *The Celestial Light of Cana*, and the old meetinghouse grew to be too small, too packed, the congregants crowded together along the aisles.

"You can see how it will look once it is finished, can't you?"

Ezekiel nods. He can see it. The meetinghouse is plain, like the other one, with room for many windows. The only difference is its size and the tower that will hold a bell with a little roof over it.

"I should like you to sketch it, a full sketch of the town, with the meetinghouse large and powerful. Make it as though all the roads are veins, all the houses organs, everything leading to the heart, which is the meetinghouse."

Ezekiel nods, though he does not understand.

"That is where your father's heart resides," Arthur adds. "It is where he chooses to keep it, so we shall draw it that way. It'll be a gift, Ezekiel. You shall give it to him when the project is finished. It will make your father very proud. Perhaps they'll frame it, hang it in the sanctuary for all to see. Perhaps they'll even put it in a later edition of *The Celestial Light*. They'll not say you're not talented then, Ezekiel. No, they won't doubt it then."

Ezekiel sets to work at once. He settles upon a boulder at the topmost part of the hill, balancing the foolscap upon his knees. Just as he does with Arthur's patients, he adds the first bold line. He has learned by now that one must begin with boldness, with a strength of spirit, or else the line will collapse from the weight of all that will be added to it. The first touch of chalk to paper must be decisive; it must speak to the intention of the artist. Indeed, it is a bold line, exaggerated out of proportion yet evoking the true spirit of the town's main thoroughfare, for this is the boldest of roads in Cana; he cannot count the number of times he and his family have traveled along it. Beside it he places faint tributaries leading to the deacons' houses, to the Munns' and the Wheelers' and the Hawkinses'. Though the houses are identical rectangles from this distance, he grants them the illusion of roundedness, of soft sponginess, through the addition of trees and shrubs, many of which he renders larger than the houses they surround. The square is the only element that is truly kept square, though only through absence of line, a bit of geometry invisible unless one traces its shape from the other buildings. The white cross at its center Ezekiel renders as a mere smudge, a hazy Star of Bethlehem seeming to hang over the space.

"Everything is so small," Arthur says, pointing to the corner of the page Ezekiel has filled. "Why, you can barely see the public house. I am not sure we can see your house at all. Or mine."

Ezekiel does not look up, does not look over his shoulder at Arthur; he does not question himself; he does not break his concentration. He finishes the square, adding with another bold stroke the rest of the main thoroughfare, winding the line through the Griggses' fields as though it were a giant serpent, adding a dot for the house where

Martha now resides with August, until coming to a stop midway up the page. The rest remains empty. He fills it with the new meeting-house, a giant structure with clapboards bent and nearly bursting, swelling from the inside with blood, a palpitating heart. The house is massive; the eye barely notices the little town cramped beneath it.

"You give life to ideas." Arthur comes up beside him to admire the drawing.

Ezekiel has not finished. At the bottom he adds the Whitfield house, and beside it, he adds dozens of little dots, no, hundreds of them, to suggest the tops of trees, the forest. He leaves a small circle where the clearing would be, and in that clearing, he adds three miniature figures. On the other end of the forest of dots, he adds the Lyman house.

Arthur grows quiet. He continues to stare at the drawing without saying a word. Then, turning away suddenly, as though searching for the clearing from this high vantage point, he says, "Do you think of it often?"

Ezekiel sets the drawing aside carefully. He stands.

"Despite your father's protests, I thought it might be possible for all of us, one day, for both families . . ." Arthur's head drops. "But the awakening changed all that. It happened so quickly, we never had a chance. We were excited by the possibility of such an awak-ening, your father and I, coming back from the mission. We spoke of it on the journey home. I told him it might mean a new life."

Arthur's hands sweep over the expanse of the town.

"What kind of a man is this Colman? Always sneaking about, probing. He says he came here last month to help finish the church. He says he raised the money for it in London and is glad to help, but

I do not know. *The Celestial Light* indeed. Here we are, Ezekiel, surrounded by so much celestial light it could blind a person. But I am rambling. I am rambling, and you have heard enough. It is good you have heard it, but it is enough."

Arthur takes a deep breath. As he sighs it out, a visible shudder runs through him. "You, at least, must be spared all that. A man like Colman is bound to come after someone like you one day, Ezekiel. But I believe we have found your path, a talent which might keep him away until the day you can manage your escape."

Ezekiel nods. What else can he do?

"I should like to show you something, young man. Let us wait a few hours before we make our rounds. No one in Cana needs us urgently."

They make their way down the side of the hill. The town grows larger and more imposing. The houses loom. Ezekiel grows smaller. Now, however, with his sketch of the town in hand, he walks in two worlds, one above and one below.

When they reach the Lyman house, no one is inside. Anne is at the sewing circle with the other women, Martha in her house by the river. The space is oddly quiet and empty without the presence of women. Ezekiel follows Arthur to his workroom. He has been here a few times, yet he is always fascinated by the glass jars surrounding them, this kingdom of plants and animals tucked away on dusty shelves, labeled for use. Sometimes he and Arthur play a game. Ezekiel points to a jar, and Arthur explains how the specimen was acquired, its rarity, its usage, what it does to the body. Then Arthur quizzes Ezekiel, naming the details once again, and Ezekiel must point to the corresponding jar. Ezekiel has never once lost the game, for unlike Mr. Shephard's hard lessons, Arthur's specimens bloom before his eyes; he sees their purposes, their climes, their journeys from one continent to another.

"There is nothing left to guess at," Arthur says, nudging Ezekiel away from the wall of jars. "You know them all by heart."

Ezekiel lets Arthur lead him to a large worktable in the center of the room.

"Stay here."

He watches as Arthur retrieves a large black box from a nearby shelf. Arthur carries the box to the table and, with some fanfare, turns a bronze key to open it. The hinges creak. Ezekiel steps round the table to peer inside.

"Maps," Arthur says. "From all over the world, or as much as we currently know of it."

The box is filled with scrolls. Arthur rifles through the stack to find one larger than the rest. He unrolls the parchment carefully.

"These maps are not nearly so interesting as the one you just made. These are practical maps, Ezekiel. Ones purchased in Boston years ago."

Ezekiel watches as hundreds of intersecting lines unfurl before him. He cannot at first tell what is water and what is land. The sight makes him dizzy.

"This," Arthur says, tracing his finger along a series of complex triangles to the edge of what Ezekiel soon sees is land, "is a drawing of the Mosquito Shore, near Honduras. I once met a man who traveled there and back. He told me they live very differently there, so differently we cannot even imagine it."

True, Ezekiel cannot imagine traveling so far. He has only been to Boston a few times. He pictures a slice of hazy shore, the prow of a ship cutting through spray, the warm water stinging his cheeks.

"It is helpful, sometimes, to imagine going someplace different, don't you think? Some place where their customs are not ours, where it would be very difficult for others to find us."

Ezekiel nods. He doesn't quite understand the intensity of the question, the look in Arthur's eyes, though he knows it has something to do with Arthur's speech on the hill.

"What if we were to leave one day? Would you enjoy traveling to such a place?"

Ezekiel nods.

Arthur's smile grows. "I know it sounds foolish, but I need to know you are willing. Nothing has to come of it, but I must know."

Ezekiel cannot form a full picture of it, but just because he cannot picture it does not mean it will not be good. He trusts Arthur, this father who is not afraid of him, who has always helped him. He matches Arthur's smile. The two men stand like this, smiling, as the morning light drifts across the room, igniting the glass jars: wonders from around the world, rare and precious spices from distant shores.

Midmorning light has already begun to enter the cabin. The room has grown hot, too hot. Sarah walks behind a thin curtain that offers little privacy from the crowd. Constance rushes to her side.

"Do you need water?" Constance asks.

"No, thank you."

"I shall tell them to wait."

"Is Martha here?" Sarah braces herself on the nearest chair. "I didn't see Martha in the crowd today. No one cares for these lessons anymore, do they, Constance?"

"Martha is not here," Constance says, her voice cautiously blank. "They were quite lively today, dear. You spoke beautifully on the wonders of the Holy Spirit. A pity you can never see how they cherish your lessons."

Sarah does not always feel the passing of time. Lately, when her lessons come to an end and she looks into the crowd gathered before her in the cramped cabin, she cannot tell whether she has been speaking for a few minutes or an hour. Constance will place a hand upon her arm, or Sarah's voice will grow so hoarse she cannot push through to the next word, or someone will sigh loudly—and suddenly, startlingly, Sarah will return to the present, sometimes midsentence, at which point she will impatiently announce that the meeting has finished and send people on their way.

When the awakening first began, she had also lost track of time; sometimes she had even spent entire afternoons swathed in rapturous visions of the Kingdom of Heaven—lips pressed to the hem of Jesus' robe, wrists bleeding furiously as the nails were driven in—but those periods had been wondrous and strange. Many others in the flock were experiencing the same visions; she was no longer an outlier someone like Deborah Inverness could mock with her irony, she was the head of a movement. But memories fade, and what was written down in a book carried more authority, even if it was only half-truth. *The Celestial Light of Cana* spoke of an awakening she could hardly recognize. In her father's words, the movement was stripped of its meaning, placed within a world in which God touched so many not through the workings of a few women and children but through a few old men whose absence had been, well, conspicuously absent from the text. This was not how she felt the truth in her soul, and she knew it was not how her father felt it either. Yet both of them had gone along with the ruse, for what else was there to do? If he had not the courage to correct the record, to break free of Colman's grip, then she certainly could not do so on her own.

The strangest aspect to her father's publication was learning that history so easily replaced reality. Those who had been there in the public house and watched as, one by one, the flock awakened, those who had seen how Sarah's words had shaped the movement and given it life, those who knew her father had been away in Kaunameek at the time, those very people were often the first to concede that after reading her father's book, the awakening was far more wide-ranging than what they had seen. But Sarah remembered. Sometimes it felt as though she alone remembered. Such isolation, such immense isolation, made her feel mad; she sometimes wondered if it was God or her own pride that urged her to remember things as they seemed to have been.

Her weekly lessons are still well attended; she has seen an increase in numbers since her father published his book. Yet, as of late, it seems she is alone in her fervor, that the others have come only to watch the spectacle of this unmarried twenty-five-year-old woman standing beside two widows with their air of sexlessness, these sisters who dare continue their lessons against the will of many who think them improper. When Sarah first noticed this change, the Anderson widows had assured her that all of the most important Biblical figures had been seen as strange, unorthodox, that her mission was to continue fighting. Even Humility, who had been cold to her at first, had come round to supporting Sarah's mission. "A husband will do you no good," Humility said. "I may not always understand your visions, dear, but I understand you. A woman must use her best talents if she is to stay unwed." So Sarah had pushed forward, secure in the knowledge that the Lord wished her to accomplish much, that the awakening could never be complete; once begun, it must continue indefinitely, for that is the nature of Christ's revelation. The flock claims to have been awakened; they claim there is no need for such excitement any longer, yet she cannot understand how they do not still feel the fire, how they do not nearly every second of the day experience the glorious and painful crucifixion as their own, how they do not sense that this town is constantly on the verge of slipping into vice, into sin, for such is her everyday experience of life within the Whitfield house.

When next Sarah looks up, Humility is at her side.

"I can tell them to leave if you'd like."

Sarah feels as though her head has been stabbed with a spear. "I do not understand why I try so hard," she says. "They do not care. They care only what my father thinks. They know that no matter what happens here it is of no importance until he writes it down."

Humility presses Sarah's hand. "Yet every week they still come to you. There is a reason for it, is there not?"

"Habit."

"I, for one, am happy things have somewhat calmed. It is not always safe for a woman to inspire so much screaming. We are not so far from Salem, after all."

Sarah raises her head, imitating a pride she does not feel at the moment. "You've never wanted me to succeed."

Humility leads Sarah to the other side of the chair. She places both hands upon the girl's shoulders, guiding her into the seat. "How many times must I say it? This is survival. I've always wanted you to survive. If you wish to last, if you wish to avoid banishment or worse, you must pace yourself. You must be patient. The truth will find its way into the world on its own time. Revelation is not so quick as you imagine."

Sarah observes Humility's face. The scar, which has grown familiar by now, seems to glow afresh in the sunlight. Something has taught her this lesson of survival. Something has led her to be careful, like Sarah's father. So God is quiet, He is slow, nearly invisible. Could this possibly be true?

"I care not for your wisdom today," Sarah says. "My ways are different from yours, from the others'. That is why we are all here."

"Stubborn girl," Humility says, laughing now, for it is clear the worst is over if Sarah is fit to argue.

"We were so near to a different way." Sarah is a little girl once more as she stares into the widow's face, pleading for a mother's comfort she has not known for many years. "I could feel it. Could you not feel it as I did?"

"Did you never stop to think that everyone in this town felt they were close to a different way, that yours was not the only awakening?"

"If Colman hadn't come, if that old man hadn't wished to have his name stamped on the movement, perhaps Father wouldn't have been such a coward."

"If Colman weren't here, it would have been someone else. There's always someone else."

In one swift movement, Sarah rises from the chair and hurries through the curtain. Without a backward glance to the widows, she opens the front door and steps outside. The sun is warm, the air teeming with pollen. The white cross at the square's center, splintered as it is, seems buoyed by the light, and Sarah approaches it carefully, with reverence. She places a hand on the surface. A prayer to remove all doubt, to reveal her path.

"You forgot your cap," Constance says, rushing to deliver it.

"Perhaps I meant to forget it. God does not wish me to hide."

"You know I care nothing for customs, dear, but we must be prudent at the moment. A woman without a cap, in spring . . ."

Sarah does not listen. This is her father's cross, the cross they built when they first discovered Cana, when they knew, by some sense they could not name, that here would be the place where the two hundred settled. She pictures her father then, young and handsome and happily married. The weather just like it is today. How frightening the future can be, how impossible to predict.

"I think I shall take a long walk," Sarah says. "I should like to enjoy one day without your orders."

She does not wait for Constance's response. She crosses the square, moving rapidly past the deacons' houses, neither knowing nor caring where her steps take her. She turns down the path leading to the Griggses' fields, the scent of the flowering apple blossoms on either side of the road, the sun unusually warm on her bare head. She shakes out her hair in the wind, clearing a few strands from her vision.

Her steps have taken her midway past the Griggses' fields. The Griggs men stand huddled in a distant corner, near the forest opening, their cream shirts like stark flags in the distance. She looks away, conscious of their eyes upon her bare head. She holds her chin high. In the distance, barely visible, shines the crest of the new meetinghouse, also bare. Her feet are not leading her to that place, thank God. She does not have to see her father and Colman, not today. Instead, she finds herself walking toward August Griggs's house, toward Martha, who did not come to the meeting today, who has not come for more than three months.

Sarah has entered this house only once. She had not enjoyed her visit; August was always lurking about as she and Martha spoke, as though ensuring nothing of confidence could be shared between the two women, that nothing could be kept from him.

Sarah knocks on the door. She knows August is not inside; he is in the fields with his brothers, but he has seen her walking by; he may return at any moment. She detects a fluttering of the curtains in the nearest window. She knocks again.

Martha opens the door, a tentative smile on her lips. Every aspect of Martha's appearance has been carefully considered. Not a strand of hair out of place. Sarah can see she has held it together with pins that have been carefully concealed. Her eyes, tired now, still carry the glow of youth, though Sarah can see something else there, too, and she knows, as though she has seen another vision, that Martha is with child.

"Sarah," Martha says, feigning surprise. "I didn't know you were coming. I would have fixed myself up."

Sarah follows her friend inside. The house, like all of the houses in Cana, is identical to her own, yet Martha has added little flourishes here and there, as her mother did at the Lyman residence, which bring life, even joy, to the rooms. Dried flowers of all colors nestled into the corners, just below the ceiling. Flickering pastels.

"I am sorry for my absence at your meetings," says Martha, as they sit together on the divan. "I've been busy with August, and—and other things."

"I already know about that," Sarah says, and for a brief moment, the expression of happiness upon Martha's face is genuine. "I saw it the minute you opened the door. Allow me to be the first to congratulate you."

"Oh, I wouldn't dare tell a soul before you, aside from Mother and Father, of course." Martha claps her hands. "But how did you know?"

"It is the logical next step," Sarah says, pressing Martha's hands in her own. She remembers how she had known of Ezekiel long before he was born; she had stood beside her mother in the garden and promised to never tell another soul of her gift. How long ago all of that seems now.

"I didn't know logic played such a large role," Martha says. "I fancy passion might have something to do with it."

"Yea, perhaps what is truly surprising is that August could be the one to inspire such passion."

"Oh, Sarah, you are impossible." Martha snatches her hands away. "You've never liked him."

"Because he took you from me," Sarah says. "It is only that I wanted you to be my pupil for much, much longer."

Sarah's words have thawed some of Martha's coldness, and she draws closer to Sarah. "I could never be so good or bold as you, Sarah. You know I am weak. Once you taught me to read, I found the Song of Songs to be the only book of the Bible I could enjoy, and even then, only because it spoke so beautifully of passion."

"I don't know what to make of that book." Sarah drops her light-hearted tone. How uncomfortable she had been when she'd first encountered those verses, shocked to find such a clear display of sexual longing in this sacred text.

"It seems I was the one who took those lessons to heart," Martha says, gesturing to her belly.

Sarah looks away. Just as she had once been jealous of her mother's pregnancy, of her mother's divided attention to the newborn in the family, she cannot help but feel jealous of the child Martha will soon make the center of her life. Such a life hardly seems easy to Sarah. Song of Songs wasn't shocking to her sensibilities merely for the fact that it spoke so openly of sexual longing; it was also shocking on a more personal level for the lack of real interest she discovered she had in the details of such longing. Once, long ago, she and Martha had promised never to marry. Now Sarah finds herself alone in her womanhood once again.

"Do you find me too strange now to be friends?" Sarah says, suddenly insecure.

"Do I find you . . . Of course not. I find you as I have always found you, as yourself."

Sarah sighs. It is a relief to possess Martha's infinite goodwill, to know it will always be available. She has missed it these past few months. "You know more than anyone else in this town that my family is not a normal one. Neither of ours is."

Martha's gaze drops to her lap. "No more peculiar, I imagine, than anyone else's, once you get to know them."

"I have often sought to correct their behavior. I've tried to rouse Mother from her bed, to ensure Ezekiel grows up properly. I have even, in my own ways, tried to convince Father of what is right."

Though Sarah and Martha have never spoken openly of the union between their fathers, Sarah believes they have an understanding. She allows the silence to speak for her.

"Today, however, I was told I must be more prudent," Sarah says. "I always thought my differences were right in the Lord's eyes, that I knew which differences were good and which were evil. I prayed on these things, and the Lord granted me freedom from a life I would have found hateful."

"My life," Martha says, without a trace of bitterness.

"Yea, Martha, though I believe it is the right one for you, being married."

"That is a new tack, friend. I felt you judged my choice."

"I did, Martha. Oh, I did. I still do at times, though I'm beginning to understand why that is not helpful for either of us."

"Each of us chooses a different life," Martha says warmly.

"You know my father does not approve of my sermons, though he turns the other way. But now there seems to be some new opposition. I believe it must be coming from Reverend Mathew Colman. Oh, I could bear the burden of Father's secret. I have learned to bear it though it has cost me dearly—I could bear our secret for both of us, Martha, the one we have never spoken of aloud, if it did not place me in Colman's debt, and in the debt of all the other men in Boston who stand behind him. For I cannot continue to strike out on my own if it will only serve to jeopardize our families."

As Sarah unburdened herself, she hadn't noticed Martha's change of demeanor, her widening eyes.

"What secret?" Martha says, her words slow, cautious.

The sight of her friend so innocently asking a question to which she assumed she already knew the answer immediately incenses Sarah. If Martha wants to hear the answer—to really hear it—Sarah will say it as plainly as possible. "The affair between your father, Arthur Lyman, and my father, the Reverend Nathaniel Whitfield."

Martha does not move. Her expression does not change. The words hang over the room, refusing to leave. The power of this truth spoken aloud is something Sarah had not understood until it was too late. If Martha had only suspected, if she had not quite known the truth . . . But her mother has known; Anne has clearly known for many years . . . Sarah cannot bear to look at her friend any longer. She studies Martha's twitching hands.

"I never truly knew until this moment," Martha says. "Oh, I suppose I did know, and you've certainly hinted at it over the years . . . Mother wanted to shield me from it, I suppose, and I always thought it was one of those things I'd made up in my mind. I've made up a great many things, Sarah. I've been wrong so many times, even when I thought I knew the truth. I have never been able to trust myself, so I didn't think it was real."

"I thought you knew. I wouldn't have said anything . . ."

"You must think me terribly stupid. You've given me far more credit than I deserve, dear friend. This life is always tricking me. It is always crueler than it pretends to be at the first."

"I thought you knew."

Martha hides her face in her hands. "August is no longer lovely. Not like he was. He hits me, you know."

Martha sobs, gasping for air. Sarah draws Martha to her, holds her as tightly as she can.

"I am a foolish girl, forever falling for surfaces when everyone around me can see plainly where things are heading. You saw it, didn't you, friend?"

"I didn't know," Sarah says honestly. "I didn't care for August, but I didn't know."

"Now we are even. One secret traded for another. It is the only time I have caught you being blind to anything, Sarah."

Martha falls against Sarah's shoulder, her tears wetting the fabric there. "Oh, it is all too awful to take in. Better if we had never said a word. Far better if we had never said any of it aloud, for now it is real. It is real, and I must face it. Can we forget we said anything, Sarah? Would you do that for me? I know I am a foolish girl, but could you humor me once more?"

"I'll do anything you wish," Sarah says.

Martha releases herself from Sarah's grip. She stands. She looks about the room as though searching for something misplaced. "August likes to return without any warning."

Sarah takes this as her cue to leave. She embraces her friend once more, but now Martha is stiff, composed, as she was when she first opened the door. It is as though nothing has happened here, nothing has been exchanged.

"Will you attend one of my meetings soon?" Sarah asks.

Martha leads her to the entry. The two women pause before the door. "August doesn't like my going. The Griggses are set against you, Sarah. You must know that by now."

"But surely you're not set against me," Sarah says, refusing to place distance between them once more. God led her to this house for a reason. "Surely August doesn't make all of your decisions for you."

"I may be allowed to have choices at the moment," Martha says. "But August ensures that they always carry a steep price. If I go to your meeting, do you have any idea what I shall face inside this house?"

"This is absurd." Sarah's voice rises to a pitch she can no longer control. "I'll not sit idly by while this happens to you."

"Please, Sarah. You promised you would not speak of it. We both promised. It only makes things worse to speak of it."

Sarah blinks away her tears. "I watched my mother hide from the truth for too many years. She withered away under the selfish desires of one man."

"For all of his faults, I don't think your father hates Catherine. I don't see her hating him. I cannot understand your father, or my own father, but I do not believe they hate their wives, not now that I know what it is to be truly despised."

"Is it really that bad? No woman should feel her husband hates her."

"And no friend should renege on her promise," Martha says, opening the door.

The sunlight is stark, blinding. Sarah does not move. She does not know where her steps will take her, but she is not so confident as she was this morning that they will lead her anywhere good.

"Do you still think me a friend?" Sarah asks.

"Now more than ever I see you as my sister."

"Oh, Martha, I never really knew what to do. I never knew what was the right thing."

"No one has ever been able to tell you what to do, Sarah. Only God has that right."

"Then I wish you would listen to Him instead of your husband." Sarah does not want to take another step.

"Do not worry after me, friend. I shall make my way to Him."

Martha closes the door. Sarah blinks. The fields cast their emptiness all about her. In the distance she can hear the slow, steady hammering of nails driven into fresh wood.

A sound coming from the children's old bedroom: sharp, like an animal cry, growing softer before breaking into quiet coughs. Despite its likeness to a laugh, Catherine does not recognize it as a sound associated with happiness. She knows such a laugh is not a laugh, for her mother's bitterness taught her well that what follows such an outburst is cruelty.

The walls are too thin. Perhaps they have always been so, but with a guest in the house, Catherine has become newly conscious of her motions throughout the rooms, concerned her every step is being recorded by a patient and exacting intellect capable of detecting her hesitations, her fears. The first time she heard the laugh, more than a month ago, only a few days after the Reverend Mathew Colman moved in to help Nathaniel complete the new meetinghouse, she felt as though she'd been jolted out of her despondency almost at once. She sat up in bed as if awakening from a nightmare, her pulse quickening. Though it hurt to walk, though every step felt like nails were being driven into her feet, she knew she could not lie about the house while that laugh continued to break the blessed silence she had worked so hard to establish. She got out of bed and walked to the hallway; as she stood there listening, the sound carved the air like a dagger thrown directly at her breast. Her heart continued to pound. She had been waiting so long for the danger to make its way to their house, and now here it was. When she first heard of the plan to build a new meetinghouse in Cana, she had pleaded with Nathaniel to keep Colman away, but Nathaniel told her he had had no choice, the man was funding the church, and besides, this was his mentor, the man who had apprenticed him in the art of the ministry, the one person in the New World who has known him the longest, all the way back to his days in London. He had finally explained what she had found all those years ago in his hidden letters, the ones from Edwin Sharpe.

"If it were not for Colman, Cana would not exist," Nathaniel told her. "He knew what I was. He saw it. He met me in that house of ill repute, yet he also saw promise within me. All my life I've been trying to escape my father's lies. Colman gave me that opportunity."

"What was he doing there in the first place? If Colman is so spotless, why did he seek out one of Edwin's boys?"

"Edwin Sharpe donated money to the Protestant cause."

"Never mind the molly house so long as you pay your tithe. That doesn't sound so different from your father's deception."

"Ours is not a perfect world."

Catherine makes her way to the children's old bedroom, now Colman's room. Through a crack in the door, she can see the man standing beside his desk, his eyes fixed on something outside the window. Even with no guests to entertain, even on days when the deacons do not arrive or when Deborah Inverness and Goody Munn do not find some excuse to call upon him, which are indeed rare, Colman wears a black double-breasted waistcoat, his polished shoes set beside the door. For a moment, Catherine imagines stealing those shoes and tossing them into the garden, his shocked gasp replacing the sound of his laughter. How satisfying it would be to startle him.

She waits quietly, watching him through the gap. She wants him to know he is also being watched. From the tensing of his shoulders, it is clear she has succeeded.

"Catherine, do come in. Have a seat."

Catherine obeys his command. Colman has rearranged the children's room so that every object is distant, the chair now in the far corner when it should be snug against the desk. The floor has been sanded, swept, and polished since he first arrived, the empty space where the bed once stood indistinguishable from the rest of the wood, so now she could hardly say this room has ever been used for any other purpose than work. She follows the sliver of sunlight cutting across the floor to the window, where the curtains have mostly been drawn shut: a meager allowance of daylight for someone whose sole purpose seems to be to gaze inward.

"You must have heard me," Colman says. "How many times has it been today?"

"I could not say."

"I am sorry, Catherine. It seems I cannot control this laugh. A tic of old age, I suppose."

Mathew Colman crosses his arms behind his back and walks to the center of the room, facing her. He is a large man, with a red face someone who did not know him might mistake for jolliness. Nathaniel, in contrast, has grown even thinner in the months since Colman arrived, thinner perhaps than when she first met him. In the mornings when she finds herself curled against her husband's warmth, she can feel his sharp hip bone, the sagging flesh of his shrinking belly. He is tenderer, smaller, than he ever was; he lets her care for him, and she finds she has the energy to do it now that they both fear the danger in their house. It is as though Colman's presence has placed them on equal footing. Nathaniel now understands how difficult it is to get out of bed, how impossible to put one foot in front of the other.

"I'm afraid I've been a terrible inconvenience to you, Catherine."

"Not at all," she lies.

Colman smiles. The smile is not warm. "You've been such a great help. It's hard for me to believe you are the same woman I met all those years ago. Something has changed, I suppose, to make you so nimble?"

"The Lord answers prayers."

"Indeed He does. Speaking of which, the new church will soon be completed, and Reverend Whitfield will be made a great figure in our history of the New World. People will write about him and this town for decades to come. How would you like that, being married to a figure?"

"I cannot say it will be very different."

"Being married to a figure makes you something of a figure yourself, does it not?"

Catherine straightens her spine. She places her hands in her lap to prevent fidgeting. "And what does that make you?"

"Ah, you see my ambition, do you? But I do not think it is pride which motivates me, or not merely pride. God has granted me the ability to find talent. I know how to find it and how to cultivate it. One must seek it out in unexpected places, places where no one else would think to look. That is the key. That is what separates me from the rest. I am able to find the diamond in the rough, and I found quite a diamond in your husband."

Catherine takes a deep breath. She must ask it. "Where did you meet my husband, if you don't mind my asking?"

"You mean he's not told you?"

Colman turns to the window once more. Catherine does not answer. She does not wish to tell an outright lie for fear of detection. She does not know how long she should remain silent. One problem with fear is that it makes one incapable of keeping time.

"Let us not pretend, Catherine," Colman says at last. "I know he has told you. It is part of the reason I respect you so much, dear. You stand by your husband. You support him because you understand that the movement is much larger than any of us, larger than where we came from."

"I do not know——"

"But I must know more. I must know he has kept his promise to me. You didn't think I was coming here merely to help you build your meetinghouse, did you? There are more than two hundred ministers traveling to Cana by midsummer to witness Reverend Mathew Colman's apprentice preach the perfected Word of God to a town of truly awakened souls. I must know this man will not ruin me."

"You are trying to have me say something, something which will——"

"Nathaniel has assured me, but I must hear it from you, the wife."

Catherine cannot think. She fears saying anything, but she must say something. "We all have sacrifices we must make," she says. "That is what it means to be Christian. God has given us foresight in the image of Christ crucified. It is not an easy path, nor should I ever presume it would be."

"Fine words," Colman says, laughing. The laugh cuts through her chest.

"They are true words."

"You've not answered me. Has Nathaniel kept his promise, or has he sought out those devilish arrangements which were present at Edwin Sharpe's manor? I have heard how the Lymans have grown close to this family, how often Nathaniel spends his time with Arthur. Reverend Thomas Alcom of Kaunameek said the physician stayed with your husband for quite some time in one of the old cabins."

"Because he was sick. You were the one who wrote to Arthur."

"Yea, but I did not ask him to stay. I did not ask him to bring about rumors."

Catherine stands. She knows the truth. Her husband confessed it the minute he returned from the mission. But the two men had put an end to their union once they learned of the awakening; they hadn't coupled since, even if they did remain close. Catherine knows her husband isn't lying anymore; she can see the difference in him. "Should a physician not remain with his patient until he is well?"

"You must understand. It is not only your family which will face ruin if such a thing ever came to light. This entire ministry would be ruined, the entire movement. People might even begin to suspect *me* of buggery."

Catherine is no longer speaking. Someone else is speaking for her, someone who has been imprisoned inside her for far too long. "Should you be surprised if they do, since you spent so much time sniffing around a molly house?"

She turns. She pauses in the doorway, fearing she has gone too far, she has ruined her family.

"Careful, dear," Colman says. "The rest of your family is not spotless. If anything should be found out, your children, their own peculiarities—it would mark them for life. People might discover sin in their odd behavior, their father's sin stamped upon their very hearts. They would never escape it."

"I do not know," Catherine says, her head dizzy now. "I do not know."

"If there was something between those two men, I need to know there is no trace of it left."

"There is nothing," she says.

"These passions must be contained. They must be placed in their proper channels. A rare talent for passion carries risks, and I have found the proper method of containment, the proper cure for it. You must trust me on this, dear. Every ounce of his passion must emerge at the pulpit. We will see to that, will we not, Catherine? Will you help me see to it?"

Catherine does not move. She does not speak. She can barely breathe. If Colman's goal is to incapacitate her once more, he has succeeded.

"And, please, feel free to tell him what I have said today. Warn him. There should be no secrets between us from here on out."

Again, Catherine says nothing, does nothing.

"And do tell our Sarah to stop preaching her services. Now that you are up and about once more, perhaps you shall have more influence on the rest of your family. We would not wish people to say you fostered a betrayal in your own house, would we?"

At this, Catherine summons the strength to turn her head. She meets Colman's eyes directly, a challenge.

"No," she says. "We would not."

Nathaniel Whitfield has tried to avoid the sight of Arthur and Ezekiel as they make their way through the streets of Cana. Something soft takes up residence beneath his ribs, a ribbon of silk slowly winding its way inside, sheathing bone until the softness begins to harden, the silk tightening, so at any moment he feels that his rib cage might splinter. But each time he looks up from his work, he sees them: Ezekiel with his bit of foolscap, Arthur beside him, buoyant. Indeed, they do resemble each other—the same hopeful bearing, as though none of their worries has surfaced, none has troubled their outward features.

Nathaniel is grateful Reverend Colman and the other builders have left early for the day. When he is in their presence, there can be no hiding the ecstatic pain written upon his face as he catches sight of the pair. He envies them. He envies his own son and his lover. What must it be like to wend these streets so freely, to appear so happy, so unselfconsciously happy, in each other's presence? A freedom and a bond at once. No, a bond offering freedom.

He remembers a line from *The Celestial Light*, perhaps the only true line in that accursed book: "Even in the midst of abundance within our town, a great and unknowable sorrow overtook my soul, and all throughout the happy days which seemed to stretch out endlessly before me, I saw only more sorrow."

Now, as he wipes his brow with his forearm and gazes out at the freshly plowed Griggses' fields, he glimpses a familiar figure walking toward him. It is Arthur, alone this time. A vision of health itself: rosy cheeks, a bit of a gut from Anne's cooking, every bit as handsome as ever. Nathaniel busies himself, hoping Arthur will take his hint. He walks to the rear of the new meetinghouse, carrying clapboards that do not need moving. Soon he hears the familiar sound of Arthur's footsteps.

"I am always meeting you in these unfinished places," Arthur says.

Nathaniel, still crouching, does not look behind him. He can feel

Arthur draw near. A cloud drifts across the sun, deepening the grass at his feet, turning it velvet.

"We shouldn't be meeting at all."

"You know best, minister. You always know best."

"Is it not enough to see him every day? I gave you that. I did not protest it."

Arthur steps over the boards and enters the unfinished church. He sets a small linen-wrapped package on some wooden steps that will one day make up part of the pulpit. He thinks of climbing those steps, of placing himself in Nathaniel's position. Perhaps it would be easier to understand the man. He thinks better of it. Nathaniel will only take it the wrong way.

"Anne brought you some biscuits," Arthur says. "She's worried about you and Catherine in that house with that man."

"Tell her not to worry. It will all be over soon."

Arthur sits upon the bottommost step. "What will be over? Another awakening? Another book? Where does this end, Nathaniel? In a few months there'll be no more meat on your bones. You'll be picked clean."

Nathaniel stands. He does not see the judgment he feared in Arthur's face.

"It is too late to change," he says. "I have already lied. I must pray that some good—whatever good yet remains within me—will come from those lies."

"There are other ways," Arthur says, standing with him. "There must be other ways. You believed that once. You told me so when we were together in the cabin."

"That was before."

Arthur cannot touch this man, not yet. He must wait for a signal. He must wait to see if Nathaniel will break. Arthur has the power to heal, yes, but sometimes he must break in order to heal. There has never been a time when Arthur cannot break Nathaniel, open him up once more; yet now, seeing Nathaniel's stricken face, a face he has never before seen, one so tormented as to be the very image of the damned, he begins to doubt his abilities. This is not like the other times. This is not like the other doubts.

"I have signed my name in the Devil's Red Book," Nathaniel says. "I signed it in blood the minute I added my name to *The Celestial Light*."

"Then release yourself from that man's hold. You will write other books. Things which are true, which have always been true. Things which come from you."

"Colman is not the enemy. He saved me. He trusted me. He had no way of knowing about us. It was I who feared discovery. It was I who wrote the false account so as to distract the world from what I have become. He did not force my hand."

"The Devil never forces a hand. He is cleverer than that. He tempts, Nathaniel. In this case, he tempted you with secrecy. You could keep your secrets if only you became more public, an even more famous figure of the movement than you ever were. No man living could have designed a better torment for someone like you because you are a good man. Deep in your heart you are a good man, and you can still be good."

Nathaniel feels his ribs constricting. He swallows. The hairs on his arms stand upright. Electric, like lightning, this current between them.

"And what would you have me do? Declare before the countless ministers who will soon come to this town that I am a man who has lain with another man? That I am a liar, that it is my daughter and the children of this town who brought about the awakening, not I? Shall I risk Sarah's life as well with this truth? Shall I risk Ezekiel's when I tell them he is your child, every bit as much your child as Catherine's? Shall I free myself by binding others to this horrible truth? Shall I confirm all of the town's suspicions? Shall I lead you to the altar and kiss you before the congregants as I once did Catherine? Ah, what a pretty sight. Then all of us may stand before the church with hands interlocked, two families united as one in pure bigamy. What would that do, Arthur? What would that do for all of these Christians I have led into this wilderness?"

Arthur places a hand upon Nathaniel's arm. He glances toward the fields, the street. No one around.

"There is another way," Arthur hears himself saying. "I've a map. I've been studying one place in particular, a place which calls out to me for reasons beyond my understanding. The Mosquito Shore, near Honduras. But it could be anywhere, really. Anywhere far enough from the English."

"What are you saying?"

"There are many ships which could take us somewhere else. I've hidden away some money. Only Anne and I know where it is. We could all leave together, both families. We would be better off anywhere else."

"You have come to despise Cana so much?"

"It was always you I wanted," Arthur says. "We can make a new Cana anywhere in the world. We can start over. This time we will be honest, we will be good."

A pained laugh escapes Nathaniel. "I always knew you were a dreamer, Arthur, but I never took you for a fool. I am Cana, and Cana is me. For all of our flaws, we deserve each other."

"Is it foolish to travel an ocean in search of a better place? If so, then you, too, are a fool."

Nathaniel walks to the other end of the meetinghouse, placing as much distance as he can between the two of them. He can hear Arthur following close behind. The trees sway in the wind. He feels the breeze upon his wetted face, a cold slap. Spring has disappeared, suddenly replaced by winter.

"Will you consider it, Nathaniel?" Arthur says. "Will you at least consider it?"

Nathaniel does not turn around. He does not say a word. He does not give way to Arthur, but he does not reject him.

2.

Summer

It is night. The night before the service that will consecrate the new meetinghouse. Nathaniel Whitfield stands barefoot in the center of the garden wearing nothing but his smallclothes, heels sinking into damp earth. He cranes his neck to the sky, following the line of stars as they flicker and fade, a careless scattering of seeds tossed from a divine hand. To the Shadows of Divine Things add: stars, the feeling of pattern without pattern, the unrecorded infinite behind all visible creation. A wolf's cry. Nathaniel follows the sound, and there above the trees, the stars begin to disappear, a perfect rounded line like the lid of a pot slowly enveloping the sky. Rainfall. He can smell it.

He takes one step forward, toward the forest path's entrance. The leaves brush his ankles. Mint, sorrel, borage. They are cool against his skin, sending gooseflesh up his calves. He might go inside, to the clearing. He might look upon it one last time, before everything changes. The carmine flowers will be in bloom, spread like a crimson carpet, waiting. Instead, he steps into the bedroom chamber of the garden and looks up at the real bedroom, a candle flickering upon the sill where he left it. Without seeing her, he knows Catherine is asleep. The house is asleep. He does not know how he knows this. Every part of himself answers to every part of the house; it is connected to him, just as every part of himself answers to every part of the town. He has built them both. They are him.

He waits. He does not know what he is waiting for. He closes his eyes. He prays: Lord, please keep my family safe. Please watch over them and guide them through the trials to come. He pictures the house from above, a view like the one in the garden, with all of them—Catherine, Sarah, Ezekiel—moving through the rooms, living out their lives. He pictures the many happy moments they have shared over the years. He has been lucky. A miracle, to possess such a family. He would not have traded anything for them, even had he known of the future when he first met Catherine.

He steps out of the garden. A sudden pain digs into the center of his left foot. He reaches down to remove a wedge of glass that sparkles in the silvered light, a dark red line running down its center where his blood has covered it. He does not cry out. The pain is distant; it belongs to someone else, someone with far greater concern for what happens to his body. The wolf cries in his stead, closer now. Faint thunder in the distance. He wipes the bottom of his foot with a leaf. The blood continues to flow. The cut is deep, though not serious. He briefly considers asking Arthur to make him a salve, any excuse to hear his idea once more, to consider it from every angle, though they have exhausted themselves over the past few weeks with endless talk of their plan and still they've been unable to decide on a date; they've been too afraid to tell their families. Instead, they've repeated their fears to each other in a kind of liturgy.

I have failed.

You have failed.

I will lose my family.

You will lose your family.

I will lose everything.

You will lose everything.

I am damned.

You are damned.

I am nothing, Arthur. Nothing.

You are nothing.

Take me from this place.

Take me from this place.

Nathaniel has prayed for some kind of miracle. Anything to prevent tomorrow from coming. Now it is here, and he must stand before these ministers and these people he has led into the wilderness and claim the fraudulent life he has claimed in writing, declare before them all that he will continue the work of spreading this awakening from one end of the continent to the other. Colman has already written the words for him, tucked them into his gown pocket.

Nathaniel places the glass on the kitchen windowsill, then enters the house. The clock. It must have been part of the heirloom clock Sarah destroyed many years ago. How funny. She had decided to destroy it, and she had never once looked back. He envies her willpower. Of the two of them, she is far stronger, a far better leader for this movement. She has more than proven it over the years, and he had been wrong; he had been arrogant, for there was a force in her that could not be denied, a force he did not entirely understand but that nevertheless declared itself with each of her actions. Was it God? He cannot be sure. Perhaps there are many sides to God that find expression through His chosen vessels. He had wanted to tell her that. He had wanted her to know he understood. Perhaps later, once he has found the right words . . .

Inside, he moves silently through the house, past Colman's door and up the stairs to the attic where both of his children are asleep on a makeshift pallet. Ezekiel has wrapped one arm around his sister, his face buried in the crook of her arm, his breathing labored, as though he knows there is some disturbance in the air. All-knowing Ezekiel. He had never taken to his studies. He had never become the man he was meant to be, but Nathaniel no longer mourns this fact. He no longer worries after the boy. No, far better to break out of this pattern once and for all, to be as unlike his father as possible, or rather, to be unlike the fraudulent father who stands upon the pulpit. Arthur had taught him this. Catherine as well. The boy will be fine because he does not follow any path but his own. Both of his children are alike in this way, even as they approach life from opposite ends. Elemental forces changing the world through the power of their wills.

He bends close enough to kiss them both. Lightning from the garret window illuminates their faces, tracing their features in chalk, freezing them in time. He leaves the room and enters his chamber. The wind has extinguished the candle, the faint scent of wax filling the room. Catherine is asleep on her side. He meets her there.

The first thing Sarah sees when she awakes is the blood patterning the wooden floor of the garret. Ghost prints. She is not alarmed, not exactly, for many of her visions begin in such a way. She does not wake Ezekiel, who sleeps on his side facing the wall. He is so slender, her brother, his shirt slipped clean off his shoulder, his pale arm smooth and uniform, hairless.

She follows the blood down the stairs past Colman's room, past the entry, to the parlor, the kitchen, and then, swallowing fear, peers into the garden, where the tracks seem to have first materialized, right there at the mouth of the forest. Not a vision, then. Real. Without thinking, she rushes to her parents' chamber, looking in through the crack in the door to see if everyone is safe. Her mother sleeps on her back, lightly snoring. In the hazy morning light her features are softened, she is at peace, she is alive, her cheeks flushed. Her father is nowhere to be found. Sarah stands outside the room for several minutes, considering the possibilities, but nothing is clear about these tracks. Nothing except the fact that she must clean them.

She sets to work at once. She starts the kitchen fire, mixing lye with hot water. She scrubs. The water turns pink. If anyone were to enter the house right now, they might think someone had died. Sarah considers: Had her father done something to himself? Had he, the night before the service? No, it is unthinkable. Her father's actions are often unthinkable, but this would be a step even he wouldn't take. Despite her instincts, she considers the possibility of his death. She cannot be certain how she would feel. She had hated him. He had seen that hatred in her eyes as she stood in his study and declared herself. She had been right. It should have felt good to be right, but instead she had felt only sadness, a sadness reflected back at her, one they shared.

Once she has finished cleaning and prepared a breakfast, setting it aside for her mother to find, Sarah walks to the square, where already a small crowd has gathered before the empty stalls. Mr. Shephard tips his hat, jollier than usual, alive to the festive atmosphere all about them. Sarah greets him, but she turns away before the women can detain her. She knows many of them judge her, that they do not approve of her actions. She has learned to keep walking. She takes one quick glance around to see if Martha is here but, of course, she is not. August has no doubt forbidden her appearance until he is ready to leave with her. Sarah wishes she could abduct Martha from that house, that such a thing were possible, but even more than that, she wishes she had been able to prevent their union. Martha had looked up to her. She had trusted her. She had placed the entirety of her faith in Sarah's instruction. Sarah's failure with Martha is just another disappointment she has learned to accept as an inevitability, another soul damned. But how had Martha not known about their fathers? There was innocence there still, an innocence that will eventually find its end in a man like August Griggs.

Inside the public house, the main hall is livelier than usual. Men, most of them dressed in black gowns and white collars, swarm the tables with bowls of Indian pudding and roasted fowl set before them. The widows scurry about, eyes trained on tables.

"They've been here three days," Humility says once she spots Sarah. "A swarm of locusts."

"Do you need a hand?" Sarah says, shouting above the din.

"I need five, ten, twenty hands," Humility says, shaking her head. "But, dear, do yourself a favor and rest. It is a hard day."

"These men do not know who I am," Sarah says, staring with outright disgust at the many faces chewing their food so sloppily. "And they'll never know it. My father's name is the one to be remembered. He is the one with the book. Real life means very little to them."

"Don't waste your time worrying over these men. That's my job. The service will begin in no time, then it will all be over."

Sarah moves to the back of the room, near the bar. The air is cleaner here, less musky. As she continues surveying the crowd, she wonders how many of these men have already met her father. She wants to ask them what he was like before he founded Cana, before he married. Would she have liked that man?

She spots a flash of color. Vermillion. The sweep of a skirt. The sharp features of Anne Lyman's face. Sarah is surprised to see her here. When Anne finally notices Sarah, she rushes over, moving awkwardly through the sea of men. In her life, Sarah has never once seen Anne move awkwardly.

"Is Martha here?" Anne says, distracted.

"I've not seen her," Sarah says. "Is something wrong?"

"I called to check on her before the service, to see if she might wish to sit with us, but she didn't answer. I thought I heard someone inside, but the door was locked and the curtains drawn."

"Shall we try again? Together?" Sarah thinks of the worst. August might have physically prevented her from leaving the house.

"I don't know what to do," Anne says, her eyes moving rapidly, unseeingly, throughout the busy room. "I know she is a woman now with her own family, but I do not like how he treats her."

Chastity Anderson, lingering nearby, leans in at the bar. "What would you say to a quick nip, Anne?"

Before Anne can answer, Chastity has already emptied a generous amount of rum into a small glass. "From the widows."

Anne eyes the glass. She looks around. No one is paying attention to these women at the back. She downs the rum in one gulp.

Sarah senses Anne waiting for her, so she takes her arm. The men hardly look up from their tables. It is clear they are expecting an event, that they hope for something to talk about for years to come. The day Reverend Nathaniel Whitfield delivered his next great speech, one that might animate the movement for decades to come.

Sarah leads them outside. The crowd is still gathered by the stalls, grown larger now. The two of them make their way across the other end of the square.

"We've time," Sarah says. "The service won't start for another hour at least."

"You are kind to help me," Anne says. "I'm sure nothing's really the matter."

Sarah stops them. Anne cannot understand why until she follows the weight of her gaze to the road before them. It is Martha, August beside her. Even from this distance, they can see her swollen belly, the hand that returns to it again and again.

"It is as you said," Sarah says. "All is safe."

But it is not as Anne said. As Martha draws nearer, Anne can see the dark bruise around her daughter's left eye. She can see the slight limp in her left leg, the tension in the way August's fingers wrap around Martha's arm. To even dare bring his wife in this poor state out of doors for everyone to see. Anne breaks away from Sarah. She rushes to her daughter's side. August delivers a hard stare, but she cannot look at him; he is a dark presence at her periphery. She pulls her daughter aside. Luckily, Sarah has swooped in on August. They are speaking about something, but Anne cannot hear.

"What happened to you?" Anne says, not even bothering to keep her voice down.

"What do you mean?"

"You know what I mean. I called upon you this morning. No one answered. And now this. How long has he—"

"It is the first time it's been this rough, Mother."

"But why?" A moan. She cannot help it. She knows the others must be looking but she no longer cares. This is her baby, her precious daughter.

"He found out. He overheard a conversation I had with Sarah, and he asked me about it. I told him everything. Everything, Mother! I'm so ashamed."

Anne does not understand. She continues to gaze into her daughter's beaten face, the violet bruise seeming to pulse in the sunlight.

"You know all of it then?" Anne says, breathless.

"Yea, Mother," Martha says, stifling a sob. "And now he does as well."

Anne embraces her daughter. She can feel the eyes upon her back, but she does not look. There is no one else here but Martha. She is all that matters. "Oh, I should have never brought us here. I should never have agreed to it."

"He said I ruined him," Martha says. "He said I should have told him before we married, but I did not know, Mother. I did not know."

"Has he told anyone else?" Anne says, whispering now. She must whisper.

"No, he will not. He knows it would ruin us both, and no one can divorce in this town."

"You're sitting with us during the service. You'll sit with your family today."

"But it will look odd."

"Martha, you are out of doors with a bruised eye. We already look odd."

Anne leads them forward in the direction of the new meetinghouse. Anne had hated walking to church all of those Sabbath mornings. She had dreaded the whole scene, all the women she would have to meet there. Now, as the two of them walk together, all she can think is how she wishes she could return to their earlier days, when Martha was but a child and that her only worry.

The great hall's emptiness grows. Freshly hewn cedar stings Ezekiel's eyes. The ceiling beams announce themselves one by one as a brash ray of sunlight enters through the upper windows lining the front of the meetinghouse. No flowers, the boy notices, but a fine garland of pine limbs encircling the altar. The new meetinghouse is indeed impressive. Ezekiel draws close to the altar, while his father continues to pace the area behind the pulpit partially obscured from view. He can see his father is worried; something is wrong. He wonders if now is the proper time to present his gift. He has kept the drawing in his pocket for days now, and it is almost too late.

"Ezekiel? Ezekiel?" his father calls out.

Ezekiel runs to his father, who stands in a new robe that has been carefully pressed, his wig freshly powdered, immaculate.

"I am glad we can share this moment," his father says. "I am glad you came early."

His father pulls him in for a hug. Ezekiel reaches into his pocket and carefully unfolds the piece of foolscap. He presents it to his father, who stares down at it with an inscrutable look upon his face. Ezekiel leans in to admire his work once more, now through the eyes of someone else. His cheeks flush. To know he is good at something. To know it is so good as to make his father stop what he is doing.

"This is our town?"

Ezekiel nods.

"Our houses are so small, and the square with its little white cross. Oh."

He has seen the forest clearing with its three figures, noticeable only if one were looking for it.

"You remember the clearing?"

Ezekiel nods. It is mostly true. Whatever he has not remembered has been told to him. The clearing has become legend, myth. A secret gospel.

"Arthur had you draw this."

A pause.

"The church has swallowed everything. This false church. You've seen everything, Ezekiel. You can see everything, can't you, my prophet?"

Ezekiel has not heard his father say that he likes the drawing. He wants to be congratulated. He wants this other father to know him as an artist as well.

"It is remarkable, Ezekiel," his father finally says, handing the drawing back to him, but Ezekiel can hear a new worry in his voice.

"Where have you learned this talent?"

Ezekiel shrugs, shy now, for he does not know what to make of his father's reaction.

"Well, it is remarkable. Truly remarkable. No amount of learning could have taught you this."

His father kisses the top of his head. Ezekiel holds back tears. His father's intensity has begun to scare him. He remembers Arthur's words: "I need to know you are willing. If the time comes, you must be willing." Still, he cannot picture it. The foreign shores, the people there, a world different from the one he has known his entire life. Will his father come with him? Who might be left behind? The thoughts crowd his mind, filling his skull with something soft yet subtly forceful. He cannot concentrate. His vision begins to swim. All about him the pews dance, row upon row. He pictures the people in them. All of them staring up at him, waiting, the pressure continuing to build behind his eyes. Once again, he is grateful he is not his father.

"Thank you, son, for this gift, but I would like you to hold on to it for a while longer. It is more yours than mine."

Ezekiel folds the map, tucks it into his worms. Once his father isn't looking, he reaches into his pocket and crumbles the paper, making sure to tear it in a few places. What good can such a map be if they cannot all share in its vision?

Nathaniel turns toward the rear of the church. He ascends the pulpit and grips its wooden sides. He stands like this until a few families enter, the Douglasses and the Stevenses. The ministers file in, their eyes meeting his. Deborah and Robert Inverness. Goody Munn and her husband, Josiah. The farming families taking up the rear. He cannot move. He cannot greet them at the entry as he normally does. He cannot bear to see in their faces the gratitude and hopefulness this church represents, though his anxiety has somewhat subsided, replaced by a sensation of weightlessness and weightiness all at once, as though he is being held within the dark hull of a ship. Now Catherine, now Sarah. Sarah looks at him as though he were a stranger. No anger, no passion in her eyes. As each family does its best to reconstitute the former order of the assembly hall, they are all of them careful to avoid staring directly at the sight of their minister frozen upon the pulpit. Nathaniel casts a general smile to the crowd, one he hopes appears genuine. He cannot feel his face.

Colman stands behind the rest of the congregation, near the entrance, hands crossed upon his chest, satisfied. Arthur has not yet arrived, though Nathaniel is surprised to see Martha with Anne. He sees Martha's left eye is bruised. He cannot make sense of it. He does not have time to take it in. Once the flock has settled down, he leads them through the singing of psalms he has chosen specifically for the occasion. He does not mention the opening of the new church; it is enough that he has seen most of these men hauling lumber with him day after day.

O Lord my God in thee
I do my trust repose,
Save and deliver me from all
My persecuting foes

He does not move for the duration of his sermon. He cannot hear himself speak for the ringing in his ears. He had been prepared to preach on Christ's sacrifice, a simple but effective message, nevertheless one that has the power to transform the world through love. He supposes this is what he is saying. He cannot hear himself. The minutes have ceased, all the day's hours gathered here in these numberless syllables. For a moment longer, he is at peace. He steps down from the pulpit to the table before him. Communion readied by the memory of his hands, mindless and absolute. Now Arthur entering, taking his place in a rear pew. Nathaniel pours the flagon of wine into ten new silver beakers, lips offering a prayer by instinct. The deacons gather the beakers and pass them among the congregants, heads bowed.

He cannot say how many seconds have passed before he remembers to breathe. The omission of breath becomes habit. He is someone who does not breathe. He is watching the beakers being passed about. He is watching Martha with her mysterious bruise like a bad dream, then Anne with her beautiful worried face. He is watching Catherine, the woman he loves, then Sarah, then Ezekiel—these perfect children. He is watching Arthur, the love of his life. He feels the flock is watching him, waiting for something. He feels Colman's eyes upon him, pinning him to the ground where he stands. How can he guide them, how can he judge them? How can he be anything to these people?

The room has grown curiously hot. His feet drive him down the aisle. Toward the entryway. He cannot believe he is moving, but he must have air. He must feel the air upon his face. Something presses against his back, then something cold and wet at his elbow. Wine spills at his feet like a pair of budding wings. He senses Arthur nearby, this man's familiar worry as he draws near. Familiar hands upon his shoulders. Cool. Soothing.

"Breathe, Nathaniel!" Arthur shouts.

Nathaniel falls to the floor, onto the wine. The wine pools out from him like blood from his gaping side. Arthur catches his head in time, just before he would have struck the pew. The flock gasps. They have breath to gasp but Nathaniel has none. As he closes his eyes, he sees his passion bending, tunneling through him, lifting him from the cold stone floor to meet Arthur's lips. When their lips part, Nathaniel can finally breathe.

TO

EZEKIEL WHITFIELD

IN HULL, PROVINCE OF GEORGIA.

———————————————————————

Boston, Massachusetts,
February 27, 1766.

Mother is ill. Anne and I care for her in the old Lyman
residence on Summer Street. If you wish to say goodbye
to Mother, come at once.

                                    Sarah Whitfield

EPILOGUE

1766

Fall

The boy traveled like an itinerant preacher, toward the unknown, just like his father. But Catherine had not been able to follow him as she had Nathaniel. God saw fit to keep Nathaniel with her even if it meant spoiling the rest. In the hour before Nathaniel hung himself in his gaol cell, he wrote her a note.

Once, long ago, you taught me the beauty of silence. I hope to meet you there once more.

She hears Anne enter. She knows when it is Anne and when it is her daughter. There is a difference in pressure. Anne is quiet and soft. Silent. Even in old age she is still beautiful. Anne, who has always been there for her. Anne, who continues to wear her dresses, dresses from that other, earlier life. Silk, the feel of silk. There are reasons to continue living. Anne had taken her to the theatre when they first moved here after they'd left Cana. They didn't even bother to hide themselves in public. They had determined to be impractical for once, to have a little fun in spite of everything. Sarah didn't approve, but she went with them anyway. Catherine wore one of Anne's dresses. Silk. Red silk. They held their heads high. Catherine enjoyed a laugh. It was a real laugh, not a false one. They had held their heads high, these women. Once Nathaniel was dead, the public did not bother them in the same way. They were to be pitied. Better than being hated, though not by much. Ezekiel had visited his father in the gaol before it happened. He had been asked to testify. Deborah Inverness, Martha Griggs, even that cold man had been asked to testify. August, of course, with his foul mouth. There were others, too, though Catherine cannot remember. It seemed everyone had been asked to provide proof of the Whitfield evil. They had spared Catherine, miraculously. She had not been well after that scene in the church. She had never recovered from the sight of her husband collapsed on the floor, barely breathing, wine pooling under him as though he'd been gored. Then there had been the kiss. A kiss she thought belonged only to her. She had not even been angry with Arthur for it. She had simply been shocked. She has been shocked since. She thought she had lost the power to be shocked, but she was wrong. The world still had surprises in store.

The theatre had been everything Anne ever said it would be. For a moment, Catherine forgot her troubles. She became someone else, sitting in the dark with those women surrounding her in the yellow glow.

"How are you today, dear?" Anne says.

The curtains open. Too much light, but Catherine cannot bear to upset Anne. Anne is doing her best. There is only so much her best can do.

Yes, she had been enough for Nathaniel in the end. But she had never been enough for her only son.

She had not known he was leaving. At first, she thought perhaps he would be gone for only a few months. Then, as the years passed, she thought perhaps he was finding a place for them where they would be safe from that cold man's watchful eye. Finally, however, she came to understand that her son was a true prophet, his work far too important and obscure to interrupt it by returning. She would have to live with this hard truth. She would have to know he was too important for her.

How ridiculous, to ask her boy to testify against his father when he could not even say a word aloud. She wonders what they said to each other in that cell. Did her boy speak then? She had been too sick to visit, and besides, no one would have allowed it. Indecent for a woman to go anywhere near that gaol. Still, she had asked her boy to tell his father she loves him. Did he say it; did he speak her wish? She does love him. She still loves him, the husband whose passion she so admired. He had returned to that passion in the end, hadn't he? He had won in all the ways that mattered. He did not let them turn him into a liar once more. He died on his own terms. They would have made him confess to things he did not believe. Still, she worries after his soul. She prays. She asks Anne to pray with her.

"Of course, Catherine dear," Anne says. "It never left my mind."

Shutting the blinds. Left my mind. There are more rhymes now, more than ever. She hears a rhyme in everything. Nothing is singular; nothing is alone.

Perhaps Catherine will still be damned for her love. Perhaps people like Deborah and that cold man and Goody Munn were right, Catherine will suffer in the pits of Hell for loving Nathaniel, but she cannot turn her back on him any more than she can willingly pluck out her own eyes, as the Bible commands of temptation. She had been saved by him from lovelessness. She wishes her daughter could understand this, that it was not weakness that killed her father but something else, a power disguised as submission and easily defeated only because it is so delicate and rare. Christ was killed not because He couldn't fight but because His love would not allow it; to fight would be to destroy it, to spoil it. You could never win the battle against those vipers. The only thing to do was to end it on your own terms. The moment she heard Nathaniel was dead, she knew why he had done it, that he had done it for all of them, his family, though she feared for his soul, for his sin of self-murder, which so many had said damned him to Hell for all eternity. It is just like that man to sacrifice himself, to sacrifice his place in Heaven, for the sake of his family. But she has never stopped fearing for his soul. She has prayed for him every day, or every day she can remember. She asks Anne to pray with her.

"Of course, Catherine dear," Anne says. "It never left my mind." *Shutting the blinds.*

But she had not known Ezekiel was leaving. At first, she thought perhaps—

Tall Man, Lady of Green Fans, Sweetly White.

"You must get this down, Mother," Sarah says, offering some soup.

"I do not want it," Catherine says.

"You must."

The room is white, all white. They are not in Cana. They haven't been in Cana for quite some time. A roof opens and rain pours in. Something about a tree. The cold is unbearable. Where did Anne go? Sarah tries to force hot down her throat.

"I do not want it," Catherine says. "Where is Ezekiel? Where is my sweet boy?"

"He's not here, Mother. I wrote to him. I asked him to come."

"Impossible. He must be doing something important."

The hot and cold confuse her. She had known things a minute ago, before the flowers came.

Smellnice, Featherneck, Sweetbonnet. What were their other names? Were there other names for flowers?

"Did we have names for flowers?" she says. "What is the other name for it?"

"I must tell you something, Mother," her daughter says. The daughter's name is gone. It will return after the cold passes.

"Did we name a rose? We had only nine years to do it, I'm afraid, then you became the woman of the house."

"I must tell you something."

"You're being silly, girl."

"Did you hear me earlier? I told you I wrote to him. He has been writing, Mother, these past few years."

"Who?"

"Ezekiel. Your son."

"I know who my son is, Daughter."

"He wrote to me. From Georgia. He may come."

"Well, are we?"

"Are we what?"

"Are we still here? Where is Anne?"

"She went to the shops. She'll be back soon."

"Where is Ezekiel?"

"In Georgia. Or on his way. I don't know, Mother. I told him to come."

"Why did you keep it from me?"

"I wanted to protect you. I didn't know what would come of it. There were parts of those letters I didn't want you to hear."

"You do not choose that, Daughter. I choose that."

"I'm sorry, Mother. I should have told you."

"Lies are no good, girl. Not anymore. Let me read them."

She doesn't know how many days pass, though she knows she has watched a hesitant mouse rush into and out of the room. The mouse pauses on her bedclothes and looks directly into her eyes, its nose twitching. Everything else becomes white and hot. She wants to kiss the mouse's tiny twitching nose. She knows it will be cold and wet, even refreshing. The physician arrives, and the mouse leaves.

"Do not kill the mouse," she says, and the physician laughs. It is a good laugh. She doesn't know why he is laughing. He takes more of her blood. He holds it up to the light and nods. He asks her if she knows the date. She says she does not, but at the last minute she remembers her son.

"Ezekiel will be here any day," she says.

The physician seems satisfied with this.

"Arthur? Is that you?"

"Arthur is gone, Catherine," Anne says. "We don't know where."

The mouse doesn't return for quite some time. Then, when Catherine turns on her side to prevent another stitch, he is waiting. The mouse doesn't say anything. He might. He runs his paws over his nose as if something is agitating him. She wants to soothe the itch, but she's afraid she'll scare him. Sarah doesn't see any of it. She is asleep. Her daughter would not approve of such things.

She thinks, I might have had a cat that would eat you. I would have let it. Please, forgive me. I did not know you were so beautiful.

The mouse pauses his routine. He stares into her eyes. In the moonlight, he is shiny. His eyes are shiny. Perhaps she will be damned for loving him. Perhaps Deborah and the cold man and Goody Munn. She hadn't known what it was to seek shelter, how like a dark pit everything is. She is sorry for not knowing the mouse's life earlier. She cries a little at the mouse. She hopes it sees and understands. She hopes it finds its way home.

Mother?"

It is her daughter's voice. The one who is older now and still un-married.

"Mother?"

"Yea, Daughter."

"Mother, I must tell you something."

Catherine tries to sit up. Her left arm is completely numb. Around her daughter's head is a shimmer of light. The light is so bright, it causes her head to pound. She must look away, though her daughter has never looked so beautiful.

"Mother, I've received a response. He says he's coming as soon as he can."

Catherine tries to sit up once more, but her arm folds under her, a clipped wing. She has a faint memory of reading the pages Sarah handed her. Her boy's voice. A man now. No, maybe a woman. There had been some confusion about that. She had been so relieved to see he still had a voice even if only in writing. The voice had been warm and gentle, exactly as it should have been. And funny, too, she seems to remember.

"Where is Anne? Where is Ezekiel?"

"Anne is right here, Mother."

Catherine closes her eyes. She smells Anne. She feels Anne's fingers running through her hair, the lullaby drifting over her.

"Everything will be better soon, dear."

"Anne, will you pray for my husband's soul?"

Sometime in the night, an old verse comes to her: *He that loveth not his brother whom he hath seen, how can he love God whom he hath not seen?*

She is proud, remembering something so difficult. She wakes her daughter and tells it to her. Her daughter weeps.

"I've tried, Mother," she says. "I've tried to love him, but he left us. He abandoned us."

"I do not understand you, child," Catherine says, laughing.

Martha is here. She remembers Martha's name, but she doesn't want to remember the second name. Martha is a Lyman, not a Griggs. That girl who is no longer a girl is someone who should have married a good man, not that Griggs boy. Has her own daughter married? No, she has not married. For the best, it seems, judging by this sad look in Martha's eyes.

"Catherine, you look lively today!" Martha says, trying her best to lighten those sad eyes.

Martha's words are the first time Catherine fears her own death. In them she can hear the lie of living.

"Do I?" Catherine manages.

"Yea, your complexion is much better today!"

The lively voice. Her daughter's voice is lively now, too, while in the presence of her friend. Catherine closes her eyes, believing in the moment, forgetting her reservations. Her girls. These are her girls, happy now.

"There's nothing left in Cana," Martha says. "But you know the Griggses, they refuse to move."

"I wish you would live here with us."

"Let us not. This isn't the time for another quarrel."

"It isn't?"

"Do you really think he'll come?"

"I don't know. He calls himself Nobody now. He doesn't want our name, it seems."

Silence. Then, "Do you remember how it felt at the end? I thought none of us would survive after . . . what happened with our fathers." A pause. "It would have been nice to cast it all aside, don't you think? To start anew?"

"Yea, would that we had been granted such an opportunity."

"No one granted it to that poor boy. He was being asked to test- ify. I don't know, Sarah, I think it's all too difficult to comprehend. He was not like the rest of us. He saw things differently. He was younger, much younger. Now that I have children of my own, I only want them to live more freely than I have lived."

"You seek to tutor me now?"

"Experience has taught me much."

"Indeed it has, Martha."

"You didn't fail him. It was not your fault."

"You have always believed the best in me."

"That is the nature of faith, is it not?"

Do it for me," Catherine says.

"What?" her daughter says.

"Love him for me."

"How?"

"Like when you were a child. Forget everything. It is easier, Daughter, and better."

The girl begins to weep.

Catherine remembers another verse. She is proud. Perhaps she is not damned. *Whosoever shall not receive the kingdom of God as a little child . . . shall not enter therein.*

The girl weeps. Her head falls. "Now you are the preacher, Mother," she says.

"No, you are, Daughter. You and your father. That passion, so much passion in both of you. Will you pray for his soul, girl?"

The girl weeps.

She has forgotten her own name. It will return to her if she stops trying to remember. She must stop trying so hard and it will come. The same was true for her son, who is coming.

After a while, she stops worrying about the name. Everyone has been so worried about names. Better to leave all of that behind. Let her be nobody then. It is a warm bath, to simply be. Hadn't her boy taught her that?

The left side has gone blank. She cannot move it. Her daughter must move her around a little each time she empties herself. She feels guilty for making the girl do it. Then, just like that, she feels no more guilt. No guilt and no shame. Nothing over her any longer. What had that been? What had been that place? They had left a town named something. Back there, something had been left. Guilt and shame, yes. They had left them there. Now even words are going.

"Remember what you taught me, Mother?" the girl says. The girl with the name that no longer matters. "Do you remember, Mother? It was a funny song."

She shakes her head.

"Use me well and keep me clean . . ."

What joy! All the little shocks one feels. Arriving at once, the song. "Use me well and keep me clean . . ."

"And I will not tell what I have seen."

"And I will not tell what I have seen."

What have we here? A little mouse? Why hello, little mouse. Nice to meet you. God be with you, little mouse.

She remembers her boy. She remembers him, and she knows she must wait. He is coming. From a place with a name. The daughter had a letter. The physician comes and drinks some blood. He is not her husband's man after all. Her husband—where is he? He is dead. Her dead husband's man must be old now, like all of them. The girl will not be quiet. The woman who is the mother she never had will not be quiet.

"Stop that crying," she says.

"I don't know what to do," the girl says.

"You have to wait like the rest of us. You think you're special?"

"I don't know how to do this. I pray and pray and pray . . ."

"Stop worrying so much. Do you not remember waiting? This is how it feels."

Her right side seizes, then something in her chest. She is jolted awake for the first time in days. It draws her out of the warm bath into pain and knowing. Her daughter is out. Anne is somewhere in the house, though not in this room.

Catherine knows this is it. She cannot cry out for anyone. She remembers pieces of her life—too many all at once. She wants to run from them, but they sink down upon her chest, smothering her. She is afraid, more afraid than ever, not because no one is with her but because she feels God's presence near. Looming. Is this a benevolent presence? She cannot be certain. She claws at the edges of her vision, holding fast to life, but life is too slippery. She wants some assurance that she has been a good person. She wants her son and daughter by her side. She reaches out. She falls from the bed. The light billows. The gap grows larger. Rain floods her mouth, her lungs. The horses are neighing somewhere outside. Soon they will be gone with her. She cannot feel her body. Only a pocket of vision remains. There, within the tapering halo: the sweetest little mouse. Ah, him again. She remembers him. He had forgiven her everything.

2

Winter

Nobody arrives in Summer Street before dawn. He pauses beside the stocks and checks the housefronts for signs. The Lyman sign is long gone, of course. He removes a hand from his muff, runs his fingers through his tangled hair. The freezing wind bites his arm.

It had been foolish to ride all night, but he had not thought of his own health in these last few weeks of travel. It had been just as windy on that fated night he had walked out of the gaol with the knowledge that his father had forgiven him for even considering testifying. "You'll be asked to do a great many things, Ezekiel," his father had said. "But they'll never be satisfied. They'll think you're willfully opposed to them if you don't speak. They'll think you commanded by some demon." Nobody had wanted to speak out, to cry with his father, to say he loved him, but instead he had only been able to hand him a scrap of paper with his mother's message. "I'll find a way," his father said. "There is a way to save you all from the worst of it, but when the time comes, Ezekiel, you'll need to care for your mother."

Nobody had not known what his father planned to do. If he had known . . . If he had even imagined . . . would he have been able to leave?

Care for your mother, Ezekiel.

That name. It no longer belonged to him. Nobody had taken one step, then another. Out of the gaol, into the street. He was to return to Anne and his mother and sister. Instead, he split into two people. The boy named Ezekiel, the dutiful son, would be the one to return. Yes, Nobody would send that dutiful boy on his way to that other life, a life of slow suffocation at the hands of charitable people who would always look at him askance, those people with their inexhaustible expectations. His instinct was to pray for his soul, for his father's soul, for all of their souls, but the minute the words left his head, a white flashing rage ignited within him. He was being asked to murder whatever was left of his soul. From that point on, he would not only cease to be Ezekiel, he would cease to be a person at all. No matter if he testified or not, the future had no place for him. No, it never had. He could see that now. The future did not want him in it: God had passed him over until now—and now that God had cornered him, He had placed him in this impossible position. One where he would never find joy, or peace, or love. God had already taken away his family, and He wouldn't stop there, that much was already clear. Why would God do such a thing? What kind of god allowed this? What kind of god asked of a son such an impossible sacrifice? What kind of god indeed, he laughed to himself, but the very same who had asked his son to die for him in order to save humanity. And if God asked such a sacrifice as this, what depravity might He ask of a person next? It would never end, Nobody could see, taking another step, then another, in the opposite direction. If one believes in Christ, then the sacrifices will never end. Better not to believe. Better to cast all of it behind him. And so he had. Unthinkingly, unbelievably—against every instinct he had been raised to feel—he had turned away in search of a shore where he might be left alone.

"Call me Brother," he says now, to an empty street. His first words in more than twenty years, practiced again and again on the ride here. Will he have the strength to say these words that others might hear, that his sister might hear?

"Call me Brother, Sarah."

Sarah cannot rest in this house, not anymore. Though Anne has been wonderful as always, as has Martha who returned from that awful husband to help her friend, the sound of their hushed talking, of their occasional laughter—it is too much to bear, any sound at all is too much to bear; she craves the silence her mother cherished. Finally, Sarah thinks, it is appropriate to have such silence in a house, the silence of death.

"We shall have to think what to do," she hears Martha saying. Then, in a whisper: "with the body."

"Let us wait for Ezekiel," Anne says.

"Do you think it wise? Will he really come, Mother?"

Sarah walks to the window. The reflection of an aging woman in black. All black. Black crepe shrouding the pictures on the wall be-hind her. She waits. She hates herself for waiting each day, listening for any sudden sound in the street. Behind her, on a bier, her moth-er's body waits in a coffin. She won't look.

A clatter below. She looks. She chides herself for looking. When her brother left, when he abandoned them, she hadn't been angry at first, she'd felt only that she had failed him. Out of all the children she led to the Lord, her own brother . . . What would people think? Then, of course, she considered what people already thought now that she was a disgraced daughter. Hatred, pity, private judgments she could sense behind their falsely sympathetic eyes but never truly see. She had had her reckoning. Reverend Colman had made sure to let her know she could never again preach in any town. Good, she thought. And neither can you. Each time he preached, he would al-ways wonder if people were thinking of his famous apprentice, the central failure of his life. Yes, she had cast that life behind her. She would never preach again, though she hadn't been able to cease her prayers at night, a habit that still brought her great comfort. But no more visions. No blinding glory, no nightly raptures. She had closed a door within herself and left it shut. On the other side of that door: fury. Blinding rage. Madness at everything she had lost. After she allowed herself to think the impossible—that her brother would never return, that he had abandoned their family just as their father had abandoned them for all eternity—she opened the door one last time, the rising heat nearly blinding her, and she shoved her brother behind that door, locking it forever.

Then the letter. The first of three. After nearly twenty years. And from a person by the name of Nobody. It was absurd. Who did he think he was, telling her about his pain, confirming all of her worst suspicions, letting her know he is just as selfish as their father was? He had followed his passion, his freedom, at the expense of everyone else. Hadn't she wanted to do the same? Hadn't she been tempted, as these men had? She had wanted to write back. She had been tempted to lay out all of her own pain, let him see how she had sacrificed her life for the sake of the mother he had abandoned. All she had ever done, since his birth, was try to protect this family. She had failed, but at least she'd tried. He had run away from them the first chance he got. Not even a word for twenty years. By his crushing silence, he let them know he never loved them. She felt betrayed. She regretted ever loving him. She wanted him to know this, to make him see, perhaps even—could she admit it to herself?—to save his soul, to save at least one final soul. But no, far better to make him suffer her silence as he had made her suffer with his silence. An eye for an eye, tongue for a tongue. She couldn't help it. She turned away from God as she cast her letter into the fire. She couldn't bear to pray for the many lost souls of the world, for she didn't want to help the one who was closest to hers, never mind how many miles were between them.

Then that second letter as Mother began to grow worse. Sarah was raw, broken inside. She saw him more fully now, even if she didn't wish for it. She saw him suffering, this lost soul. Still, she didn't write back. She kept the door firmly shut. She needed all the strength she could muster if she was going to help her mother. But her mother had not allowed her to keep the past in the past where it belonged. As her mother's mind went, so did her fear of speaking aloud the many desires she had kept hidden for twenty years. She begged for Ezekiel; she begged for Sarah to bring him back to her, if only for a

moment. She asked for a miracle, and Sarah couldn't avoid her questions any longer. She wrote to him. She didn't expect him to answer
so quickly. She still doesn't believe he is coming. He is too late, of
course, he is too late; but perhaps, perhaps he will come. She turns
from the window.

Nobody knocks. The door opens. He hardly recognizes Anne and,
behind her, Martha. He doesn't know what to do, but Anne does.

"My god," she says, embracing him, smoothing his weather-
beaten hair. "A miracle."

Martha rushes to his side. "I knew it. You're here."

They lead him to the parlor where the coffin lies. He had been
preparing for this moment, dreading the possibility of his mother's
death, and now that it is here, he can hardly feel anything. The
woman before him is not his mother. Even in rest she had been alive,
far more alive than the rest of the world. He must sit down. Anne
offers him some tea, but he can't hold the cup without spilling.
Where is his sister? Who is that woman all in black in the corner of
the room? The woman nods. She stands.

"You're too late," the woman says. "What would you have me
call you?"

Nobody looks into her eyes. She is older, yes, but the fire is still
there. He sets his tea aside and prepares himself to speak.

"Call me Brother," he says. He had not known if he would have the
strength to speak his words aloud to another person, especially her.

Sarah removes her cap, letting her gray hair fall about her shoulders. "The person with that name died twenty years ago."

"Sarah," Anne says, tutting. She leads Martha out of the room.

Sarah won't draw any closer. She remains rigid, frozen in her mourning. "So you speak now," she says. "You've waited long enough."

Nobody busies himself with a thread on his coat. "I'm speaking to you now because I have something important to say. You're the only person who can hear it, because you're the only one who could possibly understand."

"Ha!" Sarah says. "Is that so? Well, I should be delighted to be speaking with a corpse. A nobody."

He can see the pain in her eyes, the redness there.

"You are not wrong, Sister. Ezekiel died. He died in Cana."

His sister leaves the room. He is alone with his mother. The silence, it is different now.

Later, after they have spent a day in silence:

"Don't place the blame on me, Brother. I am finished with blame, with all of it. Do you know how many times I've wondered why you left us, why you abandoned me? Did you think of me at all? Did you think of me alone here with Mother?"

Nobody finds he has the strength to stand. They are in the parlor again. "I thought of you every day," Nobody says. "I've never stopped thinking of you."

"Some comfort. You've always been skilled at keeping in your head, Brother." The word is a cudgel, a curse.

"I couldn't testify," he says weakly.

His sister leaves. She has a way with leaving, with making him feel she might never return. He watches the horses at night for signs of stirring.

When you heard Father had, that—"

The parlor. Morning light this time. She has awoken early to scold him. From the looks of it, she has not slept.

He stands, ready to catch her the moment she begins to leave. "I couldn't think of returning after I'd heard. I didn't know what to do. For the first time in my life, I had a taste of freedom. No one understood me in that town, Sarah. You were the closest."

"Well, you didn't make it easy with your silence."

"No, I didn't. But I was a child, Sister."

At this, Sarah lifts her eyes to meet his. "I tried to protect you. Every day I tried to protect you. I prayed for you."

"I know." He hazards one step, then another.

"I failed."

"There was no other way, Sarah. It wasn't your fault."

"Who are you to speak to me about fault? You abandoned me. You didn't even think to ask if we were alive or dead. You didn't care. You think being a woman is easy? If I had been the one to run off, do you think I would be alive today, as you are?"

"I cared a great deal," he says. One more step. "I cared so much I couldn't bear to ask. So I kept running. I had hoped to find a place where I could settle, where I could think about everything that had happened in peace, where I could become myself—someone who could make sense of everything—but every time I stopped, the past returned with such force that I couldn't bear it any longer."

"We must find a place for Mother. We have waited too long."

"They'll not take her in Boston."

"Why are you here?"

"I thought maybe you could help me understand why."

"Find a place to bury Mother." Sarah turns abruptly to the coffin. "You can start with that."

Sarah does not leave the room this time.

Days pass. No churchyard will take Catherine, no burying ground. They close the coffin to keep out the stench, but it is powerful; it pervades every room. They will have to do something, anything. The bustle of the city confounds him. He cannot think amidst all of this noise, this smell. He and his sister do not speak. He can feel her anger smoldering through the walls. In some ways it is easier, returning to silence.

Well?" Sarah says.

"We shall have to travel somewhere," he says. "I know many routes. We will find a place to bury her and a place for us to live. I shall fare better with you by my side. Perhaps one day we may even come to call it New Cana."

His sister says nothing.

"You can use some of our money," Anne says. "I want to help."

Sarah takes a seat beside the coffin. The fire is gone from her eyes. She is quiet, contemplative. He recognizes this sister, the one who once watched over him. "That is your great plan, Brother? The one you saved up twenty years to tell me?"

"I'm afraid it's the best I can do."

"And then what? If we end in failure, as Father did?"

"Oh, Sarah," Martha calls from across the room, "your life is not over. Far from it."

"Let us begin here, Sister," he says, moving to her side. "You shall have plenty of time to save my lost soul on the ride to wherever we end up going."

Sarah shakes her head. "You aren't Nobody," she says. "You're not a lost soul. You're somebody."

"Then you shall find me a name, and save me, as you have always wished to do."

"I haven't agreed to anything. You can't come back here and tell me what to do."

"Nobody tells you what to do."

"You're not funny," she says. "You're not. Stop laughing. All of you. I mean it. Stop laughing."

3

Spring

Arthur walks the many forking paths of the pleasure gardens. He holds a knotted branch in one hand, weaving it through the dirt, sweeping aside an ivy curtain to a secluded arbor. He finds a worn bench. The air is too cold for his bones, but he persists anyway.

He waits for a stirring in the hedge. A young man emerges, his belt already loose. Arthur straightens his back and sucks in his gut, staring hard the way he knows the young like to see in the old. They don't mind his age, some even prefer it. He never tires of it, no matter how many times he visits places such as these.

The young man says nothing. Arthur bows, a courtesy before they begin. The boy drops to his knees as behind him another man emerges. Arthur closes his eyes and melts.

———————

The manor standing before Arthur, with its sweeping chimneys and broad windows and imposing Gothic stone façade, must have looked beautiful once; Nathaniel had described it as full of light and elegance.

Arthur passes through a rotting pavilion overlooking a desiccated pond, the sound of some long-forgotten leviathan sweeping through the muddied water below. No sign of a servant anywhere. The shrubs haven't been pruned in months, and a pile of leaves hugs the base of the main entrance. The abandoned house looms as he nears, an ugly thing up close. The moss along the stones adds the only touch of lightness. A crack in the marble travels the length of one of its central columns, bursting into small tributaries near the crown.

Arthur smooths his hair and knocks loudly. The door swings open without effort, unlocked. A flash of blue from above. He follows a bluebird into a long wainscoted corridor, then into an adjacent interior hallway where the only furniture is a heavy table covered in yellowed paper. He should call out, but if someone should demand he leave, he'll not see this vision of a young Nathaniel sitting at the table with his long hair parted evenly and that look of steady concentration. He has only a few days before he must leave for another coast, somewhere far from London. It was a risk to come here, but he had waited long enough, and before this moment, he wouldn't have been able to face the idea of a young Nathaniel; he wouldn't have been able to see the hope here, the future that might have been had Nathaniel not ended his life.

The bird has settled on an iron rod at the top of a bay window overlooking the garden. Arthur opens the latch and releases the bird into an overgrown rosebush. A faint path below where young Nathaniel strolls, a book of poetry dangling carelessly from his fingers. *Love, all alike, no season knowes, nor clyme, / nor houres, dayes, moneths, which are the rags of time.* If they had been here in Edwin Sharpe's manor, the two of them. Arthur yearns for an inexhaustible Nathaniel, one just out of reach, half-ephemeral. Perhaps it is easier in this way to love a dead man.

Arthur walks the length of the corridor until he arrives in a great landscape room where all of the furniture has been covered in heavy white sheets. Marble tombs. The room is dark, drapes drawn, a layer of dust coating a nearby table. Arthur runs his finger over the table and adds his initials, then Nathaniel's. Here they are. Here is the man Arthur still loves, all these years later. Nathaniel rips the sheets from the furniture and sends them flying into the air. He falls into the deep cushions of an emerald divan and crosses his legs. "Will we be staying?" he says. Within the relentless rags of time, they will require diversions, something to help them forget the lives they've left behind. Perhaps some art, some more Donne. No, someone happier. One should know more poetry, not only the classics, not only the somber poems.

Arthur turns. There, in the wall opposite, wait the drawing room doors. He bends low, crouching, one hand on the doorknob. He draws his eye to the keyhole, and waits.

The Unfathomable

———|———

A note on the research for
All the World Beside

I magine a club where a group of men get together in the evenings to gossip, fuck, dress as women, and stage outrageous performances, a place where one might adopt an over-the-top persona by the name of Princess Seraphina, Fanny Murray, or Queen Irons. The men hug, dance, play, sit on one another's laps, kiss passionately.

If you're reading this book, you already know my scenario is a setup. We're speaking of an eighteenth-century club, not one from the twenty-first century, and we must be careful not to impose our contemporary notions of identity onto the past. According to Daddy Foucault, in his *The History of Sexuality, Volume 1: An Introduction* (Pantheon Books, 1978), homosexuals were invented in the nineteenth century. But scenarios such as those described above have been documented in great detail (largely from police reports—so much of our history has been told to us by police) in *Male-Male Intimacy in Early America* by William Benemann (Harrington Park Press/Routledge, 2006).

And so.

So.

Go ahead. Walk inside. Take a closer look. For research purposes.

This club is exclusive, not just anyone can waltz in, and there's a chance that drawing too much attention will entice the police to raid, as they are wont to do when these private gatherings grow too public. A man thus arrested might—depending on race, wealth, and social status—be accused of or even charged with sodomy. He would likely be marked for life.

He may have faced similar fears when meeting a man in the pleasure gardens (think cruising spot) or at a tavern, one of those seedy establishments down by the wharves. You know the drill: sneak into a toilet, cock in hand; decide who is top (active) and who is bottom (passive). Again, this scenario is from another police report. We really kept them busy. The accounts in Benemann's book are, shall we say, steamy. Here's a brief example: "I was picked up by an individual who had his cock *[son vit]* in his hand, and asked me if I had a hard-on and approaching me wanted to put his hand in my breeches. He said that he shouldn't expose himself in this spot, and asked me if I had a room, where we could go to jack off *[branler le vit]* or to screw. He also told me that for the last 20 years he had been involved in the gay life *[la bardacherie]*, and that he knew many footmen with whom he amused himself very often, jacking off or screwing them as often as they wanted it." It sounds so much better in French, doesn't it?

Paris, London, Berlin—as an eighteenth-century gentleman, you would know where to go looking for it. Dense, crowded cities, all those bodies packed together. People whispered about it. Sometimes you could read a broadside about a particularly scandalous sodomy case. On the books, the punishment was death throughout much of the century. If you lived in France, you might only be sent to Bicêtre Hospital, where you would be watched for signs of religious conversion.

I know what you're thinking: This seems really . . . *gay*. Didn't I basically just cite what some might consider to be an early example of conversion therapy? But we're talking about sex, not love, and when it comes to queer people throughout the centuries, we as sober scholars must hold the queers to a higher standard. Desperately craving a bottom session from a rugged seaman is only one part of the equation. An act does not an identity make. For me, at least, an echo from my childhood: Hate the sin, not the sinner. Really, with all of those crowded bodies in one city, it's no wonder a few aberrations would practice sodomy. That humans have been doing it in every century in no way connotes a fixed identity.

So now we come to romantic friendships, a category that by no means suffers from broad generalizations about human life in the eighteenth-century. The reasoning goes that before the word "homosexual" muddied the waters in the late nineteenth century, same-sex relationships were often romantically expressive, dotingly physical, and entirely platonic. As important context, the term "homosexuality" was called "sexual inversion" first (1883), then "homosexual" (1892) in an English translation of Richard Freiherr von Krafft-Ebing's *Psychopathia Sexualis* (1886). Yes, that's sexual psychopath, a phrase you might hear uttered by at least a dozen politicians in 2024, the year this book is being published. Any historical letters we might find between two men that take on what we perceive as homoerotic overtones must be read primarily as part of the literary conventions of the time. Take an example from Richard Godbeer's *The Overflowing of Friendship* (Johns Hopkins University Press, 2009), citing a letter written between two men in 1800, emphases mine.

> Though we should *beware* of leaping to *unwarranted conclusions* about the kinds of intimacy that "dear chums" enjoyed when lying "warm" together, it is of course *not inconceivable* that in *some instances* "those pleasures" might have included erotic stimulation or even sexual activity. Some letters are a good deal more suggestive than others in expressing nostalgia for nights spent with a close friend. Virgil Maxcy . . . assured his "chum" William Blanding . . . that he missed sleeping with him: "I get to hugging the pillow," he declared, "instead of you . . . Sometimes," he wrote, "I think I have got hold of your doodle when in reality I have hold of the bedpost." A

"doodle" that could be confused with a bedpost was hardly in a state of repose, and Maxcy signed this particular letter "your cunt humble." *One cannot help but wonder.*

One cannot help but wonder, indeed. One might spend seven years wondering, as I have. A certain person, that is a full-grown adult, might even choose to throw caution to the wind and do the "not inconceivable" work of assuming queer people have existed in the same way historians have assumed straight people existed, and all of this despite the fact that we queers still don't have an American Girl doll. Even more inconceivable to History is the idea of queer women.

All jokes aside, this type of reading was probably a sound methodology at some point—we needed to know what the boundaries of sentimental friendship really were before we could argue for some form of queer existence in the past. It's clear what happens when we queers overstep, when we become all too visible—but there has to be a point at which we acknowledge the double standard: a man writing passionately about his physical ache for a woman is assumed to be exhibiting sexual desire, yet when it's two men . . . well, you guessed it. Though the conditions might be different for same-sex relationships throughout history, there is no reason we cannot apply a similar lens that explores the possibilities of sexual longing under a different rubric. Plenty of excellent scholars have done this work, to be sure, but outside of academia, the conversation usually goes something like, "OK, yeah, well, I'm not sure we can ever know for sure." Just as I can never know for sure whether a Jane Austen novel has any straight people in it or whether the conventions of marriage and manners at the time make it impossible to exactly map twenty-first-century straight lived experience.

My frustration with Godbeer's hedging, despite my admiration for his skill as a thorough researcher and pioneer for queer academics, pales in comparison with what Larry Kramer expressed in 2009 for *The Gay & Lesbian Review*. It's a gloriously messy rant that I hope wouldn't have met anyone's editorial standards had he not been famous playwright and activist Larry Kramer. Referencing Godbeer, Kramer writes, "Gay people are victims of an enormous con job," and by that point, you already know the rest. Kramer wants us to understand that Abraham Lincoln is a fag; he even goes so far as to reach for George Washington. And let me tell you in all earnestness: you will get lost if you choose to go down this route. If you choose to pin our identities onto specific historical figures in an attempt to justify our existence, you'll never be satisfied until you find Abraham Lincoln's dildo, and even then, you'll have some historian arguing that the presence of a dildo in that private bedroom could have meant anything, and the historian won't be wrong.

So why do any of this work at all? Why search for ourselves in the past, armed only with police reports, court documents, and, at best, private letters? If we have no eighteenth-century terms exactly matching contemporary LGBTQ identities, is the whole endeavor foolish? And think it's bad for the gays? Try searching for scholarship on anything but the G. Following this logic, queer people were never so much erased but rather born fully formed in the last century as a pathology to be dealt with.

These were the animating questions I asked myself when I first sat down to write an early draft of *All the World Beside*. I'm not sure I ever found the answers. I have my own hunches, sure, but what I've come to understand about the work of queer history is that the goal is not in finding answers but in expanding the way we think about the past, the way we make assumptions, in opening up imaginative possibilities that allow us to paint the whole human canvas with the bold, bright colors we see today. We don't have to pin all of our evidence on sex acts or sentimental declarations of love, tossing facts back and forth until the matter is no longer interesting. We can see the past as part of a larger mystery, the same mystery we see staring back at us when we look at the face of love. In my admittedly religious definition of mystery, revelation becomes possible, but the revelation will be different for each person who chooses to take the journey.

The great thing about fiction is that when you start to fill in the gaps of history the imagination grows bolder, more ambitious. After stumbling upon and falling in love with a volume of the prominent eighteenth-century minister Jonathan Edwards's sermons in my father's office about a year after the publication of my memoir, *Boy Erased*, which explored my time in conversion therapy in 2004, I began to ask myself whether it was possible for a queer eighteenth-century minister to exist. Immediately, I grew irritated at the question—what do you mean he couldn't exist?—yet I couldn't get rid of the feeling that any narrative built upon this premise couldn't be taken seriously, not even by myself.

If you don't already know, my father is a Missionary Baptist preacher. I was always to follow in my father's footsteps, one way or another. Ezekiel Whitfield was so difficult to pin down because knowing and seeing oneself is almost impossible. I'm reminded of a Nathaniel Hawthorne quote, from "The Custom House": "Doubtless, however, either of these stern and black-browed Puritans would have thought it quite a sufficient retribution for his sins, that, after so long a lapse of years, the old trunk of the family tree, with so much venerable moss upon it, should have borne, as its topmost bough, an idler like myself. No aim, that I have ever cherished, would they recognize as laudable; no success of mine—if my life, beyond its domestic scope, had ever been brightened by success—would they deem otherwise than worthless, if not positively disgraceful. . . . And yet, let them scorn me as they will, strong traits of their nature have intertwined themselves with mine." If you haven't already guessed, Hawthorne is another inspiration behind this novel.

Still, Jonathan Edwards remained a talking point between my father and me. Edwards is such a brilliant eccentric, a real writer's writer, though I'll excuse you if you find much of his theology odious. If you're at all interested in the history of the English language, read any/all of the following for a truly thrilling example of high rhetoric: *A Divine and Supernatural Light* (1734), *The Distinguishing Marks of a Work of the Spirit of God* (1741), *Some Thoughts Concerning the Present Revival of Religion in New-England* (1742), and *A Treatise Concerning Religious Affections* (1746). After I began to read these sermons, all of the doors my father and I had closed began to open up. We spoke openly of God, of revelation, of love. We entered long-sealed debates with new language, a new old language capable of breaking through defenses. We've used poetry for this as well. Nothing like having your father quote *Leaves of Grass* to warm the cockles of your gay little heart. I began to see how I might enter other sealed-off spaces with this language.

But it was only after several speaking engagements with readers that I began to see the real possibility of Nathaniel Whitfield. There were so many queer Christians who came up to me after each event to express how deeply affected they had been by my memoir, how rare it was to see themselves in a text. They spoke with me about how the language of Christianity, which most of them had heard their entire lives, was like a home to them. Though Biblical interpretations rooted in bigotry had brought them great hardship, they did not want to give up the joy they found in communing with what they believed to be God. Maybe God didn't look the same as He did to their parents, maybe God used different pronouns actually, but almost everyone I spoke with believed in restorative justice, in a better future where religion could be a great comfort to everyone regardless of gender, sexuality, race, or class. These beautiful souls knew what it was to cut off a vital portion of themselves, to lie, to live in fear—and they were unwilling to give up their religion to the bigots who harmed them.

I'm a stubborn Aries, moved by other people's stubbornness, and I love the idea of being a Christian for the sake of pissing off bigots. I joke, but sometimes I think I write about religion and sexuality so much because other people want me to shut up about them. My dad, continually: "When are you going to write a book I can share with other people?" Me: "You actually think your flock isn't reading every word I write?"

A few months after discovering my love for Jonathan Edwards, I reread Nathaniel Hawthorne's *The Scarlet Letter*, which provided an emotional landscape broad enough to capture, with great empathy, the story of adultery between a troubled Puritan minister and a brilliantly talented young woman. Through close study of the character of Arthur Dimmesdale, I was able to open the door to Nathaniel Whitfield. Through the restrained oddness of Hester Prynne and the gnostic wildness of her daughter, Pearl, I began to sketch early versions of Catherine, Sarah, and even Ezekiel Whitfield. Mathew Colman, as his name suggests, found his footing in the bitterness of Roger Chillingworth. When I first understood the power of the scarlet letter as a symbol for shame and public humiliation that, through Hester's art, is transformed into beauty, I found a corollary to my experience writing *Boy Erased*. Only through composing my experiences was I able to make something beautiful of something that had been deeply shameful. Also: Hawthorne, originally Hathorne, was deeply troubled by his Puritan family's involvement in the Salem witch trials. His themes—his obsessions—are mine.

I completed research alongside these early sketches. Despite the highly speculative nature of the material, I wanted to ensure that the novel was rooted in the material reality of the time. I knew I wanted to work from a fictional Jonathan Edwards, especially since the Great Awakening provided a dramatic backdrop for an exploration of repression and desire, as so many of our contemporary identity categories arguably arose from the era's emphasis on subjective, personal relationships with God. From there, with the help of my brilliant research assistant at Kennesaw State University, Aly Gilmore, I divided research into categories as the need arose: Early American Christianity, Great Awakening, Puritan Society, Sexuality, Native Histories, etc.

The following sources have been invaluable: *Early American Houses with a Glossary of Colonial Architecture Terms* by Norman Morrison Isham (Dover Publications, 2007); *In Small Things Forgotten: An Archaeology of Early American Life* by James Deetz (Anchor Books, 1977); *Under Their Vine and Fig Tree: Travels through America in 1797–1799, 1805* by Julian Ursyn Niemcewicz (Grassmann Publishing, 1965); *The Accomplished Housekeeper, and Universal Cook* by T. Williams (1845); *Martha Washington's Booke of Cookery and Booke of Sweetmeats*, transcribed by Karen Hess (Columbia University Press, 1981); along with near daily virtual visits to the Plymouth Colony Archive Project; the Colonial Society of Massachusetts; the 18th

Century Notebook; Townsends Journal (@Townsends, You-
Tube); and finally, a huge thank-you to the Stockbridge Library
Museum & Archives; Historic Richmond Town; the Massachu-
setts Historical Society; and the Colonial Williamsburg Founda-
tion. Also: *Worlds of Wonder, Days of Judgment* by David D. Hall
(Harvard University Press, 1989); *English Sexualities, 1700–
1800* by Tim Hitchcock (Palgrave Macmillan, 1997); *Men in
Love: Masculinity and Sexuality in the Eighteenth Century* by
George E. Haggerty (Columbia University Press, 1999); *Early
Native Literacies in New England* edited by Kristina Bross and
Hilary E. Wyss (University of Massachusetts Press, 2008); *The
Collected Writings of Samson Occom, Mohegan* by Samson Occom, edited by Joanna Brooks (Oxford University Press, 2006);
The Puritans in America: A Narrative Anthology by Alan Heimert
and Andrew Delbanco (Harvard University Press, 1985); *American Jezebel: The Uncommon Life of Anne Hutchinson, the Woman
Who Defied the Puritans* by Eve LaPlante (HarperOne, 2004);
and *The Literatures of Colonial America* edited by Susan Castillo
and Ivy Schweitzer (Wiley-Blackwell, 2001). For more research
and sources on the period, along with a full bibliography, refer to
garrardconley.com.

These early queer Christians, as they began to take shape
through the aid of research, drew my imagination to new and
unexpected places. Armed with a style inspired by Hawthorne,
Edwards, and contemporary storytelling, I began to explore the
idea of including many queer identities under the same roof,
within the same biological family. I had a hunch that this

arrangement might be in conversation with the chosen families we see today. Though I don't think categories ever entirely capture the complexity of any human being, I imagined characters with the following proto-identities: nonbinary/genderqueer, asexual, bisexual, and gay. By no means did I exhaust the possibilities of queerness, but each time I encountered those pesky questions—Could they even exist? Is it likely this many queer people knew and protected each other?—I forcibly pushed them aside. The unfathomable—the impossible—is the enemy of art and, to a certain extent, life. We push boundaries because we want to see where we stand, where we can stand, and where we have always stood. I invite others to join us in New Cana. I'm pretty sure Sarah, Ezekiel, and Arthur Lyman are already waiting.

Others already waiting in queer utopia, deserving all the thanks and praise:

My queer writing group: Meredith Talusan, Michelle Hart, Denne Michele Norris, Austen Osworth, Nick White, Torrey Peters. My fabulous agent Julie Barer at The Book Group, whose patience has been infinite. My team at Riverhead Books: Laura Perciasepe, editor extraordinaire, who helped me through many drafts; Jynne Martin, fellow ex-fundie and overall genius; Nora Alice Demick, Rebecca Reisert, Sharon Gonzalez, and Helen Yentus; my beautiful and spirited publicist, Bianca Flores. The Kennesaw State University English Department. Dear friends Ashley Campbell, Wesley Sooklall (who taught me to have confidence in my art), Edmund White, Douglas Stewart, Garth

Greenwell (thank you for the style read!), Brandon Taylor (the title! the author photo!), and Dr. Paula Backscheider. Thank you to Shahab Yunus for daring me to complete this project and for providing so much inspiration. My reading partner and cheer-leader, Wesley Sooklall; and Lisa Linsky for her infinite support. And thank you, always, to my family, to Hershel and Martha Conley, who taught me to love and forgive.